CHRONOS

AND THE

ROGUE HUNTERS

EDWARD ECK

YEAR
of the
BOOK

Year of the Book
135 Glen Avenue
Glen Rock, Pennsylvania

ISBN 13: 978-1-949150-03-2
ISBN 10: 1-949150-03-8

Library of Congress Control Number: 2018945511

To Mom and Dad

1 THE DARK FIGURE

The tunnel was dark with patchy light given off by torches every thirty feet. Barely large enough for a full grown ogre to pass, the ancient and worn rock walls appeared to go on forever. Every so often a drop of water could be heard splashing into a puddle somewhere in the distance.

A solitary man in plain black robes trudged through the corridor. The air was damp and heavy as if all the weight of the city above pressed down upon him. Not even rats ventured to this place. A thin mist whisked around the uneven dirt floor while the stench of burnt flesh permeated every inch of the passageway.

His cowl was pulled up over his head with his hands placed in the sleeve of the opposite arm. The depth of the hood allowed no light to reach his face. He wanted it that way. He dreaded reaching his destination and made no effort to increase his pace.

When he neared the end of the tunnel, he could hear the rumbling of a great fire and the scent of brimstone was strong in the air. The robed man paused in the shadows and swallowed hard before entering the larger chamber. He knew what manner of creature dwelt in this place and of its power. To displease this individual meant instant death.

He had already prepared what he would say. It wasn't his fault things hadn't gone as planned. He hadn't even been present for the part of the mission that took place in Babylon. It was the failure of another who, fortunately for him, had already met his fate.

The robed man took one final breath before stepping into the chamber. The space was a massive cavern almost the size of a gymnasium. Its ceiling rose fifty feet into the air. Hundreds of cauldrons burned with a fiery glow all around the perimeter. In the center was an earthen ring of jagged rock twenty feet in diameter, radiating unbearable heat. About ten feet below the edge of the formation sat red hot lava. The boiling magma pressed hard against a magical barrier which prevented it from rising into the chamber and incinerating everything. The lava's glow helped light the cavern, revealing a huge pentagram on the ceiling above.

Fog from the barrier rolled over the edges of the pit and covered the floor. At the far end of the chamber, flames reached twenty feet in the air and curled around a figure sitting on a huge throne. Its fiery silhouette was vaguely humanoid in form and at least ten feet tall when standing, while shapes to either side resembled huge wings.

As the robed man began his slow procession across the chamber, smaller creatures dashed between and around the many cauldrons. Occasionally he caught a glimpse of what looked like skinny little imps no more than two feet tall with leathery wings. Almost reptilian, their long tails whipped around as they moved among the stalagmites.

A sound from above caused the man to look up and see four large, human sized, bat-like creatures hanging from the ceiling. Their human heads with long white fangs glared down at him.

Upon reaching the edge of a dais surrounding the throne of fire, the man knelt on one knee. He remained there unmoving, without a sound.

The figure on the fiery throne also remained unmoving for many long minutes. "What happened?" it eventually spoke in a low booming voice. Its anger fueled the flames.

"Frederick Von Woonst has released Tiamat," replied the robed figure, "but the dragon goddess has since disappeared. As has Von Woonst. He obviously failed to convince her to attack the human population. I promise, I shall find him and destroy him myself."

The robed figure continued to kneel at the base of the dais nervously awaiting a response.

"I was monitoring his progress. Von Woonst is already dead," said the booming voice with a hint of pleasure. "The dragon was displeased with his commands and incinerated him. But you already knew this. And Cerberus?"

The robed figure hesitated then pulled back his hood to reveal the aged and worried face of Malcolm. In his late forties and of African descent, Malcolm's head was bald except for a dark goatee with a touch of grey. It had been his job to release Cerberus and he had also failed.

He remembered the young water elemental sorcerer named Max who prevented him from completing his task. The boy had shoved Hades' helm of darkness down the three-headed guard dog's gullet. Stealing that helm had been Malcolm's job—an act which would have freed the monster from the Underworld. Cerberus' acidic saliva destroyed it though, forever thwarting the hound's release from Hades' spell.

"My lord, I did as instructed." Malcolm's voice was shaky. "But there were three powerful sorcerers there from the Circle. I was outnumbered." He stared at the floor in front of him, refusing to make eye contact with his master.

The heat intensified with each excuse. "What of the Harpies, the Minotaur and Cerberus himself?" the dark voice grumbled from within the flames.

"The Harpies and the Minotaur were worthless," exclaimed Malcolm. "They barely did anything to assist me. I would have been better off with a team of water automatons." A bead of perspiration ran down the side of his face. Malcolm knew he was lying, but he was frantic at this point. He didn't want to meet the same end as Von Woonst.

"If you were as poor a sorcerer as you are a liar, I would destroy you here and now," bellowed the dark voice from within the flames.

Malcolm shuttered at the accusation.

"Fortunately for you, I still have need of your services," the voice seethed. "Besides, the third operative was successful in releasing his target creature. The dragon will play her part when the time comes, though I would have preferred to have Cerberus with me for the coming war."

His master's anger was great, but Malcolm was relieved to know he would be spared. He also knew if he failed again, his usefulness would quickly end. He could not afford to disappoint his master again. However, the fact he hadn't known about a third operative did raise concerns in his mind.

"Return to your fortress for now," commanded the voice. "I will summon you when I am ready for you to perform your next task."

The voice went silent and the flames around him increased, driving Malcolm back from the dais. He stumbled to his feet and quickly made his way back to the chamber entrance. The little demon-like creatures continued scampering around the cauldrons, stalking his departure. This made Malcolm even more nervous as he glanced from side to side watching them, preparing for an attack.

Once Malcolm made it to the corridor, he quickly pulled up the hood of his robes. In the passage, he turned and paused for a moment. One of the smaller creatures had approached the throne of fire and knelt in anticipation of orders. The others scampered around the chamber excitedly.

Malcolm heard the dark voice command, "Keep an eye on him. I don't want another failure like the last time. My next move must succeed or things will become very difficult."

The figure within the flames then made a dismissive gesture with his right hand and the little imp-like creature quickly departed.

"The wolf will keep them busy for now."

2 THE SEARCH BEGINS

It was just after sunrise in the Painted Desert of Arizona. Long morning shadows gave the barren space an eerie feel. The sheer majesty of the ancient mountains with their vivid mineral colorations made the desert look more like broad brush strokes on an artist's canvas.

A battered red pickup drove down an old dirt road, kicking up a cloud of dust and disrupting the quiet peace of a new day. Its engine ran rough and the exhaust blew clouds of white smoke. When it pulled into a nearby gas station, the driver jumped out and ran inside, looking quite anxious with his knees pressed firmly together.

The owner just sat behind the register in tattered overalls and a stained t-shirt. He lifted the rim of his red baseball cap to get a better look at Old Bob—a regular customer, overweight and obviously in need of a shower. Anyone could tell from his awkward stance he was looking for the bathroom.

The owner tossed him the restroom key and smiled as he watched Bob run to the back of the store as quickly as possible.

But when Bob opened the restroom door, two people seemingly stepped out of the mirror and landed right in the middle of the tiny room. Bob clearly forgot about bodily needs as he stood with mouth agape, a wet spot running down one leg of his jeans.

Bob then barreled through the store knocking over racks and almost crashing into the glass door on his way out. Confused by the sudden departure, the owner rushed to the restroom to find a man in his late forties and a girl in her early twenties, each carrying a small backpack. The man looked like a character from an old western movie wearing blue jeans and a button-down tan shirt with a brown leather trench coat, cowboy hat and boots. The girl looked out of place as well, but in an entirely different way.

She wore a black leather trench coat over skin tight black leather pants and a black shirt with one too many buttons undone.

The station owner was riveted by her long, bright red ponytail and dark sunglasses. "Where did you two come from?" he asked, lifting his cap and scratching a bald spot on the back of his head.

"Ah," said Vincent. "We're new in town. You wouldn't happen to know where we could rent a vehicle?"

The station owner just stood there staring with his hands on his hips. He bit his lower lip as he raised a single eyebrow. "Ya got any money on ya?"

Vincent reached into his pocket and pulled out a very fat money clip.

The owner's eyes lit up as his attention shifted to the neatly folded cash. A big grin spread across his face. "I got an old Jeep out back I'll sell ya for a thousand bucks."

Taryn watched as Vincent craned his neck in an effort to look out a back window. After straining his eyesight to no avail, Vincent placed the money clip back into his pocket with a polite smile. "Any chance I could see it first?"

The grin faded when the money disappeared. The owner turned and waved for them to follow, then made his way out of the station and around the back.

"She ain't much ta look at, I'll give ya that, but she'll get ya where yer goin'." He climbed into the Jeep and started it up.

Taryn thought the tires looked to be in fair shape and the engine sounded good. It was grey except for the rust-red left front fender. There was no top other than rusty roll bars.

"Five hundred," said Vincent, circling the Jeep.

The owner's jaw dropped. "Naw, she's a good Jeep. Make it nine hundred."

Taryn stood with her arms crossed and shifted her weight from one foot to the other while staring at the two of them over the top of her dark sunglasses.

"Seven-fifty," Vincent said with a grin. "Final offer."

Taryn could almost see the little gears in the man's head turning.

In an attempt to force his decision, she started walking away and called back with a slight Irish accent, "Ye be wastin' too much time. I'm out of here."

When Vincent moved to follow, the station owner's attention shifted yet again. "Okay, seven-fifty."

The two travelers stopped and turned around. With a smile, Vincent pulled out the money clip and began counting out the payment.

Ten minutes later after filling up the tank, they were on their way with Taryn behind the wheel.

"Ye would have given him five times that amount just so ye wouldn't have to walk. Why haggle?"

Vincent sat in the passenger seat scanning the horizon with a pair of binoculars. "I've always enjoyed negotiations and seeing how I no longer work for Malcolm, I'm probably out of a job at the investment firm."

He lowered the binoculars when they heard a rustling behind them.

As he turned around, he asked, "Is your backpack alive?"

"What?"

"There's something moving inside your backpack."

Taryn stopped the Jeep and they both climbed out, prepared for an attack. The pack continued to show movement, but nothing threatening.

Taryn eased closer and opened it. When she did, a black cat climbed out leisurely and stretched. "Oh, it's ye," she said. "Well, I hope ye like the desert 'cause we're not takin' ye back to Ravenicon castle. Ye'll just have to stay with us for now."

Vincent looked at Taryn, then at the cat, then back to Taryn. She realized he was trying to decide if she was losing her mind or if she was actually expecting the cat to understand her.

"Something I should know about?"

"He's been sneakin' around Ravenicon Castle for the past week," said Taryn. "I'm not sure how or why but the cat seems to understand us. Sometimes I even think he's tryin' to talk to us, but we don't understand cat."

The feline curled up in a ball on top of Taryn's pack and looked like it was about to take a nap so Vincent and Taryn climbed back into the Jeep and started off again.

"Based on the sketchy information from Meagan and Hank," she said, "we should be headed toward the general area where they arrived from Hades. Can you see anythin'?"

Meagan and Hank had narrowly escaped Hades, as did Max and Malcolm through an ice mirror—an unpredictable form of transport. Ending up in the clouds above the Painted Desert, they had almost fallen to their deaths if not for a levitation spell. Their hope was that Max too had appeared somewhere in the Painted Desert, but they had no idea where.

Vincent put down the binoculars and cast a spell, "*Searo teyon maku.*" He held out his hand perpendicular to the ground and moved it around in search of magical signs nearby. "Nothing yet," he said.

They had known this was not going to be an easy task. Trying to find Max in the middle of a desert was going to be like looking for a needle in a haystack the size of New York City. And that's if he was even still alive.

3 RECOVERY

Today, the training room was a long practice range, fifty feet wide and a hundred feet deep. The walls were the same grey stone as the rest of Ravenicon Castle. A fireball impacted the hovering target at the far end of the training room. Only two feet wide, the target now bore the customary scorch mark. Another fireball slammed into the bottom half of a different target, followed by a third just barely catching the top edge of the last target.

A kick at the gravel floor stirred up a wisp of dust. "Ugh," shouted Cyrus in frustration as he paced back and forth near the room's entrance. His black hair was frazzled as sweat rolled down the back of his neck. He had been practicing for over two hours that morning with the fireball bracer Elisa had given him. The latest shots were by far his best attempt with two-foot targets at a distance of fifty feet, but it still didn't please him. His sorcery couldn't keep up with the elemental powers of his friends. He was determined to make sure at least his aim had unquestionable accuracy.

It had been nearly forty-eight hours since their return from Babylon. Cyrus had been practicing almost every available minute after recovering from the poisoned spikes of a manticore. He wasn't wearing the normal sweat suit, but instead had chosen blue jeans and a white sleeveless t-shirt, revealing his muscular frame from his high school days playing quarterback. A standard punching bag hung in the corner of the room. He took a few good jabs at it to relieve tension. He was exhausted from both the mental and physical exertion, but was determined to carry on with his practice.

As he continued to pace, the door to the training room opened and Meagan walked in carrying a bottle of water. She was wearing her grey sweat suit and had her long curly blonde hair tied back in a ponytail. A bandage still covered the left temple of her forehead from injuries she sustained in the Greek Underworld.

"You need to take a break," she said, and handed him a bottle of water. "There may still be some after-effect from the poison. You're not invincible. you know."

"I know," replied Cyrus still a little disgusted with his practice session. "I just can't help feeling like we failed in Babylon. No... like *I* failed in Babylon. Taryn and I were too easily captured when approaching the ziggurat. Then she almost died from heat in the underground passage, and Amber nearly followed trying to find Tiamat in the dark chamber. All I could do was get stuck by the poisoned spikes of a manticore."

"You're only focusing on the bad parts. You did some good there too, you know," commented Meagan with a smile. "It was your idea to use parasailing to beat Frederick Von Woonst to the Khazneh in Petra. You selected the correct pillar to open the door to the dark chamber and save Taryn. And you led the charge to save Amber in Babylon. Taryn and Amber might not be alive if it weren't for you. Besides, we didn't do so well in the Greek Underworld either. While Max did prevent Cerberus' escape, he wound up being pulled through the ice mirror with Malcolm."

Cyrus knew Taryn and Vincent had already departed for Arizona in an attempt to find Max. Their only hope relied on Max truly being the immortal Chronos from Greek mythology. Otherwise, they were merely looking for his dead body.

"Thanks," sighed Cyrus as he stopped pacing and just stared at the targets. "Well, at least my aim's improving. That's better than what I did in practice before going to Babylon."

"How's Amber doing?" inquired Meagan. "I haven't seen her except for supper last evening, and she didn't seem very talkative."

"Okay, I guess," replied Cyrus. "She was still sleeping last time I checked on her." Now he was becoming concerned about his sister, too. She didn't normally sleep in this late and she had been quiet the evening before.

"Well, lunch will be ready in about an hour." Meagan turned to leave. "Oh, and you may want to consider a shower between now and then," she added with a smile. She snapped her fingers and the door closed behind her, leaving Cyrus standing in the training room to ponder his sister's solitude.

He focused on his right hand and clenched his fist. Concentrating all his anger into that one moment he snapped around to face the target and let loose one last blast from the bracer. The fireball flew from the leather arm guard and slammed into the target just shy of dead center.

When Cyrus returned to the New Circle room, he stopped in the middle to examine the crystal and found Max's Scorpio sign still flickering off and on. The circular room contained five doors besides the entrance—one for each current member of the New Circle.

He looked to one of them to find Max's name scratched out like those of the Old Circle who had died. Normally if someone dies, their sign disappears from the crystal as well. Cyrus moved closer to Max's door and inspected it again. Though the name was missing, the symbol remained. As it was explained to them by Gollnick and Elisa, it was the sign of Chronos from ancient Greek mythology. At least it gave them a little hope their friend was indeed still alive. He ran his hand over the etched symbol as he contemplated Max's fate.

Turning from the door, he approached Amber's room and knocked. "You awake in there?" Cyrus placed an ear close to the door in hope his sister had finally decided to wake up.

"Go away," she replied quietly.

It sounded like she had been crying. Cyrus became even more concerned as he reached for the door latch, but hesitated. He looked over his left shoulder at the crystal before returning his attention to the door.

"Amber, can I come in?" Even though he was her brother, no one could enter someone else's room in the New Circle without their permission. The crystal wouldn't allow it. And Cyrus didn't feel like challenging its power.

"Whatever," was Amber's only response. Cyrus took this as permission, though he wasn't sure if the crystal would see it that way. When he reached for the latch, he was cautious, but it didn't zap him. He then opened the door and entered.

Amber was lying curled up in a ball on her bed with tears in her eyes. She was still wearing her sweat suit from the night before and was holding on to her sheets for dear life.

"Amber, what's wrong?" he asked with concern as he sat down on the bed next to her.

"It's her," whimpered Amber. "Whenever I close my eyes I see her in my nightmares. I'm always falling, falling right at her. She opens her mouth and I fall in... Then I wake up in a cold sweat," she whispered as if afraid to be heard.

"Don't worry, it's only a nightmare. It can't hurt you," said Cyrus. "Who is it that's in your dream?"

"Tiamat," whispered Amber so quietly he could barely hear her.

The name stabbed at his heart. The anger he felt earlier returned. It was his fault his sister had to face that monster alone and he couldn't help but blame himself. Cyrus took her hand and as he did, she sat up and hugged him.

"She's gone," Cyrus soothed. "She disappeared to the south, most likely to the dragon colony down in Antarctica somewhere. You don't need to worry about her." But Cyrus knew Tiamat would be back one day and Amber would have to face her fears. Next time, he needed to be ready to destroy the dragon that tormented his sister's nightmares.

4 THE ROGUE HUNTERS

A few hours after arriving in the Painted Desert, Taryn and Vincent stopped for a break. Their quest to find Max—or at least his remains—was not going well. The desert was a big place and trying to find a single person dead or alive in such a vast space proved daunting.

The varied colors of the mountains with the sun directly overhead gave a majestic appearance to the towers of dirt and stone. In such a place, their only hope was that Max was still alive, so Vincent's spell could detect his magical power. However, in this part of the world, magical energies were common. But they knew Malcolm had been transported here from the Greek Underworld too, so they also had to be on guard.

They sat in the Jeep drinking water and resting from hours of driving. Vincent sat in the front passenger seat reviewing maps of the area as he attempted to get his bearings. Taryn had reclined in the back with her sunglasses still on, scanning the horizon. As she lay there, the black cat walked up on her belly and looked at her.

"Can I help ye?" she inquired, studying the feline.

The cat merely lay down with its head on her chest and fell asleep. Taryn petted it with her left hand as she took another sip of water.

"I think I finally figured out where we are," commented Vincent with enthusiasm. He scrunched the map into a ball and threw it. "We're lost."

"Wonderful," said Taryn with a dry smile. "I figured that out about an hour ago. Any suggestions as to what we do now?" She had not really expected Vincent to locate their position on the map. They were in the middle of a desert with no roads. "What about the GPS on your phone?" she questioned.

"It says we're somewhere in the blasted Gulf of Mexico."

Taryn could tell he was less than happy about the phone's inaccuracy. "Hmm, somehow I thought there'd be more water."

Taryn smiled when she realized Vincent had chosen to ignore her and was now casting his spell to search for magic once again. *"Searo te-yon maku."*

She watched as he turned in a circle then hesitated in one direction. His attention was off in the distance, but neither of them could see the source of his focus.

"There's more than one source of magic," Vincent said, rising from his seat, prepared for a battle. "Either Malcolm found Max first and they're heading this way... or we're about to get some unexpected company."

Taryn picked up the cat and placed it back in her backpack. It let out a dissatisfied meow. She then jumped out of the Jeep on the opposite side from Vincent and raised clenched fists out to either side, staring into the distance.

From behind one of the enormous rock formations, she could see a dust cloud heading in their direction. It wasn't big enough to be a dust storm, but it also wasn't small enough to be a single vehicle. As they stood there preparing for the unexpected, the dust cloud continued to draw near. Taryn heard the motorcycles before she saw them. They weren't heading right at the Jeep, but passed about a mile south of their position.

"I'm bettin' they know where they're goin'," she suggested. "Maybe we should follow 'em, at least get out of this desert and try again later this evenin' with a better search plan." She was hopeful Vincent would agree. Also if the passersby had a magical member in their group, perhaps they could provide some assistance.

"You drive," he replied. "I'll keep an eye on our friends over there."

Taryn was glad to have found a way out of the desert, but was unsure about the magical motorcyclists. They weren't aware of any unfriendly sorcerers in the area, but then they weren't aware of any friendly sorcerer activity either. This was a strange puzzle, but the group would most likely lead the way out of the desert, which was the main objective right now.

If the motorcyclists noticed they were being followed, they did not give any indication. They continued on at the same speed and direction. After about an hour's drive, they came upon a small town. When the Jeep neared the place where the bikes were parked, Taryn noticed the name of the restaurant in big red and blue letters—The Desert Windstorm. It was a small white diner with a few siding panels pulling away from the bottom of one wall. The parking area was covered in sand with a line of twenty motorcycles along the front of the building. Taryn parked, then grabbed her backpack and started for the entrance.

"Wait," called Vincent as he rushed to block her path. "We don't know if these people will be friend or foe. Let me go in first. I'll let you know if the coast is clear. I want to make sure we're not walking into a trap."

"A trap?" questioned Taryn. "In all likelihood, these guys are rogue sorcerers. They will probably care less who we are or why we're here so long as we don't stay too long. Let's just go in, get somethin' to eat and see if we can identify the sorcerers among them. If we can make peaceful contact we will, otherwise we leave."

"Fine, but I'm still going in first," Vincent insisted. "Stay behind me." He turned and started for the door.

As they approached the entrance, a man stepped out and stood blocking the door with his arms crossed in front of him. African-American and about six and a half feet tall, he was very muscular with short black hair. He wore a jean jacket with no sleeves, an old pair of jeans and black boots. It was evident he had just come across the desert as he was covered in dust from head to toe.

"Ah, hello," said Vincent with a bit of surprise. "We were uh…" He looked the man up and down, but let his sentence trail off.

"We were just goin' in for a bite to eat," said Taryn, pushing her way past Vincent and the tall man, who merely looked at her and let her pass.

The two men just stood there in amazement at her lack of intimidation. Vincent gave a half-hearted smiled and slowly stepped around the tall man, following Taryn inside.

There were ten booths along the outer walls with a bar on the opposite wall. Other tables were scattered around the room. At the back of the diner was a larger table with ten people seated around it. Four other booths were also occupied. The sizzle of frying food could be heard from the back and the smell of breakfast whetted Taryn's appetite. It was still early in the day and the blinds were closed. The dim lights made it difficult to see until her eyes adjusted.

"Are you insane?" questioned Vincent as he caught up to Taryn, placing a hand on her shoulder. But then he stood there like a deer in the headlights. Everyone in the place was now looking directly at Taryn and Vincent. He lowered his hand to his side.

The customers were all dressed like the man who had attempted to block the door. Most were Hispanic with a few African-Americans and some Native Americans. The tall man stepped inside and stood directly behind them, once again crossing his arms.

With a quick glance, Taryn spotted a logo on the back of one of their jackets that read *Rogue Hunters*—obviously the name of their motorcycle gang.

"Maybe we should go somewhere else," suggested Vincent.

Taryn was not dissuaded. She walked to an empty booth and sat down. Out of the corner of her eye, she saw Vincent pause before following her. She picked up a menu and looked it over. Vincent didn't take his eyes off everyone else in the room as they continued to stare.

"Taryn?" he questioned in a higher pitch than normal, "I'm not sure this is such a good idea."

"I think I might try the fried chicken. What do ye think?" she asked, not paying any attention to the multitude of eyes now focused in their direction.

Vincent made no reply.

One among the gathered congregation stood. An older man, a little older than Vincent, with long grey hair tied in a ponytail, appeared Native American and wore a white t-shirt under his sleeveless denim jacket and brown leather pants with brown boots.

As he approached their table, he pulled up a chair and turned it backwards. Straddling it, he used the chair back as an armrest while he eyed the two of them.

Taryn continued to look over her menu and Vincent sat back in his seat, locking eyes on the stranger.

The man looked from Vincent to Taryn and back. "Why are you here?" he asked in a dry elderly voice.

Taryn watched a bead of sweat roll down the side of Vincent's face. If these were normal people, they would be reluctant to use magic. But she knew if things became dangerous, she and Vincent could use it to escape. In this case, she knew there were at least two sorcerers among them, possibly more. An attack could come from any direction at any time.

"We, uh... We're looking—" stuttered Vincent.

"We're lookin' to get somethin' to eat. Is that alright with ye?" Taryn interrupted, not even looking up from her menu. Unlike Vincent, she appeared calm and unfazed by the attention they were attracting.

The man just looked at Taryn then redirected his attention. "You followed us out of the desert. What were you looking for?" His eyes narrowed on Vincent.

"We, uh, we were lost," stuttered Vincent. "We followed you hoping you knew where you were going." He gave a weak smile.

Taryn realized this could turn ugly if things went wrong. It was only the two of them against a gang with two or more sorcerers. She knew Vincent liked to haggle, but she couldn't understand why he was faltering at a time like this.

The man continued to study Vincent. He opened his mouth to inquire more.

"Are ye daft?" Taryn raised her voice. "We're here for a bite and then we'll be on our way. We mean ye no harm. By this point, ye know what we're capable of and we know what yer capable of. Why not just let us eat in peace and then we'll be on our way? Okay?"

"You have spirit, young one. I like that, but we must be cautious about strangers in our territory. Another stranger came through here recently and killed two of our friends," said the man with a stern face. "We will not allow that to happen again."

Taryn and Vincent looked at one another with concern and shock.

The man's eyes darted between the two of them. "You know this man I speak of?"

"African descent? And about my age?" Vincent asked.

"Yes," replied the man, leaning closer.

"With a greying goatee, and dressed completely in black? He might have a slight limp from a leg injury?"

"Yes, that's the man we seek. You know him?" questioned the stranger with even greater interest.

"His name is Malcolm, he's a dark sor..." but then Vincent stopped and started looking around the room at the others.

The man looked over his shoulder then back to Vincent. "My brothers and sisters are aware of magic and those who possess the ability to control it... such as you two," he said.

"His name is Malcolm, he's a dark sorcerer from New York City," said Vincent. "We are good sorcerers and members of the Circle. And you are?"

"I am Qaletaqa, and this is my adopted son Jayden," he said, pointing to the large muscular man who had met them at the door. "And my daughter Sheelin." He turned to a beautiful Native American girl standing behind Vincent with a knife already drawn, ready to strike.

Sheelin sheathed her weapon and placed it in a belt at her waist. She was around seventeen and wore a tan t-shirt under a black vest. Her brown eyes continued to keep watch over them even while she brushed back her long black hair with a feather fastened to the left side just below her ear.

"And are you dark sorcerers or good sorcerers?" questioned Vincent cautiously.

"We are what you would consider... *rogue* sorcerers." Qaletaqa looked around to those present in the room. "We take no sides in your war. I am a shaman and leader of our company. My daughter and I were the sorcerers you detected when following us out of the desert. Oh, and our other young friend— Alex Desert Walker." Qaletaqa turned and pointed to the back of the restaurant. A young man rose from his seat in acknowledgment.

Taryn turned to see him. "Max!" she yelled in astonishment, rising from her seat. As she did so, the entire gang rose as well... in preparation for an attack.

5   MAX, BUT NOT

Taryn faced Max from across the room. She realized he was now part of the motorcycle gang... and they would protect their own. She stood there a moment hoping Max would realize who she was and attempt to calm the others, but this did not happen.

Along with the rest of the gang, Max was prepared for a fight—magical or otherwise.

Taryn couldn't understand why he didn't recognize her. It had only been a few days since they met in Vincent's office in Miami. Sure, their meeting wasn't the friendliest, but he had rescued her from a fire and carried her back to the castle in Baltimore.

"Max? Don't ye recognize me?" asked Taryn hoping that hearing her voice and his name, might jog his memory.

The young man just stood there. "My name is Alex Desert Walker. You must have me confused with someone else."

Qaletaqa looked at Taryn with a furrowed brow. "How do you know Alex?"

"His name is Max and he's my friend, and a member of the Circle. He's the leader of our group," answered Taryn trying to put some authority behind her speech this time. She was beginning to get concerned about the situation now. If this gang had adopted Max, they might not be willing to let him go. Rogue sorcerers would have no reason to help either the Circle or the dark sorcerers.

Qaletaqa looked at Taryn and Vincent then stood and headed for the door. "Come with me." The others started to follow, but he waved them to remain where they were.

Qaletaqa, Taryn and Vincent exited the restaurant. Sheelin mumbled something under her breath and then followed the other three out.

In the parking area, Qaletaqa turned to face them in the hot dry afternoon sun. "You claim to know Alex. You also claim to know the man who murdered our two friends, and now you claim to belong to the Circle. What proof do you have of any of this?"

"As I said, his name is Max and he is my friend," replied Taryn. "Why does he believe his name is Alex Desert Walker?" She couldn't help but wonder why they had to leave the restaurant to have this discussion? And why had only Qaletaqa and Sheelin come out with them?

"As you probably suspect, we found Alex wandering the desert yesterday. His clothes were a shamble and he had no memory, but we took him in as one of our own. We know he is a powerful sorcerer. I'm not sure it's a wise idea to let anyone have that kind of power... dark sorcerer or Circle. For now, he will continue to believe he has been a long-time member of the Rogue Hunters."

Taryn was not about to back down. "What does that even mean? What do ye hunt?" She looked out of the corner of her eye to see Sheelin still behind them, eyes closed. Taryn wasn't sure of her intention, but it raised concern.

Qaletaqa cleared his throat to regain Taryn's attention. "While we let your Circle and dark sorcerers battle over the creatures of the Nightmare Realm, we try to keep the creatures born of this world and the spirit world in check—those creatures that affect the crops, hunting, illnesses, and just plain mischief."

"Look," said Vincent, breaking the tension, "we came here for Max. He defeated Malcolm in the Greek Underworld while trying to prevent the release of Cerberus. Max was injured, but Malcolm drug him along through an ice mirror during his escape and ended up here. We were concerned for Max's life."

"So you say," responded Qaletaqa. "Why should we believe anything you tell us?"

Taryn met his eyes. "As I said, we mean ye no harm. We just want our friend back."

Sheelin stepped forward between Taryn and Vincent. "Father, they speak the truth, even if they do not speak all they know."

Taryn now realized what Sheelin had been doing. "Ye cast a truth hearin' spell before ye left the restaurant. That's why ye were standin' back there listenin' to us."

"It was important to know you were being honest."

Qaletaqa placed a hand on Sheelin's shoulder. "It takes about an hour for her truth spell to wear off. She will continue to know if you speak the truth. So, where is this Malcolm?"

"If he's not here anymore, then he's most likely returned to his fortress in New York City," answered Vincent. "I know where it is located, but New York is a dangerous place. I wouldn't recommend attacking him there. He's too powerful and commands too many sorcerers."

"Even if we wished to leave now, we could not," replied Qaletaqa. "There are other matters that demand our attention, but rest assured, one day we will have our vengeance."

"Is there anythin' we can do to help?" questioned Taryn. If they could find a reason to stay with the Rogue Hunters, they might have the opportunity to convince Max to return with them to Baltimore.

"Perhaps," replied Qaletaqa as he studied her.

"Hello? Is anyone there?" came a voice from Taryn's backpack. Everyone including Taryn and Vincent jumped at the sound.

Taryn remembered the small mirror they had brought along for communication. She set the backpack down on the ground and opened it to look for the mirror. As she did the black cat jumped out, startling everyone further.

Grabbing the mirror, she said, "Gollnick, now is not a good time. We'll have to call ye back later." She then waved her hand over the mirror's surface and stuffed it back into her pack.

As she returned her gaze to Qaletaqa, she realized he was craning his neck to look behind her at Sheelin. Taryn turned to find the girl had moved away to follow the black cat.

"Never seen a cat before?" questioned Taryn.

"My daughter has the powers of the Shaman, as I do. She senses something unusual about your feline friend. Sheelin, what's wrong?"

"There's something unnatural about that cat," she stated.

Taryn wasn't sure what was unnatural about their black cat, other than its odd personality, but it didn't seem to improve their situation. She noticed Qaletaqa made no move to stop Sheelin, but looked at them with a furrowed brow.

After a few moments, Sheelin returned to the group without the cat. Wide eyed, she glared at Taryn and Vincent. "What gives you the right to trap someone like that?"

"Wait, what?" Taryn's eyes shot wide open.

"It's a person trapped in the form of a cat!" exclaimed Sheelin.

"That animal found us. We didn't do that to anyone." Taryn recalled the cat had mysteriously turned up in the castle days before she joined the New Circle, but no one knew where it had come from. The cat now came strolling back to the group and sat facing everyone, as if waiting.

"I still sense you speak the truth," replied Sheelin. "But that doesn't change the fact you are in the company of someone trapped in animal form. I tried releasing the person, but the spell must have been cast by a powerful sorcerer. More powerful than I have the ability to reverse."

Taryn became concerned, not just for the cat, but also for the cat's real identity. Was it a criminal whose punishment was to stay in animal form for the rest of its life? Or someone being punished by an angry spouse, or worse? Either way, they needed to find a way to break the spell.

"Father," said Sheelin as she turned to Qaletaqa. "You are much more powerful than me. Perhaps you can release the trapped person."

After a few failed attempts by Qaletaqa, Taryn and Vincent each took turns at trying the same. Finally the cat lay down, crossed its paws and looked away from the humans.

As they were about to give up, Max—now known as Alex—came walking out of the restaurant. They all turned to stare at him as he looked from person to person, then to the cat, and back to everyone. "You've been out here for quite a while, and since I got the impression it had something to do with me, I thought I should be here to have my say."

Sheelin approached Alex. "His memory is gone, but he does have serious power within."

"What?" said Alex as he looked from one to the other as if waiting for an explanation.

"Alex, we'd like you to attempt to remove a spell from this cat," said Qaletaqa, as he pointed to the cat lying on the ground in front of them.

Alex knelt down to get a better look, but the feline didn't move other than to stare back into Alex's eyes. From his crouched position Alex looked up to Qaletaqa. "Let me get this straight, there's a spell on this cat? And you want me to remove it?"

Qaletaqa just nodded and motioned for Alex to give it a try.

Alex raised his right hand over the cat. *"Dim-tar mai secul,"* he said absentmindedly. As the words rolled out, the form of the cat stretched on the ground before them. Its black fur thinned and faded. In less than a minute, the small animal was replaced by a fairly large and muscular man who continued to lay face down in the dirt, exhausted by the transformation.

Sheelin ran back into the restaurant and quickly returned with a tablecloth which she placed over the naked man.

Once covered, the large man propped himself up on his forearms, but remained on the ground. "My name Radimir Rasputin. I thank you for freeing," he said in a thick Russian accent.

If he had been standing, Radimir probably would have been over six feet tall, maybe even more muscular than Cyrus. His big brown eyes looked weary as he beheld his rescuers, sweat glistening off his bald head. The transformation had clearly taken a lot out of him as he faded off to sleep and collapsed to the ground once more.

6 A New Threat

Just before lunch, Meagan went to the library in search of a tome regarding defensive spells. The huge semi-circular double doors opened at her approach. There were stacks of books and shelves of scrolls scattered throughout the room. These weren't normal books. Hundreds of tomes were almost two feet in height containing ancient magical spells. The disorganized and irregular piles created a maze of narrow rows and pathways, completely blocking view of the grey stone walls.

She navigated past an old wooden table that had seen better days and four big overstuffed chairs. At the other end of the room was a large oval-shaped mirror with bronze trim that hovered in midair. She remembered seeing the tome on one of the stacks off to its left.

When Meagan approached the stack of books, she had not taken notice of the image in the mirror, but now a voice spoke, "Meagan Strom!"

Wide eyed, she spun to face the mirror, swallowing a scream. Staring back at her was the image of Veena, one of the members of the Sisterhood of the Muses. An attractive girl in her early twenties, she had her brunette hair up in a bun and looked like a librarian with her reading glasses. Veena was a descendant of Clio, the muse of historical literature. She had been trying to locate old scrolls or tomes regarding the ancient prisons in an attempt to aid the New Circle.

"Veena," said Meagan still trying to catch her breath. "Nice to see you again. What can I do for you?"

"I have urgent news," replied Veena. The bags under her eyes and drained look on her face revealed she had put in long hours reading and researching.

Meagan was certain that *urgent news* couldn't mean good news.

Veena continued, "Another prison has been attacked and this time the creature within was released."

A chill ran through Meagan as she realized the dark sorcerers were still on the move even after being defeated in the Greek Underworld and an unsuccessful attempt to enlist the aid of Tiamat in Babylon.

"How bad is it?"

"None of the creatures placed in prisons are any good, but it took the Norse gods, err... sorcerers, many years to find a way to bind this one."

It was just before noon and everyone at the castle was gathered for lunch. The kitchen had the standard grey stone décor. Its modern appliances looked out of place in an old castle, but then, Cyrus appeared grateful for the microwave from time to time. Gollnick was getting around better now after being attacked by a demon in New York City, though he made use of a cane for added support. He had grown anxious to join the search for Max, but Meagan had insisted he continue to rest a few more days as his leg was not healing as fast as it should. Elisa—Gollnick's ex-wife and member of the Old Circle—had departed for Philadelphia in an attempt to gather information on the dark sorcerer situation now that Frederick Von Woonst was dead and Malcolm had failed in his mission to release Cerberus. They could only hope Malcolm had fallen from grace and the dark sorcerers were in disarray.

Cyrus was seated at the table looking through a comic book about sorcerers as he devoured a sandwich he'd made for himself. Amber was sitting quietly at the table barely nibbling at some food her brother must have given her. Hank remained in the infirmary after recovering from a broken leg. What would have normally taken months to heal was mending in days with the aid of magic, but Meagan had insisted he also remain in bed for at least a few more days.

They were all seated around the large circular table when Meagan rushed into the kitchen and everyone's attention shifted to her. "We have a problem. The dark sorcerers found another prison. And this time they've already opened it."

The room fell silent.

"How do you know this?" questioned Gollnick with wide eyes and a lump in his throat.

"I just spoke with Veena in the library mirror. It seems that while we were recuperating from our battles, the dark sorcerers were still busy. She said there have been reports in Norway about a giant wolf terrorizing the countryside. She believes the dark sorcerers somehow found a way to release Fenrir from his prison."

"Okay, I'll bite," said Cyrus as everyone rolled their eyes at the comment. "Who or what is Fenrir?"

"According to Norse mythology," continued Meagan, "Fenrir was a giant wolf that even the Norse gods feared. He was so strong, no bonds could hold him. They tried several times to imprison him, but he always broke free. It wasn't until the dwarves gave them a magical ribbon called Gleipnir that they were finally able to bind Fenrir so he could not escape, but Fenrir wasn't stupid. When the Asgardians suggested binding him with a mere ribbon, he grew suspicious and insisted one of the gods place their own hand in Fenrir's mouth as an act of trust. Tyr, who had raised Fenrir from a pup, was the only one brave enough to do so. When Fenrir realized he couldn't break free, he bit off Tyr's hand."

"Okay, so it's a bad idea to stick your hand in the mouth of a giant wolf," commented Cyrus. "Got it."

"This is serious," growled Gollnick. "If Fenrir is loose, we need to find a way to re-imprison him. Did Veena give you any idea how we can capture this monster?"

"She suggested trying to find Gleipnir," answered Meagan. "Or at least whatever is left of the ancient ribbon. It was the only magical item strong enough to bind Fenrir the first time. It may be the only thing that can hold him now."

"So where do we find this Gleeper?" asked Cyrus, still not taking the situation seriously.

"It's called Gleipnir," said Gollnick with a scowl. "And if the dark sorcerers released Fenrir, they may still have it. It's also possible they destroyed it in the hope that we can never re-imprison the beast."

Cyrus put the comic book aside and straightened up. "We should probably start checking the place where Fenrir was imprisoned and see if we can figure out what happened. Meagan, Amber and I will go to Norway and see if we can find the prison and any traces of this Gleipnir."

Gollnick raised a single eyebrow as he glanced at Cyrus. "I'll be coming along as well."

"No, you won't," stated Meagan with authority in her voice, which seemed to surprise everyone. "You're still having problems with that leg."

"Besides," added Cyrus, "we may need you here in case Elisa calls with new information, or if Taryn and Vincent find Max. Worst case, we may need you as backup in case things go wrong."

Meagan wasn't sure if Cyrus was attempting to make Gollnick feel better about being left behind or if he really thought they would need backup. It was also possible that Cyrus still wanted to lead—and with Max missing, this was his way of taking charge.

Gollnick slouched in his seat and Meagan knew he was disappointed, but couldn't argue.

Meagan couldn't stand to see her uncle depressed. "If Taryn and Vincent find Max, we'll also need you here to contact me telepathically. Otherwise they won't know how or where to meet up with us."

"You're right," sighed Gollnick. "I'd just be in the way. I'll contact Veena and see if she can give us any better information on where the prison might've been. The Norse sorcerers were worshiped by the Vikings of Scandinavia. We'll need to narrow down the search area a bit. I also have a contact in Norway who may be able to provide some assistance." Gollnick sat quietly for a moment. "This could be the beginning of a much larger problem. We thought the attempts to release Cerberus and Tiamat were just a case of the dark sorcerers stumbling on information accidentally. But if they know about even more prisons, we could end up dealing with some very powerful creatures. I'm concerned they know more than we were giving them credit."

7 THE DEPARTURE

Later that afternoon, Gollnick hobbled into the training room with the aid of his cane, to find Cyrus practicing with the fireball bracer Elisa had given him. He had obviously been drilling for a while as he was covered in sweat. Upon noticing Gollnick's entrance, Cyrus stopped and grabbed a towel from a nearby table and swung it around his neck after wiping the sweat from his brow.

"You may want to focus on your spells as well as target practice," Gollnick advised. "It's great your aim is getting better, but there are other things you need to learn, too."

"We're fighting a war against the dark sorcerers," Cyrus said, still breathing hard. "I'd love to keep up with all of the studies you want us to learn, but right now, combat spells and accuracy are what we need most."

"And what if something happens to that bracer? It could be damaged or destroyed, and then what will you do?"

Cyrus grinned. "If my aim's good, they'll never even get close enough to touch it."

"Let me guess, the best defense is a good offense? What if Taryn had thought the same and never studied magical healing? You'd be dead right now from the manticore poison. And what about the spell she used to find that magic carpet?"

"I know," agreed Cyrus reluctantly. "But right now, I need to be able to protect my friends. I failed in Babylon and the dark sorcerers released Tiamat. I almost died, Taryn was almost fried, and Amber had to endure the dark chamber. I can't let something like that happen again. I need to be able to protect my sister and the others."

Gollnick shook his head. "Cyrus, you didn't fail. Yes, Tiamat was freed, but she has since disappeared. You, Amber and Taryn made it out alive and you even brought Vincent with you. For only a week's training, I'd say you did a pretty good job."

Cyrus contemplated Gollnick's comments for a while without saying a word. He had to admit the old man had a point. Yet he knew one day they would have to face Tiamat again; but not yet. For now, he couldn't afford to dwell on the past.

"Think about this," Gollnick began. "What would you do if it were just you and Amber and she had been the one poisoned by the manticore?"

Cyrus' vision dropped to the floor. He had no idea how to deal with manticore poison or any other kind. There were many other dangers that could have happened, too. Perhaps learning other spells had merit... but that was not his strength, combat was.

"Look, you have a point." Cyrus raised his eyes to meet Gollnick. "And when we get back from dealing with Fenrir, I promise to focus more on my other studies. For now, we need to pack for Norway." Cyrus looked at the paper Gollnick was carrying and decided to change the subject. "So, what did you dig up on this Fenrir?"

"According to Norse history, after the Asgardians bound Fenrir using Gleipnir, he was chained to the Gioll rock and placed a mile deep in the Earth." Gollnick flipped through the pages he carried. "Unfortunately, we don't yet know where this Gioll rock was located. Veena is searching through ancient scrolls in the library of the muses on Mount Helicon, and Elisa is trying to get information from her contacts in New York City to see how and where the dark sorcerers found Fenrir."

"Whether we can find this Gioll rock or not," said Cyrus, "we leave in about two hours for Norway. That giant wolf isn't going to wait while we come up with a way to re-imprison him. We need you and Veena to come up with some ideas."

On the way back to his room, Cyrus stopped in the kitchen and found Meagan there packing rations for the trip: dried fruit, nuts, beef jerky and some canned soups.

"What's all this?" Cyrus spread his hands toward the food preparations. "Are you planning on staying in Norway for a month?"

She had already packed many small bags of food and was filling three backpacks with some of each kind. Along the one wall were three sleeping bags and portable tents.

"In order to search for Fenrir, we'll be going into some remote parts of Norway and possibly Sweden," she replied. "It all depends on how far Fenrir has traveled. We can't be sure there will be a place to stay, so I thought it best to be prepared. Most of the larger stuff we can shrink down and put in the packs to make it easier to carry, but I wanted to make sure we had enough food for an extended stay... just in case."

Cyrus shrugged then took a seat on a nearby stool. "Can you do me a favor? Amber is having nightmares about Tiamat and being in that blasted dark room in Babylon. I tried reassuring her that the dragon won't bother her anymore, but I don't think I was very convincing. Tiamat is still on the loose and until that fire breathing monstrosity is defeated permanently, I'm concerned about Amber's frame of mind." He left it unspoken that he put the blame on himself.

"I'll talk to her," replied Meagan with a gentle smile. "Are you sure you want to bring her along on this search for Fenrir? Maybe she just needs some time to herself to rest and sort things out."

"I'll be fine," said a voice from the kitchen entrance. Cyrus and Meagan turned quickly to find Amber standing there in her sweat pants and sweat shirt looking tired. "I just came to grab a bite to eat. I guess I didn't have much at supper time last evening and I was still hungry."

"Amber—" began Meagan.

"I know," interrupted Amber. "You're just concerned and I appreciate the thought, but I need to do this. I need to get back out there and continue to fight these things. Otherwise, Tiamat wins." As she said this, she straightened and took a deep breath.

Two hours later, Amber was in the library waiting as Meagan and Cyrus strolled in. Once inside, the doors quietly closed behind them. The scent of incense was strong in the air. At the far end of the room where Amber stood, was the hovering bronze-trimmed mirror. Next to it was a coat rack holding three trench coats.

Amber was in her jeans and a white long-sleeved shirt with black boots, her brown hair hanging just below her shoulders. She leaned against a nearby table staring at the mirror like she was expecting to see something other than her reflection.

Cyrus had the Johnny Cash – Man in Black look going today with two backpacks, one over each shoulder. The packs were full, but not overly stuffed. With the larger items inside shrunk down, they did not require much space.

Meagan's blue jeans and black boots complimented her burgundy long sleeve shirt. Her hair was pulled back in a ponytail revealing her slightly pointed ears. She wore the black baseball cap from the security guard uniform she'd acquired on their trip to Miami.

"Why didn't you meet us in the kitchen, sis?" questioned Cyrus. "We don't know how much food we'll be able to get along the way. You should really eat something."

"I can go get you something if you'd like lunch," offered Meagan placing her backpack on a table and starting to turn around.

"No, I ate in my room," replied Amber. "Let's get going."

"Are you sure you're up for this?" asked Cyrus one last time before their departure.

Amber just nodded and smiled at the two of them.

When they reached for their trench coats, the little knobby arms of the coat stand extended to each of them in turn. As they each took their coat, the knobby little arms retracted and the coat rack again became still.

Before they could depart, the library doors swung open and Gollnick came hobbling into the room using his cane, struggling to maintain control of the mess of papers and a book he was carrying under one arm.

"I'm glad I caught you before you left. Here, take these," said Gollnick as he offered the items to his niece. "The book contains information on Norse history from a sorcerer's point of view—not what mythology tells us. The paper is a map of the area where Fenrir was last spotted along with the locations of all known attacks." He then pulled a small mirror out of his pocket and handed it to Meagan. "Also take this. It's too small for transport, but it can still be used for communication. Remember when you get to Skåbu, Norway, my friend Sven will take you to the location at the edge of town where the third attack took place. He is not a sorcerer, but he does know about magic. His transportation and local information are invaluable, though he will be of little help in a magical battle."

Meagan accepted the items and placed them in her backpack. She then hugged her uncle. "Thanks Nick, we'll be safe. Don't worry."

"I always worry. That's part of the job description of being an uncle." Gollnick then turned to the others and smiled. "You two be safe as well."

"We'll keep in contact and let you know of our progress as often as we can," said Cyrus. He turned to the mirror and spoke the magical spell to transport them to Norway, *"Mirtor tolanga se-atum."* The image began to swirl like a whirlpool. Cyrus was the first to enter the portal followed by Amber and finally Meagan.

With the three of them now gone, the image returned to normal leaving Gollnick standing there looking at his own reflection. "Am I getting too old for this?" He paused a moment. "Nah," he said, shaking his head as he turned around and walked out of the room with the aid of his cane.

8 NORWAY

Amber, Cyrus and Meagan stepped out of a corner mirror with wrought iron framing into an old log cabin. The walls were made of roughhewn logs, and the plank floor was dusty and in need of a good cleaning, as was most of the cabin. An old stone fireplace along one wall had a warm fire burning. Hanging above the fire was a pot of boiling water. In one corner, was an unmade bed and along the opposite wall, a table with four chairs. Next to the fire sat two comfortable looking chairs with a large worn carpet between them.

Seated in one of the comfy chairs was an elderly man, perhaps in his late seventies. His face was lined with wrinkles and his pale blue eyes looked almost ghostly. His tattered brown cap and heavy brown jacket had obviously been patched more than once. He sat there watching the fire as the trio emerged, but showed no sign of surprise at their arrival.

"Care for something hot to drink before we head out?" he asked. The man walked to the fireplace and using a mitt, pulled out the pot of boiling water and proceed to carry it to the table where four cups were already waiting.

"You're Sven, right?" Cyrus set down his pack then followed the old man to the table. Amber and Meagan relinquished their packs to join them.

"Aye, Sven is me," replied the man with a bit of an accent. He poured the hot water into the four cups then set the pot down on the table. From a little jar of fine grey powder, he scooped a bit into each cup, stirred the mixture, then handed one to each of his guests before sipping from his own mug.

Amber's eyes lit up upon tasting the drink. "Hot chocolate!" The pleasant taste brought a smile that Cyrus had not seen in many days.

Meagan sniffed her cup before taking a sip. "No, it's herbal tea."

"Tastes more like coffee to me," said Cyrus, now confused. "How did you know what we each like to drink?"

Sven smiled over the rim of his cup as he took one more warming sip. "I may not have magical powers, but I know people who do. The proto-essence powder makes your drink smell and taste like whatever you most desire—a concoction Elisa first introduced me to many years ago. By the way, if you happen to see her anytime soon, please ask her to send more. It's hard to get in these parts." He then took another sip of his own drink and smiled as it warmed him from the inside.

Cyrus set down his cup. "So, what can you tell us about the attacks?"

"Homes were destroyed and the occupants are missing. No idea if they were targeted attacks or if the beastie was just hungry."

"Has anyone actually seen the creature?"

Sven looked out of the corner of his eye at Cyrus. "Yes, but he was drunk at the time so no one believes him. And it's a good thing. Norse myths are well known in these parts. If it got out that the legends were true, there'd be a panic."

"Are we sure it's Fenrir?"

"Your Muse friend seems to think so. And the evidence supports it." Sven chuckled to himself. "Even though the authorities are baffled by the attacks. They don't suspect a giant wolf." Sven took another sip of his drink. "Finish your coffee and I'll take you to the site of the nearest attack."

After the four of them had emptied their cups, they went outside. A cold wind blew and Cyrus felt the frigid temperatures down to his bones. Wrapped in their trench coats with hands tucked in their pockets to keep warm, Sven led them north through the little village.

At the edge of town, they spotted another cabin, but this one was in ruins. Huge logs were shattered and what remained of the roof was a pile of broken shingles. One wall appeared to have a huge bite taken out of the logs. From the sheer size, Cyrus estimated the creature must have been fifty to sixty feet tall.

Sven picked up a broken board from the wreckage. "A drunk neighbor claimed it was a huge mountain wolf, but the authorities say it was an explosion. They claim the homeowners must have been experimenting with explosives and blew themselves up. Only there's no sign of burn marks... and the building collapsed inward."

Cyrus kicked over a few boards and shingles as he searched the ground. "Any tracks leading to or away from the building?"

"Aye," replied Sven, "over this way." He then led the trio to a nearby wooded area. Cyrus looked up as he made his way into the woods. The tree branches higher up were broken and devoid of the snow that still clung to other non-broken branches.

Sven guided them to a set of immense paw prints on the ground. "Authorities say this was just a prank by some of the neighbors to make people think it was a big monster."

Meagan stooped to examine and measure the paw prints. "Have there been other reports?"

Amber just stood near the edge of the woods, looking up into the trees at the broken branches.

Cyrus watched as she trembled then lowered her head and closed her eyes. He could only imagine what was going through her mind. "You okay, sis? You look cold." He started to take off his trench coat, but she stopped him.

"No, it's not the cold." She looked at the tree tops once again. "Do you think it's as big as Tiamat?"

Cyrus immediately knew where her thoughts were. "Amber, this is a wolf. Admittedly, a large wolf, but a wolf nonetheless. You need to stop thinking about that blasted dragon. We need you in the here and now. Please."

"Tracks head south-southeast from here toward Oslo, the capital," said Sven as he pointed. "I've had no word yet, but there are other villages along that trek. Easy prey for an enormous hungry wolf."

Meagan approached to get a better view of the trail. "If this is Fenrir, any idea where he came from?"

Sven didn't respond right away, but then shook his head. "There have been five attacks that I've heard of. All of them coming in a somewhat southerly direction away from the mountains. If the pit where Fenrir was bound is up in the mountains, it will be almost impossible to find even in the best of weather. There's a lot of rough terrain up there." He pointed northwest above the treetops toward a mountain range many miles away.

"We should get started," suggested Meagan. "If this cold front is bringing any snow with it, it may cover whatever tracks are still visible. We need to find the pit and the Gioll rock where Fenrir was chained."

"I'm too old for a trek into those mountains," said Sven, "but if you can get word to me, I'll do what I can to help upon your return."

Meagan pulled a compact mirror from her pocket. "We can use this to communicate. I also have a telepathic link with Nick. If we can't get word to you by mirror, it'll come by way of Ravenicon castle."

They all thanked Sven before he returned home. Cyrus kept an eye on his sister as the three of them began following Fenrir's tracks back up into the mountains. For the most part, the trail was not difficult to follow. Not many creatures are large enough to break the top branches of trees or leave footprints three feet long.

Meagan had taken the lead while Cyrus hung back to walk with his sister. Amber kept pace with them, but Cyrus needed to get her mind off Tiamat. He knew if she continued to dwell on the dark chamber and the giant dragon, she might freeze up if they encountered danger.

"This cold front could slow us down, especially if it starts to snow. Any chance you can change the weather and warm things up a bit?" asked Cyrus cheerfully. He figured it would at least get her thinking about her powers rather than her problems.

"As an air elemental sorceress, I can affect the weather to a point, but not the temperature," she said with a degree of exasperation. "Besides you know what happened last time I tried to manipulate a weather front this large. I created a storm in Petra and you had to put me to sleep in order to stop it."

Cyrus realized in addition to her nightmares of Tiamat, she still didn't trust using her elemental powers. "Amber, you need to forget about Petra and Babylon," he said. "Your powers are developing faster than mine. You need to be confident in your abilities. Don't be afraid of them. You control them, not the other way around."

She picked up her pace to move ahead of him.

Cyrus could tell the conversation was over for the time being and it was best to leave her be for now. But sooner or later, Amber and her powers would be required and he needed her to be up to the challenge... both for her sake as well as his and Meagan's.

9 AN UNEXPECTED CALL

Less than half an hour after the departure of Amber, Cyrus and Meagan, Gollnick had returned to the library and pulled a large overstuffed chair in front of the mirror. Stacks of books towered over him as he sank in the comfortable seat. After a brief moment to relax, his mind turned to the reason for his return to the library. They needed information and it was going to be up to him to find it.

He piled a few books on a table next to the chair. A pen and tablet were placed there along with a glass of water. Wanting to be near the mirror in case anyone needed him, he adjusted his seat for a long stay. It had taken the ancient Norse gods years to find a way to imprison Fenrir; he had only days.

"Mirtor a mirtor tong-la Elisa." Gollnick would start with Elisa and see if she had any new information for him. The mirror became all fuzzy then a picture emerged in the center. It was dark and he couldn't hear a thing. "Elisa? Hello? Are you there?"

A moment later the dark form in the center was replaced by a bright light, followed by Elisa's face. Gollnick was glad to see her again. Even though she was his ex-wife they still maintained a friendly relationship.

"Nick, why didn't you just contact me telepathically?" she inquired with a furrowed brow.

"Maybe I wanted to see your beautiful face." Gollnick smiled. Normally a face to face communication was an indication of a level of urgency. In this case it couldn't have been more true as he thought about the trouble in Norway.

"Now I'm really concerned. What's the emergency?" Elisa crossed her arms as she tilted her head to one side.

He recognized the body language. It was what she always did when she expected to hear bad news. Gollnick let out a quiet sigh.

"The dark sorcerers. They've released Fenrir, the giant wolf from Norse mythology."

Elisa's head straightened as her jaw slowly dropped and her posture began to slump.

Gollnick continued, "He's randomly attacking villages in Norway. Amber, Cyrus and Meagan have gone there to see if they can find out how he escaped and if there's any possibility to re-imprison him."

"Not quite the bad news I was expecting, but it's bad enough."

Gollnick now realized what news she had anticipated. It occurred to him they'd had no communication from Arizona. "I haven't heard from Taryn or Vincent yet. I tried contacting them earlier, but they were busy. I'll check in with them next. In any case, I may need to recall Vincent to examine the Tablets of Destiny to see if they contain any information regarding Fenrir."

"I'm concerned, Nick. It's been many years since the dark sorcerers even attempted to open one prison... and now in the span of less than a week they've found three? Something's not right. They must be getting information from somewhere."

Gollnick felt the concern, too. This couldn't be a coincidence. "Have you been able to find out any more about what the dark sorcerers are up to?" He didn't like being in the dark, yet that was exactly how he was feeling right now.

"No. All of my New York City contacts have gone underground. No one is talking. It's like someone placed a stranglehold on the entire city."

"Keep trying to see what you can find out, and especially if they know about any other prisons. We need to figure out how to stop them." Gollnick glanced at his blank notepad. "And it would also be nice to know where they're getting their information."

"I'll stay in touch." Elisa waved her hand across her mirror and it went dark, the connection gone.

And be careful, Gollnick mentally finished. He was about to contact Vincent next when the image in the mirror went fuzzy followed by Malcolm's face staring directly at him.

"Gollnick," Malcolm said with a surprised smile, "I hadn't expected you to be waiting by the mirror like this. I take it you've heard about Fenrir and sent one of your little teams off in search of him."

The grin on Malcolm's face almost made Gollnick sick. "What do you want? Calling to gloat?" he said with disgust.

Malcolm pursed his lips. "It seems I have a little problem of my own and I'm in need of your assistance."

Gollnick's eyes opened wide. He couldn't believe his ears. Malcolm, the leader of the dark sorcerers was asking him for help?

"You see, there are these two upstart young sorcerers here in New York who seem to think they can take over the city and destroy me." Malcolm almost chuckled at the thought.

"Best news I've heard all day." Gollnick grinned widely, though he couldn't help wonder why Malcolm was telling him this. "So, what's the catch?"

Malcolm's smile disappeared. "Actually, I thought you might be inclined to help me out."

Gollnick's eyes widened. "Why would I do something crazy like that?"

"Well you see, each of these two sorcerers have a considerable number of followers," started Malcolm. "Emboldened by the fact I failed to release Cerberus from the underworld, thanks to your apprentices, they are gaining support. Enough to actually challenge me. If this turns into a sorcerer civil war, who knows how many innocent people might be caught in the crossfire?"

Gollnick's face drained of emotion at the thought. He had experienced a sorcerer's duel in Philadelphia a little over a week ago, and that was only a single battle between two sorcerers. Others had joined in to make it look like a severe storm, but in this case it could be hundreds battling in the Big Apple with no one trying to cover it up.

"What exactly do you think I can do to stop this? I don't have hundreds of sorcerers at my disposal like you." Gollnick didn't really want to hear the answer. Malcolm was going to somehow manipulate the situation and force him to get involved.

"If for some reason the Circle chooses to take out these two upstarts, the war will fade before it even begins. Of course, everyone's attention would be on you then, but at least no innocent people would get hurt."

"Instead, everyone would rally behind you and solidify your position as leader of all dark sorcerers in New York."

Malcolm's face brightened. "Perhaps, but wouldn't it be better to deal with just me rather than multiple factions of dark sorcerers? It would make Elisa's spying so much easier."

As expected, Malcolm had manipulated the situation like the snake he was. A full-scale sorcerer's war could devastate the city. As Gollnick had discovered the week before, the rules were changing—dark sorcerers were no longer concerned about hiding their presence. Regular people were not ready to accept magic still existed in the world... especially when many leaders of business and industry were among those who possessed such magical powers. It could devastate economies and political relations the world over.

"Who are these troublemakers? And how do I find them?" asked Gollnick reluctantly.

"Excellent, then you'll help me?" Malcolm's grin widened.

"I didn't say that," replied Gollnick. "I want to know who they are before I make any kind of move. I'm not going to do your dirty work only to find out I would've been better off supporting them instead."

"I see." Malcolm's expression darkened as he pursed his lips. He let out a sigh. "Their names are Francois LeRain and Duestoff Von Woonst."

Gollnick sat up a little straighter in his chair. "Von Woonst?"

"Yes, Frederick's younger brother. Duestoff is located in the Bronx and Francois is somewhere in Manhattan. I'm sure Elisa will be all too happy to feed you whatever information you feel you need to deal with these wannabes. I—"

"I'll be in touch," Gollnick interrupted, then waved his hand over the mirror to end the conversation.

Gollnick sat back in his chair. He knew Malcolm was up to something else, something he wasn't saying. He would have to proceed with caution. This was very likely a trap, but if Malcolm was telling the truth, then it was his responsibility to do something to protect the innocent.

10 LOCAL TROUBLES

Inside the Desert Windstorm restaurant, Qaletaqa had gathered spare clothing from others among their group and put together a decent looking outfit large enough for Radimir. The white t-shirt fit very snug under a denim vest. A cowboy hat protected his bald head from the hot sun.

Radimir sat at a round table with Taryn, Vincent, Sheelin, Qaletaqa and Alex, devouring food and drink like he hadn't eaten in years. Tensions had calmed slightly, but no one was ready to embrace the others in friendship quite yet... and no one knew what to make of Radimir. Was he a friend, a foe, or something else?

"How is it ye were trapped in the shape of a cat?"

Taryn didn't know much about Native American culture, but she did know that the spirits would occasionally take animal form, though she was fairly certain he was not a spirit.

"Sorcerer named Malcolm captured me in Russia," replied Radimir in his thick Russian accent. "He said I do as he say or else. I refuse. I escape by becoming cat, but he cast spell prevent me from changing back. I stuck in cat shape." The broken English along with his accent made him difficult to understand, but everyone seemed to get the idea of his story.

"How did ye get into Ravenicon in Baltimore?" questioned Taryn. "The castle is protected by many powerful spells. You couldn't have just walked in the front door." This represented a major security breach.

"I wander around clothing store at Inner Harbor. One day I notice Gollnick exit mirror," said Radimir thickly. "I follow him to hospital where he find Max. I was very fast, very quiet. After battle, they escape through mirror in bathroom. I follow back to castle. They more concerned about Max and never notice me. I stay hidden in books until it safe to explore. I hoped someone realize I was trapped in cat form and help, but instead they thought I was bad sorcerer. Not until I help with problems around castle that Taryn start trusting me. That reason I stow away in you backpack when you come here for Max." He gave Taryn a timid smile.

Just realizing all the implications, Taryn recoiled. "Ye curled up on my chest out in the desert earlier today," she said in an accusatory tone.

"Sorry." Radimir looked wide eyed at Taryn. Even with his bulky frame, he shrunk into his chair. "Seemed good at time, but now back to human form, maybe not best idea I had."

Taryn said nothing more. She didn't know what to do with Radimir quite yet and they still had the issue of Max and the Rogue Hunters to deal with. She could only handle one crisis at a time and right now stabilizing their relationship with Qaletaqa was the more pressing issue.

"We'll figure this out later." She turned her attention to the leader of the Rogue Hunters. "Qaletaqa, ye said there were other matters demandin' your attention. Our offer to help still stands. What kind of problem are ye havin'?"

Qaletaqa didn't answer immediately. He looked from Radimir to Vincent and finally to Taryn. She could see he was still unsure if they were trustworthy.

"There is an old Algonquian legend of a creature who stalks my people," he began. "My son and a few others have seen it with their own eyes, but it is a powerful and dangerous creature. The Wendigo is an emaciated beast that feeds on human flesh. It is too strong to fight hand-to-hand, and being bitten by a Wendigo will cause its victim to become a Wendigo as well. I fear only magic can capture or destroy such a creature."

"Can it even be destroyed?" questioned Taryn.

"I know what you are thinking, young one," replied Qaletaqa. "While the creatures from the Nightmare Realm cannot be eradicated while in our world, creatures brought forth by this world such as a Wendigo *can* be. The monsters you and the dark sorcerers seek can only be imprisoned until the day when a way is discovered to send them back to their place of origin."

"How is that possible?" asked Vincent now speaking up for the first time in a while.

"According to one of your ancient legends," replied Qaletaqa, "there are three immortals in this world, and only they know how to open the portal through which these monsters came. Only they can send them back."

"And who are these three immortals?" questioned Vincent.

Taryn looked to Max, hoping the discussion might jog his memory. The Circle was under the belief that he was really Chronos of Greek mythology, and one of the three immortals, but now was not the time or place to discuss such things.

"I do not know. I may be a Shaman of a Navajo tribe, but I study other legends in case I must deal with such creatures to protect my people," replied Qaletaqa. "What I have told you was told to me by one of the elf people living in the woods of Yellowstone National Park."

"I see," said Taryn. "So, how can we help against this Wendigo?" Even though the information Qaletaqa had just provided confirmed what they already knew, it could still be invaluable in the coming battles with the dark sorcerers. Still, she hadn't forgotten why they had come—to retrieve Max. For now that meant helping the Rogue Hunters deal with this Wendigo. Hopefully it would also provide the opportunity for them to talk with Max and get him to return with them to Baltimore.

"We could use your assistance in capturing this creature," begged Qaletaqa. "I do not wish to kill any living being unless absolutely necessary, but I fear in this case we may have few options as there is no way to undo the curse of the Wendigo."

"Hello? Anyone there?" came a voice from Taryn's backpack once again. She and Vincent exchanged an unhappy look as she pulled out the tiny mirror. Vincent took it and exited the restaurant to have a private conversation.

* * *

"Nick, this is not really a good time," said Vincent impatiently. "We've found Max, but there's a complication. He doesn't remember any of us. He joined a motorcycle gang called the Rogue Hunters. Oh, and we also seem to have a stowaway—turns out your black cat is a shape-shifter named Radimir Rasputin."

Gollnick looked back with a dull stare, his mouth hanging open. "Well, that would explain what I found in the New Circle room," he said. "I checked on the crystal to make sure everyone was alright, but to my surprise, there are new symbols there now. Seems we've found *two* new members for the Circle, somewhere."

"What are their signs?" inquired Vincent. They had met many young people in the past hour, but only two who were sorcerers.

"Sagittarius and Virgo," replied Gollnick happily. "The other three have already left for Norway, but I doubt they've met anyone yet. Which means the new members of the Circle would have to be in Arizona. Have you met anyone?"

"I know of two possibilities—your black cat and the daughter of the leader of the Rogue Hunters. I'll see what I can find out," he replied, still in a hurry to get back to the discussion with Qaletaqa and Taryn.

"In addition," continued Gollnick to Vincent's dismay, "we have a couple of situations here ourselves. Seems while we were trying to prevent the release of Cerberus and Tiamat, another sorcerer succeeded in freeing Fenrir, the wolf of Norse mythology. But that's not the best part; Malcolm called. He's being overrun by two competing dark sorcerers and wants our help. I need you to return to Baltimore as soon as possible."

"What?" replied Vincent in utter shock. "Why would we help that monster? I say let them have him." The mere thought of helping the man who had manipulated his every move up until a few days ago when the control amulet was destroyed in Babylon, just turned Vincent's stomach.

"It's complicated," Gollnick replied. "I know you don't like this idea, but I'm going to need your help. I also need you to check the Tablets of Destiny to see if there is anything about re-imprisoning Fenrir. Can Taryn handle things on her own for a bit?"

Vincent pursed his lips and exhaled. "She seems to be up to the task more than I am. Let me discuss this with her and I'll be back in touch."

"Please do what you can to expedite things. I don't know how much time we have."

Vincent made no further comment and just waved his hand over the mirror to sever the connection. He paced back and forth in front of the restaurant as he considered Gollnick's request. Why should he help Malcolm? He knew the scoundrel was up to something and he was sure Gollnick could sense the same thing. It was most likely a trap, but why now?

11   THE COLD NORTH

After a good night's sleep at a local motel, Taryn met Vincent and Radimir at the Desert Windstorm restaurant for breakfast. They were still wary about the Russian, but didn't really know what else to do with him for the moment. Taryn had proven resourceful and able to handle herself in a battle, and now with Radimir's added strength and powers, she almost pitied the Wendigo. Almost.

Vincent informed her privately about the two new signs in the crystal at Ravenicon—the Virgo and the Sagittarius—and said he needed to return to Baltimore briefly. After breakfast, he opened a portal in the bathroom mirror, but left Taryn the keys to the Jeep.

About an hour later, Taryn and Radimir were joined by Qaletaqa, Sheelin, Alex Desert Walker and five other members of the Rogue Hunters, ready to begin their search for the Wendigo. The others brought along backpacks of camping gear.

Qaletaqa turned to Taryn. "Our search for the creature begins near the last known point of attack. We must travel to where the Wendigo is terrorizing our Algonquian brothers and sisters. They have a mirror prepared for us and are awaiting our arrival."

"I thought the Wendigo was around here." The change in location without warning bothered Taryn. Vincent had just left and now he would have no idea where to meet them. She did have Radimir with her, but she wasn't even sure she could trust him. She would have to use the little mirror in her pack to contact Vincent later.

"No," replied Qaletaqa. "A friend of mine was killed by the creature in Canada, near Manitoba. That is where we are headed. I trust you still plan to accompany us on this quest?"

"Yes, but it would've been nice to know about the location change."

"You never asked."

Taryn knew Qaletaqa had wanted to keep Alex away from the dark sorcerers as well as the Circle, but this did little to improve her trust in the Rogue Hunters' leader.

They entered the restroom to use the mirror for their trek. Even Alex, who stood wide eyed near the entrance, seemed surprised by the unexpected deviation. As Qaletaqa cast the transportation spell, Alex stepped aside to speak with Taryn. "Sorry about the change in plans. I didn't realize we were going to Canada either. I guess you must be a little apprehensive... being a fire elemental sorceress."

Her eyes widened beneath a raised brow. "I never said I was a fire elemental sorceress." Taryn was both pleased and surprised that Max... or Alex... remembered her natural abilities.

"Sorry, my mistake." Alex's brow furrowed as he turned away.

"Don't apologize." Taryn placed a hand on his arm, pleased by his recollection. "Ye're correct. It's just that I haven't told anyone yet. Are ye rememberin' somethin'?" She was hopeful, but didn't want to alienate him. He was still a member of the Rogue Hunters and until he willingly decided to join her, she had to be careful.

Before he could answer, the spell was finished and everyone started passing through the mirror. Qaletaqa ushered Alex to join the others. Before Taryn could follow, he pulled her aside. "I know you have offered, and I do appreciate any help we can get at the moment, but be aware that I will protect my own. And that includes Alex. There is great power in him and I will protect that power from any who would seek to abuse it."

"I mean him no harm. He's my friend. I only wish to help him remember that. He saved my life once, though I've never admitted it to anyone. I owe him and I intend to repay that debt." She couldn't help but think back to the attack on Vincent's office in Miami when Max had knocked her out with a blast of water from two huge aquariums. The office was on fire, but Max refused to leave her unconscious in a burning room. She may be a fire elemental, but while unconscious, she could have burned to death.

Qaletaqa straightened his posture. "I can tell by your determination you mean what you say, and you have every intention of repaying your debt. That is something I can understand and respect. The coming days will prove your intentions." Qaletaqa then stepped aside, allowing Taryn to pass through the mirror. He followed close behind.

When they arrived in Canada, Taryn stepped out into a small campsite. Others were already gathered around a fire, warming themselves from the long winter chill. Snow on the ground indicated spring had not yet arrived in this part of the world. There were tents pitched in a circle around the fire where at least twenty members of other groups stood talking and telling stories. It seemed more like a reunion—except for the camouflage jackets and hunting rifles.

Taryn stayed near the edge of camp, keeping to herself, trying her best not to reveal her distress in dealing with the cold.

Alex too stayed near the edge of the firelight and made little attempt at getting to know anyone.

When he caught her stare, she didn't turn away. Their eyes locked for a moment before he made a motion to approach her. Taryn's hopes spiked until Qaletaqa intervened, and taking Alex by the arm, guided him toward the fire and the other hunters. Alex glanced back at Taryn as if to say sorry for abandoning her.

Taryn stood there in the frigid cold, until Sheelin walked up beside her, offering a warm hooded coat and gloves. "Sorry you weren't better prepared for this climate. My father hadn't planned on additional sorcerers joining us when he made the plans to come here."

"Thanks," replied Taryn. Looking around she now realized that someone was missing. "Have ye seen Radimir?"

"Oh, he was one of the first through. I don't think the cold is bothering him too much. He's still wearing the same clothes we gave him yesterday." Pointing over toward the fire, they could see Radimir enjoying himself. "It seems your friend has already found the food. Why don't we join him?"

Taryn and Sheelin made their way over and sat down beside Radimir who offered them a spit of beef. Sheelin took out a knife and cut a piece for each of them.

Taryn looked from the meat to her new Russian friend. "So, Radimir, ye never did get a chance to tell us how ye ended up stuck as a cat wanderin' around Baltimore."

Radimir finished chewing down a chuck of beef and swallowed before responding. "In Baltimore I hunt man who took sister." His English had not improved.

"Who took your sister?" Sheelin chimed in.

"Man with no hair, beard and..." then he made an up and down motion with open hands along his side as he was trying to think of the word, "...suit."

"Do ye know his name?" asked Taryn hopefully.

"Malcolm."

Taryn and Sheelin exchanged a glance. Taryn regarded the Russian. "It seems our African adversary strikes again."

"So what happened?" questioned Sheelin.

"Find man near Falls Tip."

"I think you mean Fells Point," corrected Taryn.

"Yes, there. He find old things. I attack. He men stop me. He laugh. I change cat get away. He cast spell. I run fast. Try change back, not work. I stuck. I wander many days. Find Gollnick near hospital. I follow."

Though his story was choppy and difficult to understand, they were at least grateful it was short.

Taryn placed a hand on his shoulder. "He still has yer sister?"

Radimir just nodded.

"Don't worry, we'll find a way to get her back."

After some thought, Taryn pondered Malcolm's actions. "I know there are some antique stores near Fells Point, but what was Malcolm lookin' for?" Taryn knew the area. There were many stores, but none that dealt with magic—at least none she knew. She could not understand why he would have been in that part of town.

The topic had hit a pause. She decided to change the subject. "So, Sheelin. What's yer story? These are yer relatives, aren't they? Or do ye just enjoy our company that much?" Taryn couldn't help but wonder if Qaletaqa had sent her to spy and gather information.

"These people are friends of my father, not relatives. Besides my brother, father, Alex and you two, I don't know anyone else either. This was Qaletaqa's idea to hunt the Wendigo. He lost a friend up here about a week ago and we just lost two more members to that Malcolm you spoke of. He's looking for vengeance and I'm afraid we won't be able to stop him until he finds it."

Taryn looked around then sighed. "I need to ask each of ye a question, but it might be better if Qaletaqa didn't know."

"I don't keep secrets from my father," replied Sheelin.

Taryn pursed her lips then continued, "You might want to keep this one."

Sheelin and Radimir both nodded.

"Ye're familiar with the Zodiac Crystal in the chamber of the New Circle?" Taryn wanted to see if she could trust these two.

They each nodded in acknowledgment. As sorcerers, the stories and legends of the Circle, though its location changed every few centuries, should be familiar.

"Two new symbols appeared in the crystal yesterday. I need to ask each of ye what yer zodiac sign is."

"Sagittarius," replied Radimir without hesitation then bit off another piece of meat.

Sheelin was not so quick to respond. "I know the crystal uses a form of clairvoyance to predict the future, but my father would be furious if he found out I had been offered a place in the New Circle." She hesitated a moment longer before responding. "Beaver."

"Beaver? Is that some Native American zodiac symbol?"

After another moment's hesitation Sheelin said, "Virgo." She looked sideways at Taryn like she was afraid to hear the response.

Taryn could see her reluctance, but nodded confirmation to both of them.

Sheelin smiled, but then looked over her shoulder to see her father on the other side of camp. "He won't be happy to hear this news, but I'm tired of sitting on the sidelines while the battle between good and evil rages on. I want to help people. I know of the dangers in this world. I've wanted to join the fight, but my father keeps holding us back. I need some time to think about this. Please don't say anything to him yet."

Taryn could see Sheelin's inner struggle. However, now was not the time to force a decision.

"We know Alex is a Scorpio... and you are?" Sheelin asked.

"Ares," Taryn replied.

"God of war. You seem good warrior," commented Radimir.

"Are there other members of the Circle?" Sheelin asked.

"We also have our Taurus, Leo and Aquarius."

"Where are the other—" Sheelin wanted to continue her questions when Qaletaqa approached.

"You two should grab a bite before Radimir eats everything. We have a long day ahead of us." Qaletaqa looked at each of them. "The monster normally hunts after dark. We plan to split into groups of three to track this creature. Perhaps you three would care to work together."

Taryn could tell this was Qaletaqa's way of keeping her away from Alex, at least for now. She still had her suspicions Sheelin was instructed to keep an eye on her. Perhaps if she could make the Native American sorceress see that Max was needed in the Circle, then maybe Sheelin could help get Max to remember the past week and the battles fought.

While the others were eating, Taryn decided to make one last attempt at contacting Alex before departing for the hunt. She walked through camp, keeping an eye out for both him and Qaletaqa. She spotted Qaletaqa talking with some other members of the group discussing directions. Alex was standing by a tent staring off into the cold wilderness that surrounded them. Evening approached and the sun was beginning to set.

"Penny for yer thoughts?" Taryn was curious if the revelation of her powers earlier had sparked a memory.

"I was just thinking about what this creature looks like," replied Alex as he looked over his shoulder at her. "Qaletaqa has tried describing it, but I want to see it for myself."

Realizing she had little idea of the creature's appearance either, she felt it was at least a safe topic of conversation. "So what is it supposed to look like?"

"From what I've been told, it's around eight feet tall, skinny, almost emaciated, but with incredible strength. It has long white hair and is covered in a thin white fur, long sharp teeth and sharp claws. And it's very fast. It also prefers the cold which is why it's in Canada."

There was a long silence between the two of them. Alex appeared deep in thought as he stared off into the distance.

"Who all is in the Circle?"

Taryn's eyes popped open at the change in subject. "Well, there's me, Cyrus, Meagan, and Amber." She intentionally ended with Amber, hoping that hearing her name might ring a bell. They'd had a strong interest in one another—even to the point that Amber insisted on casting the telepathic link spell. It hadn't worked, but the fact that they wanted to try meant they at least had some kind of interest in one another. "As I understood from Meagan, ye were plannin' on askin' Amber for a date."

"A what?"

"Never mind." Taryn shook her head. "Do ye remember Amber?"

Before he could answer, she spotted Qaletaqa advancing in their direction. "Looks like our time is up." Taryn turned and slowly meandered away. She knew Qaletaqa's approach was her cue to leave, but she didn't want him to think she was afraid of him, just respectful of his presence. There would be other opportunities to talk with Alex. If she could convince Sheelin to help then maybe she would have a chance with both of them.

* * *

Qaletaqa placed a hand on Alex's shoulder as the young man stared at the stars once more. "Alex, I need you to be careful in dealing with Taryn. Her intensions appear honorable, but she is holding something back. We need to be cautious."

Alex looked over his shoulder at the old shaman. "Who am I, really?"

Qaletaqa straightened his posture and looked to the sky. "You are Alex Desert Walker. And you are exactly where you belong. I know you've lost your memory and that is scary, but Taryn is trying to fill it with information she wants you to believe. Trust me, Alex, you are one of us."

Alex looked into Qaletaqa's eyes. He saw a proud man with a strong resolve, but couldn't help wonder who was telling the truth. His memories started two days ago wandering the desert. It was Qaletaqa who took him in and gave him clothes and a place to stay. He claimed to be his adopted father. But the words of the fiery Irish girl felt right.

Alex knew he belonged somewhere, but he couldn't remember where. While the name 'Alex' didn't feel right, the name 'Max' didn't have a familiar ring either. Something was missing, but he didn't know what.

With a gentle slap on the back, Qaletaqa steered Alex back toward the camp. "Come. You'll be joining my group in the hunt. It's going to be a cold night."

12   DARK PLANS

The cavern where his master resided gave Malcolm the creeps whenever he had to go down there to speak with the dark creature. As he entered the sweltering hot chamber once again, his sense of dread drained his strength. He didn't know where this monster had originated, but he knew what power it possessed. And he knew he wouldn't stand a chance in a battle against it. For now at least, he was content to do as his master commanded even if it meant not understanding the reason for the commands.

He knelt before the dais of the fiery throne. "It is done. As you have commanded, I contacted Gollnick and requested his help in fighting off the subversive sorcerers." Malcolm spoke through gritted teeth and a bad taste in his mouth. "I don't understand why I need Gollnick's help. I can dispose of this minor inconvenience myself. I've been doing it for years."

"Fortunately, my plans do not require your understanding, just that you follow instructions," said the deep booming voice from within the fire surrounding the ancient throne.

Malcolm's eyes drifted to the floor. "He is to contact me shortly with his answer." There was a quiver to his voice. "What happens if he decides not to help?"

"If he doesn't, then you are no longer of any use to me," the voice growled louder. "And I would think you know what that means."

"Y-y-yes, my lord," stammered Malcolm. He knew all too well what uselessness meant to his master. It meant his expected life span would suddenly become drastically shorter.

"Send one of your best sorcerers with a team of automatons to Norway," commanded the voice as the anger leveled off. "It seems a group from the New Circle have gone there to recapture Fenrir. I have need of the wolf. Whomever you send must be the best. If they fail, they had better die in the process. For if they don't, I will destroy that sorcerer myself."

"Why not send the one who released Fenrir in the first place?" Malcolm asked, puzzled. "I would think the wolf would owe that sorcerer a debt of gratitude."

"Gratitude toward a human?" The dark creature's voice grew louder with each word. "For what, freeing him from a mortal prison? Denying him the right to attack and destroy as he chose? Fenrir owes no one gratitude, least of all the corpse who freed him." The fiery creature paused a moment then spoke in a softer voice. "Oh, did I forget to mention? The sorcerer who freed Fenrir was the wolf's first meal in centuries."

"I have the perfect person in mind," Malcolm sneered. "Her name is Alexis Malkin and she is an enchantress. She will have them begging to die at her hand." He had dealt with her once before and had almost been seduced himself, if not for an unexpected explosion in the dungeons of his fortress.

"Since you no longer control Vincent, what automatons do you plan on sending with her to Scandinavia?" questioned the dark voice.

Malcolm had left the amulet with Frederick Von Woonst who died at the hands of Tiamat. Now with it lost, they no longer had control over the water automatons.

"My people have spent the last twenty-four hours destroying Vincent's water automatons. They could no longer be trusted." Malcolm was a little disgusted by the situation and shifted his lower jaw from side to side as if trying to get rid of a bad taste in his mouth. "I will be sending my two new earth automatons with her. They take more time to make than Vincent's water automatons, but they're also harder to destroy."

"For your sake, I hope you are correct," said the mysterious creature within the flames. "One among the group from the New Circle is an earth elemental. If your powers are not stronger than hers, she may be able to take control of your automatons and use them against this Alexis of yours."

"I guarantee, she will not be able to control them." Malcolm spoke with a great degree of certainty. "I will provide Alexis with a control bracelet—only the wearer may control them. She will have no excuse for failure. I promise."

"Take care what you promise. For now her failure will become yours."

The dark figure went silent and the flames around his throne rose with a roar, driving Malcolm back from the dais. He crashed to the floor on his backside with a surprised expression, but quickly got to his feet and hurried out of the chamber.

An hour later, Malcolm arrived at his private office in his fortress. The room was spacious and had a high vaulted ceiling. It looked more like an art studio with dark walls and lights shining down in certain areas to define the spaces. Three of the walls displayed expensive paintings with a single light shining on each. Opposite the impressive double doors, the entire wall was covered in video monitors. Some listed stock exchange rates, others displayed business and government news, still others showed sports programs. The largest was the center screen which currently showed a map of the city of New York indicating the areas of his control and those controlled by the subversive sorcerers attempting to challenge his authority.

Alexis Malkin was already there waiting for him. She was relaxing in a large overstuffed leather recliner near the center of the room watching the video monitors. She didn't bother to stand as Malcolm entered the room. Her low cut, tight fitting black pants suit with loosely knotted tie made her look like a runway model with perfectly styled short black hair and a copper tan giving her a radiant glow.

"I take it I'm here for a reason?" she inquired, almost as if she couldn't care less. Then her eyes thinned and she gave a crooked smile. "Or did you just miss me?"

Now she was just teasing him. Malcolm knew she would try again to seduce him if she had the opportunity. She desired power just like he did, but the power she wanted came from controlling individuals... not cities or nations or even the world. Her desire was to control the people who controlled the world.

"How are you with Norse mythology?" Malcolm knew she preferred the high fashion of New York and history wasn't her best subject, but she was smart enough to keep up to date on current events. At least magical current events.

"Asgardians, Yggdrasil, Thor, Odin, Loki, what exactly do I need to know?" Alexis rattled off the common names, but seemed more preoccupied with her fingernails.

"Have you ever heard of Fenrir?" Malcolm continued to walk past the sitting area where she reclined and moved to a control desk in front of the wall of monitors.

"Is he an underwear model?"

Malcolm knew she would never admit her ignorance. She detested signs of weakness.

"Fenrir is a giant wolf," corrected Malcolm. "I took the liberty of writing up some useful notes about the creature, its location and its former prison." He almost seemed pleased with himself for knowing something Alexis did not. "You will depart immediately for Norway. Three members of the New Circle are there now trying to track down and re-imprison Fenrir. You will stop them or die trying, there are no other options."

"And if I choose to turn down this little trip of yours?" Alexis continued to buff and re-examine her nails with little interest in Malcolm's command. "New York is where I need to be at the moment. Had you suggested a place like Paris, I might have considered it, but not Norway."

"As I said, you will stop them or die trying, there are no... other... options." Malcolm emphasized his last three words to make it perfectly clear she was going whether she wanted to or not.

Alexis stood and slowly walked over to Malcolm. Running a hand over his bald head and down his back, she whispered into his ear, "Wouldn't you rather have me here with you? We could— "

"Save your breath." Malcolm sprung up and grabbed her arm. On his other hand he flashed her the ring he had on his index finger. "This ring is meant to protect its wearer from your spells of enchantment. You are going on this mission and you will succeed or you will die. Do I make myself perfectly clear?" He then picked up the notes he had prepared for her and shoved them in her direction.

"Crystal," said Alexis with a snarl on her otherwise straight face. She snatched the notes from his hand and turned to leave.

He smiled with the knowledge his ring had protected him from her powers. "One other thing," Malcolm called as she started to walk away. "Stop by the dungeon level and pick up the two earth automatons and their control bracelet, just in case you need some muscle in dealing with these three young sorcerers."

She didn't respond or even turn around to acknowledge his comments. She continued on her way to the doors, glancing at the notes. "Why couldn't this Fenrir be imprisoned somewhere like the Caribbean or the Bahamas?"

13 This Is A Bad Idea

Arriving in the library of Ravenicon castle, Vincent was met by his old friend Gollnick who was still using a cane to get around. The wound from the demon attack at the warehouse in New York City wasn't healing as well as he had hoped, but Gollnick was determined not to let that slow him down. He had a job to do and it was to mentor the New Circle, but right now it was a more distasteful job he had to perform. His chief pain in the neck and leader of the dark sorcerers was asking for his help.

"Nick, I'm telling you, this is a trap," Vincent said, displeased with the situation. "I say let them have him. Even if we end up with ten new dark sorcerer lords in New York, it will still be better than Malcolm."

"And what about all the innocent bystanders who will be caught in the crossfire? The dark sorcerers are not playing by the same rules anymore. They're openly displaying their magic in broad daylight."

"Okay, I'll admit I don't want to see anyone get hurt, but this is a trap! As soon as we get there and start trying to stop this civil war, they'll turn on us and we'll be outnumbered."

"I know, which is why we're not going up there alone. I'm calling in every favor I can think of. If we go to New York City, I plan on taking an army with me."

Marching into New York with their own army appealed to Vincent. Wiping out all the dark sorcerers at once would make the world a better place. They wouldn't need to worry about protecting the remaining prisons around the world continuing to entomb the great monsters of myth. Unfortunately, he knew it wouldn't solve anything. Other dark sorcerers would rise up to take their place. With a quick shake of his head, he brushed the sneer from his face and snapped back to reality.

"Wait a minute, you want to take another army? I know the place is big, but how many armies do you think that city can hold? The more sorcerers, the greater the risk to the innocents."

"What do you suggest?" Gollnick responded, clearly frustrated.

Vincent raised a question. "What do we know about these sorcerers who are attacking Malcolm? Would they be willing to talk to us? Maybe we can reach an agreement with one or more of them."

With a sigh, Gollnick seemed to calm down to consider Vincent's suggestion. If they could talk their way out of a civil war then fewer people would be at risk. Perhaps some research into who was attacking Malcolm was worthwhile, but time was against them.

"Vincent, none of this is making sense. You worked for the dark sorcerers for a time, albeit against your will," Gollnick challenged. "You must have some idea why they're doing all of this. The civil war, releasing the monsters of myth, what are they trying to accomplish?"

Vincent paused to gather his thoughts. "The general idea is to remake the world as they see fit. They're not just interested in controlling the countries of the world, they want to wipe everything out, civilization as we know it. Start the world over with maybe a hundred thousand people across the entire planet, less than one percent of the world's current population. Each and every one of the survivors would be sorcerers. Magic would once again rule the world. Of course with the dark sorcerers in charge of everything, the monsters of myth would be their pets... slaves to control the remaining masses. They'd reset everything back to the dark ages. It's their version of population control."

"Not the most entertaining thought," replied Gollnick. "Okay, Malcolm said the opposing forces were Deustoff Von Woonst and Francois LeRain. Let's see what we can find out about these dark sorcerers, but we can't spend too much time doing it. The longer we wait, the more people might get hurt. Agreed?"

Vincent smiled as he took Gollnick's hand and nodded approval.

"We'll do this together. I may no longer work for Malcolm, but I still have contacts in both New York and Miami who will talk with me. Maybe we can find an alternative to this war."

"I've already alerted Elisa and Hank. Hank won't be much help in a battle until his leg heals completely, but he's already able to walk without crutches. Apparently magical healing works better on a broken leg than one speared by a demon like mine. Regardless, he may be able to round up some other sorcerers in Cairo who might be willing to help if it comes to a fight."

Vincent had another thought. "I'll also contact the Muses and see what they can tell us about the situation in New York."

"Fine, but first I need you to do something else. Right now I need you to look through the Tablets of Destiny. We need to find a way to re-imprison Fenrir. You're the only one I know who can read the cuneiform. Cyrus and the others are going to need ideas on how to stop that monster."

14 GIOLL

After a long day's walk, Cyrus, Amber and Meagan found themselves camping in a clearing not far from tracks made by Fenrir. The sun had set and a light snow was falling, along with their hopes of finding the giant wolf's prison. The ghostly glow of moonlight behind a patch of clouds gave a cold light to their surroundings. They had pitched tents for each of them and built a campfire in the center of the clearing. Flames danced among the logs, causing shadows along the tree line, giving a false sense of movement. They were constantly on edge as each sound sent their senses whirling, looking for danger.

They endeavored to stay warm and dared to relax. Meagan, the only one to study any kind of magic other than combat, had set a series of magical crystals around the camp's perimeter. "The crystals are enchanted to emit a high-pitched tone if anyone or anything comes near." No one made any comment as she took a seat near the fire to warm herself.

Cyrus sat on the cold hard ground with his arms wrapped around himself, staring at the fire. His gaze drifted up until it came to rest on his sister. He could see Amber staring into the flames, lost in thought. Still concerned for her mental state, he got up and walked over to her.

"I'm fine," she said as he sat down next to her.

"I didn't say a thing, did I?"

Cyrus glanced at Meagan meaningfully, and she stood and stretched. "I think I'm going to turn in for the night. I'll see you two in the morning." She went into her tent and closed the flap.

"Sis, I know you're still troubled by the nightmares," Cyrus consoled. "I can't pretend to know what happened in the dark chamber, but you can't dwell on it. Tiamat has fled south. She won't bother you anymore."

"She'll be back," said Amber with a straight face and determined look in her eyes. "She haunts my dreams, I'm afraid to fall asleep. I know I'll see her again." A tear slid down the side of her face, but she quickly wiped it away.

"If she ever does come back, we'll face her together," Cyrus reassured. "We'll have our Circle and together we'll find a way to destroy that dragon, for good this time." He was doing his best to sound confident, but knew what he was proposing was impossible. Their best bet was to search the Tablets of Destiny to find a way to re-imprison her.

Cyrus put his arm around Amber and she placed her head on his shoulder as she closed her eyes, daring to fall asleep and hoping not to dream.

* * *

A little later, Meagan stepped out of her tent and noticed the two of them sitting by the fire with their eyes shut. She walked over and pulled a blanket over Amber. As she started to do the same for Cyrus, his eyes popped open.

"I'm fine." He looked down at his sister's face then gently kissed her on the forehead.

Cyrus picked up his sister and carried her to her tent. Meagan held the tent flap open as he laid Amber inside and re-covered her with the blanket. Afterward, Cyrus and Meagan returned to the fire still burning at the center of their campsite.

Cyrus added another log. "I'm concerned about Amber."

Meagan sat down opposite him as she watched him stare into the flames. "She's stronger than either you or she realizes. She willingly went into the dark chamber in Babylon to save you and Taryn. She's done some amazing things with her air elemental powers. Air is a difficult element to control and she's doing as well as any air sorceress I've ever met. I knew a druid in California with air elemental powers and it was always a struggle for him to keep them under control."

"I believe in my sister and I know she's strong." Cyrus sounded confident. "The problem is, she doesn't seem to realize it."

"She will soon enough. Depending on what we find at Gioll, we may need her powers sooner than you or she realizes." She looked to the north toward the nearest mountain. "We're not far away from a fissure in the mountain and the tracks seem to be leading right to it."

"Can you tell how deep it is?" Cyrus must have realized Meagan's earth elemental powers could allow her to sense the fissure some distance away.

"Not at this distance. It's deep, but I can't be sure how deep." She could tell they were thinking the same thing. The fissure might be the pit they were looking for and at the bottom of the pit would be the Gioll rock where Fenrir was previously chained.

Meagan continued, "If it is the pit of Fenrir, legend says it's one whole mile to the bottom."

"Can you create some way down?" Cyrus almost begged.

Meagan realized he would not want to force Amber to use her powers in a similar manner as she had in Babylon when she descended into the dark room to find Tiamat. "What? No hot air balloon in one of your packs?"

Cyrus just chuckled.

She grew more serious as she pursed her lips and stared into the fire. "It will depend on the structure of the pit. If the walls are fairly flat, I might be able to make some stairs. But if it really is a mile deep, that's going to be a lot of stairs... and I'll only be able to make about ten to fifteen at a time. I'd be exhausted by the time we reach bottom, assuming we don't take the express way down and fall to our deaths."

"Encouraging thought. We may need to come up with some other options. Let's just get to the fissure first."

"We'll also need to consider a way out."

Cyrus sat silently for a few seconds. "There's no way a giant wolf could climb out of a one-mile pit. Fenrir must've had help from the dark sorcerers. We may find there's already another way out."

Meagan nodded. She could only imagine what the next day would bring. Stairs or not, they would eventually need Amber and her powers. Cyrus and Meagan said nothing more as they each went to their tents for the night.

* * *

The next morning, Cyrus and Amber awoke to the smell of breakfast cooking on the fire. As always Meagan had prepared the morning meal. They all had a bite to eat before packing up camp and getting ready for their journey to the Gioll rock.

As they neared the fissure, Meagan began to describe the size and depth of the crack in the earth. "This must be the pit where Fenrir was chained," she said. "I lost the tracks at the base of the mountain, but this must be it. Even standing next to it, it's hard to tell the exact depth of the fissure, but I'd estimate it's at least a mile down."

Cyrus examined the jagged rock walls and knew it would be difficult to climb up or down. "What do you think?"

Meagan looked over the side. "The walls are too irregular. The stairs idea won't work, at least not here. Maybe further down."

He figured there had to be another way down, then it hit him. "Amber," called Cyrus, but she never gave him the chance to finish his statement.

"No!" said Amber in a raspy voice. "I had a hard enough time keeping myself aloft in the dark chamber in Babylon. There is no way I can float the three of us down there without killing us all." She wrapped her arms around herself and backed away from the edge of the fissure. The color had drained from her face and she stood there staring at the great crack in the earth.

"Amber, we need to get down there," Cyrus pleaded. "Once we get deep enough, maybe Meagan could create stairs or something, but it would be a long and dangerous way down. And an even slower, more dangerous climb getting back up. You can do this, I know you can."

"What if I try and fail? One or both of you could fall to your death." Tears were already beginning to well up in Amber's eyes. "I can't risk it."

Cyrus reevaluated the pit for a moment. "Meagan, have you ever heard of base jumping?"

Meagan raised a single eyebrow as she looked out of the corner of her eye at Cyrus. "You're kidding, right? Even if you have parachutes in that pack of yours, I'm not about to go jumping freefall into a giant pit and hope I don't impale myself on a rock or outcropping somewhere in that deep dark hole. I don't know the skill level of you and Amber, but that's dangerous even for professional sky divers."

"It was just a thought." Cyrus returned his attention to the pit for a while then another idea hit him. "Well then, do you know a levitation spell?"

Meagan's eyebrows shot up. "Yes, but just a basic one. It's only good for one person and wasn't meant for descending a mile into a giant pit. It'll take over an hour to get to the bottom using that spell. And it will only last as long as the caster maintains their concentration. I don't know about you... but maintaining concentration on one spell for over an hour would be a daunting task."

"Do you think you can teach it to me?"

"Well, it's better than any other option we've come up with so far. I think I can, but it won't be easy."

Cyrus lowered his pack then reached inside and pulled out what looked like a small coil of string. "We'll tie this rope to each of us and each cast the levitation spell. Amber can use her air elemental powers to control our descent. That way as long as we don't all lose concentration at the same time, we won't fall to our deaths. It might work."

Cyrus could see Meagan was thinking out the problem as he explained what to do. After a moment, she nodded her acceptance.

"Amber?" asked Cyrus, hoping this would satisfy her concerns. With this option, she would only need to support her own weight using her elemental powers and she'd have Cyrus and Meagan to help if she lost concentration.

"Okay," she said. Cyrus could tell she still wasn't happy about the idea, but at least it provided a safety net of sorts.

They did as Cyrus had suggested. Once they returned the rope to normal size, they tied it from Meagan to Amber to Cyrus. With Amber in the middle, she would be able to control their descent into the fissure while relying on the other two to catch her if she failed.

Once the ropes were attached, they moved to the edge and cast their spells. Cyrus and Meagan began to float just a few inches off the ground. Amber took a deep breath then raised her arms outward as the gentle breeze began to pick up. The wind continued to increase as it moved them out over the great crack and slowly began their descent. As they lowered into the fissure, the winds died away and each was left to concentrate on their spells.

"Amber, we're getting too close to the side," called Cyrus as he noticed himself dangerously close to the rock face. He could see the concentration on Amber's face. A sudden burst of wind pushed them out to the center of the rocky and jagged fissure once again where they continued their descent.

After about fifteen minutes, they had lowered only a quarter of the total distance. They were all tired and Amber's control of air currents was becoming shaky and erratic.

"Meagan," called Cyrus.

She merely looked at him without a word. The strain on her face made it obvious she was totally focused on her levitation spell.

He too needed to maintain concentration so he made a motion like his right hand was coming out of his left wrist perpendicular to his arm. Though a little crude, Meagan seemed to get the idea and she nodded her head to confirm the suggestion.

She looked down and just below their position, the rock face started growing out toward them. Meagan's concentration was now split between her elemental powers and the levitation spell. Ultimately, the levitation spell failed, and she dropped, landing on the newly formed ledge a little harder than she would've liked, twisting her left ankle in the process. "Ow!"

The little ledge was just large enough for the three of them to stand. Amber saw the ledge and gently lowered herself then collapsed. She was exhausted and in need of a rest.

Cyrus too landed then lowered to his knees to catch his breath. Looking around he could see they had further to go than they had already travelled.

Meagan held her hand over her left ankle and cast a healing spell, "*Hema toe-zie fume.*" By the look on her face, the pain in the ankle quickly faded.

"We've gone about a quarter mile so far..." said Meagan as she looked up. Then looking down into the darkness, she continued, "...and I estimate at least three quarters of a mile to go. There's a fairly large cavern at the bottom. That's probably where we'll find the Gioll rock."

Cyrus could see the other two were tired and so was he, but they had made good progress with few incidents so far. After a five-minute break, Cyrus and Meagan cast their levitation spells again. Amber seemed reluctant to continue, but had few options. She motioned for the wind to pick up and they resumed their descent.

They made another rest stop around the half-mile mark. A tiny speck of light from the top of the fissure was barely noticeable. The darkness was taking over. They could see Amber looking quickly from side to side, up and down. Her breathing grew more rapid and the wind became more erratic.

Cyrus put his arms around her and spoke in a calm voice. "You okay? Don't worry, we're right here."

Amber whispered, "The darkness is closing in. I can't breathe."

From the dark, they could hear Meagan's voice, "*Alecto orona na-see.*" A little orb of light appeared above their heads and hovered there. It wasn't a blinding light, but they could at least see one another and their immediate surroundings.

Amber looked at Meagan and whispered, "Thank you," then held tight to her brother once again.

Cyrus was concerned so he decided to rest fifteen minutes this time. Looking down into the darkness, he knew it was only going to get harder the further they travelled, but he didn't know what else to do at this point. They couldn't go back. He began to question if bringing his sister along was such a good idea, but then pushed the thought from his mind. He knew he couldn't leave her behind. They needed her and she needed to face her fears.

Once Amber had calmed down and everyone had regained their strength, they continued on their way. Meagan had moved the little glowing orb a few feet below to help guide them. This time the descent was slower. The increasing darkness made it more difficult to navigate oncoming obstacles. Amber's guiding winds knocked a few rocks loose and the occasional jagged outcropping posed a minor challenge in direction.

As they neared the three-quarter mark, Amber's guiding winds grew stronger and erratic once again. They were all glad for the next rest stop. This time, they all felt a little uneasy. Even with the glowing orb, the sides of the fissure were getting further apart.

Meagan stretched a hand out over the side of the makeshift ledge she had created. As she moved her hand around, Cyrus grew concerned. Based on the supposed size of Fenrir, he estimated the cavern was probably large. His fears were confirmed when Meagan finished her search.

She leaned in and whispered to him in the hope Amber would not hear. "We have a quarter mile to go to reach the bottom, but the fissure stretches out in all directions from here. There won't be any walls to guide us to the bottom from this point on. It's just going to be darkness."

Cyrus whispered in return, "Do you think it's safe enough to parachute to the bottom from here?"

Meagan looked at Cyrus through squinted eyes. "We have no idea what the floor of this cavern looks like. And you want to jump into the darkness?"

"So, we continue with the levitation spell?"

"I don't see any other options."

"The echo in here is a little too loud," said Amber sitting on the edge of the ledge staring into the darkness. "I can hear you. I knew we would get to this part sooner or later. It's the dark chamber all over again."

Cyrus moved next to her and put his hands on her shoulders. "Just remember, we're here with you. We won't let you fall."

Amber looked over her shoulder and smiled. "I know. And Tiamat isn't here either. But it doesn't change the fact that I know I'm going to hear and feel her in the darkness." Amber looked down into the fissure. "Whether she's here or not, she's always with me, in my mind."

For the fourth and final time, they each cast their spells. "*Levas mon see-tor.*"

They lifted off from the ledge and descended into the black void. The light from above was now gone. The glow from Meagan's orb touched nothing in their vast surroundings. The walls had disappeared along with any air current. No longer needing Amber's power to move them away from the crevice walls, they descended into dark silence.

Meagan shifted her orb into the center of their triangular rope connection so they could see one another.

Cyrus noted his sister's white knuckles as she gripped tightly to the ropes. Her eyes were squeezed shut and she gritted her teeth. He reached out his hand to take hers, and her eyes popped open at his touch. She grasped his hand and smiled weakly.

A small object flew by them. Cyrus was startled at the motion, but quickly realized it was only a small bat. When he returned his attention to Amber, her eyes were squeezed shut and the winds had picked up and were growing. He knew she must be thinking of Tiamat.

"Amber!" he called out to her, but the winds drowned out his voice.

"Cyrus!" he heard Meagan call, but he couldn't make out what she said. She pointed at Amber, but all he could do was cup his hands around his ears and shake his head as the wind intensity grew.

Meagan grabbed on to Amber and lost focus on her levitation spell. She called out something in the howling wind. Within seconds, Amber fell asleep and the two of them dropped. The rope connecting them to Cyrus was the only thing keeping them from plummeting to their deaths.

Cyrus held tight to his section of rope, maintaining focus on his levitation spell. He knew it was now up to him alone to get them to the bottom of the cavern alive. He looked down to see Meagan holding the limp body of Amber as she grasped the rope binding them all together.

It was ten minutes more until Meagan's orb finally caught a glimpse of something below. Cyrus looked down just as Meagan stretched out her legs to kick off of a huge stalagmite rising up into the darkness. "Watch out!" she called, and shifted their descent away from the jagged rock formation.

Cyrus knew the bottom had to be close. His attention was being pulled from their descent as he looked around for other signs of their destination.

Meagan called up to him, "Keep your focus. Let me worry about the bottom."

Her little orb of light descended faster than they did in an attempt to locate the cavern floor. The orb was twenty feet below them when it hit ground.

Cyrus lowered them the final distance and gently placed Amber and Meagan on the ground before dropping the final few feet himself to join them.

Cyrus and Meagan collapsed in exhaustion, joining the already unconscious Amber. They remained there in silence as each needed time to regain strength. After a ten-minute rest, they awoke Amber and assessed their situation.

All light was gone save for Meagan's little glowing orb, but it did little to illuminate the enormous cavern. The space was huge and the crack in the ceiling that had led them to the fissure was thousands of feet above their heads. The cavern extended before them, where stalagmites of all shapes and sizes littered the cavern floor like a mouth full of sharp teeth.

"*Alecto orona na-see*," Cyrus cast a light spell. A small orb followed him around, just enough to illuminate twenty feet in all directions.

"This way." Meagan pointed off to their left.

Cyrus led the way with his light just above his position.

They walked about a hundred yards until they came to a gigantic boulder at least a hundred feet high.

"This must be it," suggested Meagan. "The rock has been worn smooth in a few places like something big had been rubbing against it for years."

Cyrus observed the large patches of smooth rock, still in awe of the enormous size the wolf must have been. "Look around for Gleipnir," he instructed. "We need to find that magical ribbon if we're going to re-imprison this giant wolf."

They all started looking around the area near the rock. As they spread out, Amber cast her own light orb spell so they could each see better in the area they searched. "I found it," she exclaimed.

"I found it," exclaimed Cyrus.

"I found it," exclaimed Meagan.

All at once they realized what they had found was not Gleipnir, but only shredded fragments of the whole. Gleipnir had been sliced and ripped into many pieces. They gathered the fragments into a pile of nearly a hundred pieces, as well as the giant sword that had been placed in Fenrir's mouth to prevent him from biting at Gleipnir.

"What do we do now?" asked Amber, staring at her brother.

They had come all this way to retrieve Gleipnir in the hope of using it to imprison Fenrir once again, but the shreds would never hold such a creature. And they all knew it.

15 Questions of the Past

Alex was beginning to wonder about who he was and where he came from. From the first moment he met Qaletaqa, he had been told he was a member of the Rogue Hunters, but now he was beginning to wonder about the validity of that statement. They had encountered a young redhead named Taryn who claimed to be his friend, but she knew him as Max and informed him they lived in Baltimore, Maryland—not Arizona. Confused by the debate, he decided it was time he got some straight answers.

People were breaking off into groups of three and preparing for the hunt. Some carried rifles, others knives. Some like Taryn, Sheelin and Radimir carried no weapons at all. Their weapon was the power within. A power Alex too shared. He could feel it, but he was still learning how to use it. He knew many spells, but was having a difficult time remembering them. His attention snapped to the present when he heard Qaletaqa call his name.

"Alex, come on. We should get ready to head out."

Alex reluctantly approached with questions heavy on his mind. "Was I really part of the Circle before joining the Rogue Hunters?"

The shaman took in a deep breath then let out a long sigh through pursed lips. "Now is not a good time for this discussion."

"Qaletaqa, I need to know."

The old shaman sighed. "Honestly, I don't know. Taryn seems to think so, but it's possible she's just after you for your power. You will be a force to be reckoned with one day and I don't want to see that strength fall into the wrong hands. For now, it's best you stay close to me."

"So I wasn't always a member of the Rogue Hunters?"

"We found you wandering the desert two days ago, hence your name. But this Malcolm that Taryn and Vincent spoke of was torturing people to find out where you were. I knew I had to keep you safe. We found you in shredded and blood-stained clothing. You had no memory, but even then Sheelin and I could sense your power."

"Why didn't you tell me the truth? Why make me think I was a member of the Rogue Hunters for years? And tell me I was your adopted son?"

Qaletaqa remained silent for a moment. "I said what I needed to in order to save your life. You were delusional and dehydrated. If I hadn't convinced you to come with us, you would have died. After that, I should have told you the truth, but I was afraid you were with this Malcolm, who killed our friends. I couldn't let power like yours go back into the hands of those who would seek to destroy this world."

"And now that Taryn is here?"

"For all we know she could be working for this Malcolm person. She seems to have a good heart, but I'm not ready to blindly trust her just because she claims friendship... nor should you."

"What about Sheelin's truth spell?"

"Sheelin's spell indicated they were speaking the truth, but not the entire truth. Taryn's holding something back and until I know what that is, I can't trust her completely."

"Every time she and I try having a conversation, you keep interrupting. Why?"

"I'm only looking out for you, Alex. She could be trying to fill your head with lies, trying to convince you to go with her regardless of what I say. The power you possess must be protected."

"I understand, but I also understand if I want to know who I am, I need to talk with people who knew me. I need to find out what she knows."

"In time, we will discover the truth together. For now there are more pressing issues to deal with."

Alex nodded in agreement, but in the back of his mind, he was beginning to wonder. *Who am I and where do I belong?* These were questions he would need to get answered, and he had a strong feeling Taryn was indeed the one to answer them.

* * *

Later that evening, Taryn, Radimir and Sheelin started out on the path set for them by Qaletaqa. As they left camp, Taryn noticed Qaletaqa kept Alex in his hunting party. He wasn't going to make it easy for them to speak privately. He guarded Alex as if protecting him from an enemy. But Taryn wasn't their enemy. If only she could figure out how to convince Qaletaqa of this fact.

Sheelin was a skilled tracker and an apprentice shaman. After a couple of hours in the frozen wilderness, she indicated unfamiliar tracks leading into a tree line west of their position. Perhaps it was their quarry, the Wendigo.

Taryn did her best to cope with the cold. As a fire elemental sorceress, she could deal with extreme temperatures of heat, but her tolerance for the cold was lacking. Even the heavy winter jacket Sheelin had provided did not offer the warmth Taryn preferred.

Radimir on the other hand tolerated the cold with ease. Living in Russia must have accustomed him to the colder climates.

"You make fire, keep you warm," he said.

Taryn wasn't sure if Radimir was making a suggestion or asking a question, but either way she knew it wasn't an option. "The f-firelight will give away our p-position and alert the Wendigo of our approach." Her speech was shaky and her teeth kept chattering.

"Shh..." admonished Sheelin, placing a finger to her lips while she crouched beside a bush. She pointed to some broken branches and tracks in the snow. She then pointed further into the woods indicating the direction of the tracks.

They continued to follow the trail deeper into the woods until at last, the tracks disappeared. Sheelin searched around trying to figure out how the trail simply disappeared and where their quarry had gone.

"Wendigo go up." Radimir was pointing upward at a section of bark that had been torn from a nearby tree. Claw marks in the bark indicated something big and heavy had climbed the tree at that point.

As they continued looking around, the claw marks kept climbing until it was too high for them to clearly make out the direction of the Wendigo's path.

Radimir fell to his knees and put his head down, shaking briefly before he began to shrink in size. The other two stood back, observing what was happening to their Russian friend. His clothes collapsed inward and from the pile of discarded clothing arose a hawk. The reddish-brown bird of prey took flight with one thrust of his mighty wings and soared into the sky. He circled the trees many times before landing on a downed tree limb not far from the girls' position. The hawk took one look at them then turned and flew off into the woods.

Sheelin grabbed Radimir's clothing, then they followed the shape-shifter amongst the trees and woodland debris. At one point, the hawk disappeared from sight around a large tree. As the girls approached, Radimir poked his head out from behind the great tree.

"Clothes?" Other than his head, he remained behind the tree. Sheelin tossed his pile of clothing over to him and the girls waited. Once dressed again, Radimir stepped out of concealment and pointed off to his right. "Tracks, there."

"I take it ye can shape-shift at will like I can control fire?" asked Taryn.

"Change easy." Radimir smiled, proud of his ability. "When not trapped."

"The Wendigo is back on the ground again," said Sheelin as she examined the tracks, "but it's found the tracks of something else now. It looks like another one of the hunting parties. There are three individual sets of prints besides the Wendigo. They may be hunting him, but now he's hunting them as well. We'd better pick up the pace if we're going to catch him before he catches them."

Taryn took a step, but then fell to one knee. Her face was white and she couldn't stop shivering. The cold was affecting her more than anticipated. Sheelin and Radimir rushed to her side, but she waved them off as she struggled back to her feet.

"I'm okay. I just tripped over a root sticking up out of the ground."

The temperature was just below freezing, but Taryn felt like it was twenty below zero. Right now, she would've liked nothing better than to be standing in the middle of a burning fire.

The other two clearly weren't fooled. "Perhaps you should return home to your castle in Baltimore," suggested Sheelin.

"I promised I would help catch this creature." Taryn's determination was evident in her voice if not in her appearance. "That's what members of the Circle do—we protect the world from monsters like this, no matter the cost to ourselves. Max believes that too, which is why we almost lost him and why he's here now."

Sheelin studied Taryn for a moment then opened a pouch at her side and pulled out a small bottle. "Drink this."

Taryn looked at the bottle and then at the pouch before accepting the bottled liquid.

"It's a multi-dimensional pouch," commented Sheelin as she caught Taryn's gaze. "I have a few hundred potions in there in case of emergency. This one is for health, but it will also keep you warm, at least for a while. It will wear off in a few hours."

Taryn unstopped the cork from the small bottle and drank the potion. Within seconds, she could feel the warmth returning through her body and reenergizing her. It warmed her so well, she felt like she could take off the heavy winter clothes and wear her normal bikini top in the middle of a snow storm. Even if the effects were temporary, it felt good for now.

They continued off in the direction of the tracks at a brisk pace, but still slow enough that Sheelin wouldn't lose the trail. After about an hour, the screams of two men and the howling of their quarry was unmistakable.

A battle was in progress, and the three broke into a run hoping to arrive in time to capture the beast. A few gun shots were heard followed by another howl, then silence.

When they arrived at the scene, the snow-covered ground was soaked with the blood of at least one from the hunting party. There were signs of a struggle, but no bodies... alive or dead. Whatever had happened, they hadn't killed the beast.

Sheelin began searching the fringes of the battle scene for more tracks. Taryn and Radimir waited patiently as she made her rounds.

"One man headed off to the east by himself," Sheelin announced. "Another headed south. The third was the one whose blood this is. Based on the amount, he's most likely already dead. The Wendigo must have gotten him and dragged him away to the southwest."

"If it's draggin' a body, it should be easy to track down," said Taryn. "And if the creature has just fed, it shouldn't be hungry anymore."

"Not this beast," corrected Sheelin. "When a Wendigo eats, it grows... so it's always hungry."

Taryn gulped. "I just hope we're not its next meal."

16   YGGDRASIL

After shrinking down the remnants of Gleipnir and placing them in her pack, Meagan joined the other two in looking for a way back up to the top of the crevice, or for another way out of the chasm. They each had a light spell providing them with glowing orbs, but the cavern was so large they could barely see each other.

Though exhausted, Amber felt a slight breeze and followed it. Rounding a corner, she discovered a tunnel and the smell of fresh air. Obviously created to allow Fenrir's escape, she followed it for a few hundred feet before it rounded another corner and opened up to a hole in the side of the mountain. There was a twenty-foot drop to ground level, but for a creature the size of Fenrir, it would have been a small leap.

She quickly ran back to find the others. After the three emerged out in the open, Amber realized the one chance of recapturing the great wolf was gone. They had no way to imprison it again.

"I guess it's time we inform Gollnick we failed," Cyrus said with slumped shoulders.

Amber knew he was upset that another creature of myth had escaped into the world.

"We didn't fail," corrected Meagan. "Fenrir was released long before we arrived. There was nothing we could have done to stop it. Besides, we were battling other creatures when the wolf was freed. What we need to do is find another way to imprison it."

"Oh, yeah. I think I have a ball of string in my pack, maybe we can tie him up with that," Cyrus chided. After hanging his head for a few seconds, he turned to Meagan again. "I'm sorry. I know you mean well, but we're out of options."

"Maybe not."

"Maybe not, what? You have a plan?"

A loud howling sound echoed through the mountains. Scanning the horizon, Amber could see the monstrous shape of a giant wolf standing shoulders above the treetops. The creature was still a few miles off and downhill from their position, but it was returning their gaze. Fenrir had doubled back and was hunting them. Standing beside the wolf was a figure they could not make out at such a distance, but it was wearing heavy winter clothing. The silhouette was either a child or... Fenrir was larger than they had expected... because the human wasn't even the height of the knee of Fenrir's front legs.

If they were going to make an attempt at Meagan's plan, they would need to act quickly. It wouldn't take long for a creature as large as the wolf to cross such a distance.

Amber hesitated, but Meagan's gaze never left the wolf. "Gleipnir was made by the dwarves of Norse mythology."

"Mythology being the keyword," added Amber. "We know mythology was based on the actions of ancient sorcerers, though I have no idea how Norse dwarves fit into the picture."

"Some myths were true," replied Meagan, "at least to a point. We need to find the rainbow bridge through Yggdrasil to get to Nidavellir, the home of the dwarves."

Amber just stood there staring at Meagan, not quite sure how to respond.

"Ne-da-velour?" Cyrus stumbled over the name.

The idea of leaving Earth to find dwarves by way of a rainbow bridge had Amber a little confused. She knew a bit about Norse mythology herself, but had no idea which parts were true and which were fantasy. Based on Meagan's suggestion, she was beginning to believe perhaps the rainbow bridge was the former.

"The nine realms of Norse mythology are real," started Meagan, "and there is a real rainbow bridge connecting them all through Yggdrasil, the world tree. According to Norse mythology, it was the dwarves who made Gleipnir for the Asgardians."

"And how exactly do you know all of this?" questioned Cyrus.

Meagan hesitated for a few seconds before responding. "I read books." She raised an eyebrow at Cyrus.

Amber giggled, knowing her brother's love of books, or more precisely, his lack of love for them.

"So where do we find this rainbow bridge?" he asked.

"That's the thing," replied Meagan. "I know a spell that will open the Bifrost to Asgard, but in order for it to work, we need an actual rainbow." She then slowly turned to look at Amber.

"What's a Bifrost?" Amber asked. "And why are you looking at me? I control the air, not rainbows."

"Bifrost is what the Asgardians called the rainbow bridge," replied Meagan.

"I think I know what she's thinking, sis," Cyrus said. "We need a big storm. Once it clears, we should get a rainbow. It might also keep Fenrir at bay rather than attacking."

"No! No way! I'm too tired. I won't be able to control it. If I start a hurricane in Norway, I could kill people." Amber backed away, shaking. The mere thought of using her powers like that terrified her.

"You controlled your power in Babylon, remember? You used your air elemental power to keep you aloft in the dark chamber."

As soon as Cyrus mentioned the chamber Amber winced. She had been trying to forget what happened there, and the giant dragon Tiamat that now haunted her dreams. "After what we just went through, you did not just say that!" she screamed. In the blink of an eye, a streak of lightning was followed by the crack of thunder in the sky above them. Clouds quickly began forming overhead as the afternoon sky darkened.

Cyrus had gotten what he wanted. Now if she could only keep from killing him.

The lightning continued flashing as the downpour of rain began to drench the three friends where they stood.

Meagan backed into the tunnel opening while Cyrus remained standing, allowing Amber to thoroughly drench him as punishment. He deserved it.

After a few minutes of focusing her anger at her brother, Amber realized she couldn't stay mad at him for long. As her anger drained away, the storm's strength died with it.

Though they were both soaking wet, Cyrus looked up to see the tears welling in her eyes. He took a step toward her, but she ran to him and hugged him close. "Don't ever make me do that again," she sobbed. "I can't stand being angry at you. Don't do that."

Meagan stepped out of the tunnel as the sky began to clear, a rainbow arching its way across the sky. The bright colors were a cheerful result of the storm and a welcome sight. Meagan cast the spell, "*Reslectum tolanga be-frost atume.*"

A great howl echoed once again from the valley below as Fenrir had already launched itself from the tree line, accelerating toward them. Teeth bared, it looked hungry for a meal.

The brilliant rainbow that arched across the sky bent in an irregular shape as it redirected from its normal path. One end slammed into the ground at their feet. It looked like a translucent column of colored light.

Meagan approached the column of light, grabbing Amber's hand on one side and Cyrus on the other. Upon entering the rainbow, the world around them was lost from sight. Shooting up into the air as if fired from a cannon, they began travelling through corridor after corridor of light and energy, one leading to another like the branches of a tree ascending into the vastness of time and space.

Amber looked up as if searching for their intended destination. She noticed Cyrus looking around at visible energy waves and side branches shooting off in other directions. Amber clutched Meagan with both hands and closed her eyes. She prayed she wouldn't lose contact and be lost on some other world, stranded alone.

A few seconds later, they came to an abrupt stop. As the Bifrost faded, they found themselves standing on a platform at the edge of a vast golden city. Towers spired skyward as arches framed central locations, with bridges and roads providing access throughout the great city. It would have been an impressive sight except for the dilapidation of the place. Many bridges were damaged, arches collapsed, buildings crumbled into ruins. Even the main spire at the heart of the city appeared to have great holes in its side. The panorama was both awe inspiring and depressing at the same time.

As they walked through the city streets, Amber noticed weeds and vines had overgrown the walkways. Intricately painted pots and vases lining the intersections had met with a shattered ending. Cracks shot through walls and compromised many structures, as if the city had barely survived an enormous earthquake.

The obvious thing missing were the people. Asgard was supposedly the home of the Asgardians of Norse mythology. Even though they were mortal sorcerers, the trio had at least expected to find the descendants of the original Norse gods still living there.

"What happened?" Amber asked.

"Ragnarock," replied Meagan, "the great battle of good versus evil at the end of the reign of the Norse gods. Many were killed, some survived, but those who did fled to Midgard or other realms. Asgard used to be a beautiful golden city that glimmered in the sunlight. People built their lives here, serving the Norse gods and raising their families. It was a peaceful place, once."

"You're starting to sound like Max," commented Cyrus. "Please don't tell me you're immortal too and have lived hundreds of lives over the years."

"No." Meagan shot Cyrus an irritated look. "I'm still on my first life. It's just that I've seen pictures of this place when it was in its prime. And I've heard stories. Not the ones told in myth, but stories about the people who actually lived here once."

Cyrus didn't push. Instead he continued leading the way through the streets toward the central spire.

Even at a distance, Amber could see the main gates to the central building had been ripped from their hinges and lay at odd angles to the entryway.

"I thought we needed to find the dwarves on their world of Needa-Vellr?" Amber questioned. "Why are we going further into Asgard?"

"I don't know the spell to get us directly to Nidavellir." Meagan took time to carefully pronounce the world's name slowly and clearly.

"So where do you suppose they kept their spell books?" Amber asked as they neared the entrance to the main spire.

The great doors were as fractured and bent as the gate. It would have taken something big and strong to mangle the doors in this way. Like the rest of Asgard, the central spire was overgrown with plant life and severely damaged, but the structure still looked stable enough to enter.

"Somewhere in here," replied Meagan. "Maybe in a vault or library. We'll have to search around until we find something that might help."

A hinge creaked as Cyrus pulled on a broken section of door. "We could always go back and get Fenrir to come sniff out the spell books."

17 NIDO

After hours searching the different levels and chambers of the central spire of Asgard, Cyrus led Amber and Meagan into a large open room filled with banquet tables and chairs. Some had been smashed, others flipped on their sides. Plates and mugs lay strewn about on the floor. Drapes that once covered the many windows hung in tattered shreds. At the far end of the chamber atop a large dais sat a golden throne. Upon the throne sat a solitary individual. This single person was the first they had encountered throughout all of Asgard.

With Cyrus in the lead, they approached. The individual sat with his right hand covering his face and slouched as if resting his head against the side of the throne. He gave no indication he was aware of their presence. In fact Cyrus had the distinct impression he was asleep. His long white beard hung down over the scrawny frame of an old man whose robes were torn and streaked with dirt and stains.

Cyrus climbed the dais and approached cautiously. He gave the man a gentle nudge, but received no response. He tried again, but still nothing. He then shook the man's shoulder a few times. "Hey! Old man, wake up."

Groggy at first, the individual dropped his hand from his face revealing a patch over one eye. Lines streaked his face from old age, and his long unkempt hair was white as snow. The man took a few seconds to become fully aware he had company. Once he did, he looked up at Cyrus with anger in his eyes. "How dare I stand there," yelled the old man. Then in a calmer tone, he corrected himself. "Or you stand there, somewhere. Who are you?"

Surprised by the old man's confusion, Cyrus answered, "My name is Cyrus Marx." Then he pointed toward the bottom of the dais. "This is my sister Amber Marx and our friend Meagan Strom. Who are you?"

"I am he who commands and not the listener." The grizzled old man just sat on the throne and stared off into space for a few seconds. "Who are you?"

Cyrus turned and started down the steps toward Amber and Meagan. "I don't think this guy's playing with a full deck."

"I am Nido!" The old man was now on his feet and holding a long golden spear.

Cyrus and his friends stepped back. He hadn't noticed the spear before, and was unsure what this guy planned on doing with such a weapon.

The man stood tall with feet spaced apart and the spear butt end to the floor at arm's length, with his left hand on his hip. He appeared fully aware now and ready to deal with his intruders. "Speak my business or leave your kingdom."

Cyrus glanced at the girls who were staring at the old man, slack-jawed, apparently trying to figure out what he was trying to say.

"What happened here?" Cyrus asked cautiously.

"What happened where? Who are you?"

"My name is Cyrus."

"And who am I?"

Cyrus just rolled his eyes. This guy was clearly not going to be able to provide any help to them on their quest to find the Bifrost spell to Nidavellir. He waved a hand at the guy and turned to leave.

No sooner was his back turned than a lightning bolt hit the floor near his feet. Cyrus jumped in surprise and spun around. The man was now pointing the spear directly at the spot on the floor where the lightning hit.

"You are the supreme ruler of this place." The man then corrected himself, "No, I am the supreme place of this ruler."

"Whoa there, Nido." Cyrus raised his hands to show he was unarmed even though he still wore the fireball bracer Elisa had given him before going off to Petra and Babylon. "We mean you no harm."

"Who's Nido?" questioned the old man.

"You said your name was Nido." Cyrus looked back to Amber and Meagan for confirmation.

"I am Odin of Asgard." The man stood tall once again as if proud of his name and title, but the confidence in his attitude faded quickly. "Where are we?"

Meagan approached the base of the dais, raising her hands peacefully as well. "But the sorcerer Odin of Asgard died hundreds of years ago."

"I should have died hundreds of years ago." The old man flopped down on the throne and hung his head. A tear started down his cheek from his good eye. The spear disappeared in a puff of smoke.

Cyrus, Amber and Meagan slowly climbed the stairs to stand before Nido. Cyrus wasn't ready to believe this was truly Odin.

The old man made no move to stop their approach. In a lower voice he conceded, "I really am Odin. Unlike the others of Asgard, I am cursed with immortality." He seemed sorrowful about this admission. "I pose no threat to you. Take what you want and leave me be."

"Sir," began Amber. "If you really are Odin, do you know our friend Max? I mean Chronos?"

The sadness in his eyes was replaced by anger at the mere mention of the name. Rising to his feet once more, he held out a hand and the spear reappeared in a puff of smoke. The three of them backed off a little, but did not retreat down the stairs.

"It is because of Chronos and his spell that I am cursed this way." Odin's speech rose in volume with each word. "We should've let the world burn rather than be cursed like this."

"Sir, please," Meagan begged. "Just tell us what exactly happened? How did you get cursed this way?"

Once again he took a seat on his throne, though he maintained a grasp on his spear this time. The sadness returned to his eye as he leaned his head back against the backrest. "We tried to stop dark sorcerers from siphoning magic from other realms, but they succeeded in ripping a hole in the fabric of reality and created a portal to the Nightmare Realm. All sorts of creatures flooded Midgard and the nine realms. Chronos, Ra and myself tried to hold back the flow of monsters, but each of us couldn't do it alone. It was Chronos who came up with the spell to seal the portal. It took all three of us to cast it... but he made a mistake. It cursed us with immortality."

"Some people would consider that a gift," said Cyrus.

He peered out the corner of his eye. "Not when it comes with a price. Each of us had to pay a price for our immortality. Mine was being trapped in a frail old body growing weaker by the year, but I will never die. Even if I want to."

"What about Chronos and Ra?" asked Amber. "What price did they have to pay?"

"Who are you?" asked the old man, clearly confused. "How did you get here? Where are we?" In the blink of an eye and a puff of smoke, his spear was replaced by a spoon. "I command thee to loosen the tables from the main catapult and eat your stew."

Amber, Cyrus and Meagan looked from one to another. Odin was making less sense now than when he'd awoken. The many years trapped in a feeble old body had clearly taken a toll on his mind as well, but perhaps he knew enough to tell them where to find the spell to get to the realm of the dwarves.

"Sir, do you know where we can find the Bifrost spell to get to Nidavellir?" asked Meagan in a calm and polite voice.

Odin just stared at her for a moment. "Bifrost? Spell? Nidavellir?" He was repeating words that Meagan had said, but offered no answer.

"We need to find the dwarves," added Cyrus impatiently.

Amber kept silent, but took the frail old man's hand in hers and looked into his eye as she knelt before him. Closing her eyes she began muttering to herself so quietly Cyrus couldn't hear.

Amber opened her eyes and smiled at Odin before standing up and turning to leave. "The spells are in the vault, two levels down."

Cyrus exchanged a confused look with Meagan before returning his attention to his sister.

"Are you coming?" asked Amber as she walked past him.

"How?" replied Cyrus in even more confusion as he pointed at Odin.

"Clairvoyance, remember? I could see him going there in the near future, just to look around and try to remember the past. It was actually kind of sad."

Within minutes they had reached the vault. Here too, the vault doors like the main doors to the spire were ripped from their hinges. The vault had been looted over the centuries, but a few things still remained. Mjolnir, the great stone hammer of Thor, lay on the floor in the middle of the room with its handle up in the air as if pleading for someone to take it, an overhead light shining down upon it. Around the perimeter of the room were many empty chests and broken weapons. This was obviously the site of a battle, but few things remained.

As the girls began digging through the remnants of the chests, Cyrus approached Mjolnir. He knew the power of the mighty hammer. However, no one but Thor could lift it and he was long since dead. Still, he remained transfixed on the weapon.

After a few minutes, Meagan called out, "I found it. The Bifrost spell to Nidavellir."

As Meagan and Amber ran for the exit, his sister grabbed Cyrus by the arm to encourage his departure and he reluctantly followed. Before leaving the room, Cyrus stopped. It was his one chance to gain the power of Thor. He had to at least try.

Going back to the center of the room, he gripped the leather wrapped handle of the legendary hammer. He lifted with all his might, but no luck. He couldn't even budge it. Probably the most prized weapon in all of Norse mythology was sitting out in plain view and not a person alive could lift it.

18   THE WENDIGO

After tracking the Wendigo for almost an hour, Sheelin caught the hint of a noise off to their left. There was a waterfall nearby that masked some of the sound, but she was still able to discern a slight noise of movement. She quickly signaled the other two to get down and be quiet. Taryn ducked behind a tree and prepared for an attack in the direction Sheelin was watching. Radimir dove behind some bushes and started shape-shifting into a grizzly bear, but remained still, waiting for the creature to approach.

Seconds later a figure stepped into view, but still in the shadows. Taryn stepped from behind the tree with a fireball in each hand. Radimir launched himself up toward the figure and growled a fearsome growl. The figure was startled yet not badly enough to be paralyzed by the shock of a bear attack. It raised a shotgun toward the grizzly, but paused when Sheelin ran out, putting herself between the figure and the bear.

"Wait!" she called.

Both the grizzly and figure stood motionless. Taryn raised a hand with one of the fireballs to cast a little more light. The figure was Wallace, a Rogue Hunter member who'd come along on the hunt. Within seconds, Qaletaqa and Alex ran forward into the light as well. Upon seeing each other, everyone relaxed their postures. Radimir returned to the brush and shrank back down to human size.

"What have you found?" asked Qaletaqa, visibly relieved.

"The creature ambushed a hunting party about a mile back," replied Sheelin. "Two appear to have escaped, but the third was dragged off by the creature. Based on the amount of blood in the snow, he's probably dead."

"Let's hope so," replied Qaletaqa.

"Excuse me," interrupted Taryn. "You hope he's dead? If he's alive, there may still be a chance to save him."

Qaletaqa shook his head. "Once bitten by the Wendigo, the curse is spread to the victim. He will soon desire the flesh of another human. Once he kills, he will become a Wendigo as well. It's better he die than become one of those creatures."

"Is there no way to lift the curse?"

"There is," replied Sheelin giving her father an angry stare. "If we can kill the original Wendigo before the victim consumes human flesh, the curse will be lifted. If not, we have another Wendigo to deal with."

"So far we haven't had any luck with that," said Qaletaqa matching his daughter's stare. "It's better he die now than us having to hunt him down later."

"With the six of us here," interrupted Alex, "now might be a good time to take a break and relax a bit before heading off again."

Tensions remained high while they sat down to eat a bite. Everyone had packed provisions and now took places around the small clearing, facing outward so they could watch for trouble while they ate. Qaletaqa and Sheelin sat together to talk.

Taryn looked across the meager encampment to find Alex. He glanced at Qaletaqa before crossing the campsite and sitting down next to her. "Hope you don't mind."

"Not at all," replied Taryn. "How's the hunt going?"

"It seems like you've had more luck than us. We haven't seen any traces of the creature so far. Not that I'm really anxious to come face to face with something that can turn me into a Wendigo with a bite."

"Another piece of info that Qaletaqa hadn't shared."

"So tell me about this Amber that I apparently like," requested Alex.

Taryn smiled. She was happy to see that Alex was at least interested in the events of the past week even if he didn't remember it. She realized all she could really tell him was what she had been told herself. She had only known him for a day or so, but before his disappearance, Amber couldn't stop talking about him. She relayed as much information as she could about

Amber and their relationship, including the fact they tried the mind link even though it didn't work.

"Max, err Alex…" Taryn hesitated. "Sorry, I still think of you as Max."

"I understand."

"There's one more thing I think you should know. I believe Qaletaqa already suspected there's another important fact I was holding back about you. We have reason to believe your real name is not Alex nor Max." She paused a moment. "We think your real identity is Chronos, the Greek god of time and one of the three immortals. Which would make you one of the three most powerful sorcerers in the world."

Alex sat wide eyed, not saying a word.

She continued to relay the events of the past week and the battles in Hades and Babylon. When she got to the part where Max was an elemental water sorcerer, he sat up a little straighter and cocked his head.

"I never tried using elemental powers before."

Reaching out his hand toward some snow, Taryn watched as he stared at it for a brief moment. Within seconds a large patch had melted into a puddle. Then with a quick snap of his hand, the puddle grew into an ice stalagmite shooting up out of the ground. Releasing his grip and relaxing his hand, the ice returned to a puddle of water.

"Cool," said Alex as he smiled at Taryn.

"Actually it is getting cool again." After shivering a bit, she continued, "Fire elemental sorceresses don't like the cold very much."

"I have an idea. Try casting *Magna me-low torum*."

"What does it do?"

Alex paused before replying. "I'm not sure. I just thought it might help you. I have no idea why."

Taryn looked at Alex cautiously and then decided to try the spell to see what it did. She trusted that Alex, like Max, wouldn't do anything to hurt her. "*Magna me-low torum*." Within seconds, Taryn felt warmer, as if the air around her were suddenly heated. She smiled at Alex just before she noticed Qaletaqa's approach. "I think our time it up."

"Alex, it's time we get going. Oh and Taryn, when were you planning on telling us that you were a fire elemental?"

"You never asked." She wasn't sure if he had figured it out when the two groups encountered one another or if Sheelin had informed him during their chat. For now, she decided to give Sheelin the benefit of the doubt.

No sooner did Alex stand up to join Qaletaqa than they heard a loud howl coming from somewhere nearby. Everybody immediately rose to their feet, ready for an attack. It was close. They could hear twigs snapping in the forest around them, but they couldn't see the creature. Six of them gathered together must have looked like a feast for a creature who could never sate its hunger.

From out of nowhere, a ghostly white figure lunged at the group. It was incredibly quick and agile for such a large beast. White skin wrapped around bone and lean muscle. A blast of wind kicked up snow, obscuring Taryn's vision as the creature ripped through their temporary camp. Huge claws slashed across Radimir's chest sending him sprawling to the ground. Alex was launched through the air landing on Qaletaqa. Sheelin was thrown from the circle into the trees surrounding camp. Wallace was thrown from the clearing, landing head first on a large rock just outside of camp.

Taryn turned toward the movement just in time to feel a searing pain in her left shoulder. No sooner did the pain start than she realized the creature had bitten into her shoulder and was now dragging her from the clearing. The pain was so intense she passed out within seconds.

Moments later she regained consciousness only to find she was being dragged by one leg through the snow. She could still feel the pain in her shoulder. Her coat was stained with blood and she knew it was her own. Looking up she could see the large white skeletal figure of the Wendigo dragging her.

As difficult as it was to focus through the pain, she launched a fireball at the creature who dropped her leg and scampered quickly away. Stopping a good twenty feet from her, it turned and growled, bearing its fanged teeth in an angry snarl, preparing to attack. Taryn scrambled to her feet, her legs wobbly and uncertain, but she needed to defend herself.

Launching another fireball at the Wendigo, it easily dodged the throw. She could tell it sensed her weakness, but kept its distance. It would wait her out; her loss of blood would soon do her in and then it would have her. She needed to escape. She remembered the sound of a waterfall nearby at the clearing and listened for it now. It was close. If she could make it to the waterfall, maybe she could lose the beast.

She started walking away as best she could with uncertain steps. The creature kept her in sight, but far enough to avoid her fireballs. Once it realized where she was headed, it made a move to cut her off, but a quick fireball changed its mind. Taryn quickened her pace. As she reached a cliff overlooking the waterfall, the creature made one last attempt at rushing her only to be deterred by one last fireball. She jumped into the churning water below.

Fire and water don't mix, which was the reason she had never learned to swim. The pain in her lungs was not due to fire, she knew, but rather because of the icy cold water as she gulped for air. Grasping hand over hand, she attempted a doggy paddle to reach the safety of land. As she latched on to the nearest rock in the middle of the river, she looked back. It was only a thirty-foot drop, but the Wendigo did not follow. Whether because of the icy cold water or the churning rapids, Taryn didn't know and didn't care. It was no longer following her.

The temperature of the water began to seep into her bones. The warming spell Alex had taught her had worn off when she lost consciousness. She needed to make it to land and cast the spell again or she would freeze to death. Struggling as she did to reach a low hanging tree limb, she pulled herself ashore. The cold helped numb the pain in her shoulder, but now she worried about frostbite. Clearing her head as best she could, she cast the warmth spell. The sudden rush of heat helped ease her pain, but she knew she was still in trouble. The Wendigo was out there... she was separated from the group and if it was up to Qaletaqa, he would just kill her now. She had been bitten, and soon she would start to crave human flesh. Then she would become a Wendigo. She knew she needed to find help quickly. She could only hope Alex, Radimir or Sheelin found her first.

19 TARYN'S ESCAPE

After recovering from the swift Wendigo attack, Alex realized Wallace was still unconscious—bleeding from a head wound, but alive. Sheelin cast a few healing spells and the bleeding stopped. A few minutes later, Wallace regained consciousness, though still a little lightheaded.

Alex was more concerned about Taryn at this point. Sheelin examined the blood trail leading away from the camp. They all knew Taryn had been bitten, but the trail was minimal... meaning she was probably still alive.

"We need to find Taryn before the creature kills her," Alex said, hurriedly packing his things.

"No," replied Qaletaqa. "If she's not dead yet, then the sooner the creature finishes her the better."

"What?" Alex blustered. "Look, I know you two have a difference of opinion over me, but we can't just let her die."

"If she lives, she will become another Wendigo. She's been bitten. It's only a matter of time."

"What if it were me, Father?" asked Sheelin, moving to Alex's side. Radimir fell in behind as well.

"The window of opportunity is small," replied Qaletaqa. "With her powers, she'll be able to kill easily. I can't risk letting her live. It may end up costing us more lives."

"There is a spell to help her resist the curse," said Sheelin. "Isn't there?"

"It has been lost through time," answered Qaletaqa, his temper obviously growing.

Alex could see he was not accustomed to people arguing with his decisions. Alex lowered his gaze for a few seconds as he pondered the idea of a spell to resist the hunger of the Wendigo. "I think I might know it. At least, I think I knew it at one time."

"We can't take that risk," said Qaletaqa.

"I can." Alex was determined to help Taryn even if that meant defying Qaletaqa. He couldn't remember Taryn in particular, but he did remember being part of the Circle. This much he was sure. He knew he had to at least try. He couldn't stand by and just let someone die.

"I'm sorry, Father," said Sheelin, "but I'm going with Alex to find Taryn. It's the right thing to do. I'm tired of sitting on the sidelines while others fight the battle between good and evil. Taryn offered me a place in the Circle and I intend to accept. Once we find her."

"I go too," said Radimir with his thick Russian accent as he puffed up his chest like his decision was very important.

Qaletaqa sighed and stood staring at the determined trio. "I wish you all good luck. I don't want to see another person die because of the Wendigo, but if I find her first, I must kill her."

"Then let's hope we find her before you do," replied Alex.

Qaletaqa quickly packed up his things and helped Wallace to his feet. He was not moving fast and needed further medical attention, but he was able to walk. After some quick farewells, Qaletaqa and Wallace headed back to their original base camp.

Sheelin started following Taryn's blood trail with Alex and Radimir close behind. The trail was spotty, but the path from Taryn's limp body being dragged through the snow was better defined. Unfortunately, it had begun to snow again. The continued lack of blood meant there was a good chance Taryn might still be alive.

After almost a mile, they spotted what looked like a large patch of matted snow. Sheelin moved closer to make sense of the patterns, while Alex and Radimir continued scouting the surrounding area. After finding a few scorch marks on nearby trees, Alex was even more hopeful Taryn still lived.

"There's two sets of prints," said Sheelin. "Taryn went off to the southwest and the Wendigo headed due west. We need to find them both. But which one do we follow?"

"We follow Taryn," replied Alex. "If we can cast the spell to help her resist the hunger, then we can buy ourselves more time to track down the beast and kill it. Also, we need to protect her from Qaletaqa and the other hunters."

"Taryn," said Radimir.

It took little convincing as Sheelin nodded and started following Taryn's tracks.

Alex knew her father and the other hunters could track as well if not better than her. It was important they reached Taryn first.

Traveling southwest from their position, Alex could hear the sounds of rushing water getting closer. Sheelin noticed the Wendigo had also followed Taryn which did not improve their spirits.

Once they arrived at the cliff overlooking the waterfall, Sheelin continued to search the area. "It looks like Taryn must have jumped into the waterfall below. On the positive side, the Wendigo did not follow. It paced here for a while before heading off to the northwest. If she survived the jump, she might still be alive. Unfortunately this makes tracking her more difficult. We have no idea where she came ashore downstream or on which side of the river. Since the Wendigo didn't follow, she probably came ashore on the opposite side."

"I don't know about you two," said Alex, "but I don't see a way across."

"Jump," replied Radimir.

Sheelin stretched her neck to look over the side. "That water is going to be freezing cold. We could get hypothermia."

"Well," smiled Alex, "if we make it to the other side, I know a warming spell we can use to keep us from freezing. I taught it to Taryn right before the Wendigo attacked, which means she knows it too. I just hope she remembers to use it."

Alex inched toward the edge as he peered over the side. "Taryn seemed to think I was a water elemental sorcerer. Let's see if she was right." He reached his hand over the side and a column of water rose from the maelstrom below. He stepped onto the waterspout and steadied himself.

Radimir transformed into a hawk and flew to the opposite side of the river below. After gathering his clothes in her pack, Sheelin took an uneasy step toward the cliff edge. Alex reached out a hand to help her onto the spout.

As the geyser lowered to the river below, Alex noticed movement on the opposite shore. Unsure of what he saw, his concentration faltered. The column collapsed and they plunged into the icy water below. Surfacing, they gradually made their way to the other shore and Alex cast the warmth spell. After drying off a bit, they resumed their search, but without any idea where to start. It would be many hours before sunrise and tracking Taryn was going to be difficult.

After searching the shoreline for some time, Radimir in wolf form, caught Taryn's scent. Even with Sheelin's help finding the tracks again, they were tired and wet and knew the Wendigo was still around. Alex decided it would be better to set up camp for a few hours than risk running into the creature while drowsy and half asleep.

Sheelin started a fire and they sat down for a meal before turning in.

"Any idea where she might be headed?" asked Alex as he took a bite of dried meat from their food rations.

"None of us know this area very well, including Taryn," replied Sheelin. "My father would've been able to provide some help with the terrain if he weren't so stubborn, but since Taryn doesn't know the area she wouldn't know where to go anyway. Our best bet is to follow her tracks and hope we find her before the Wendigo does."

"Hope we find Taryn before Wendigo find us, too," added Radimir.

Sheelin and Alex agreed. They continued to sit in silence eating their meager meal.

"Alex," said Sheelin, "have you been able to remember anything about your past? Anything about the Circle?"

Alex had to ponder the questions before answering. He'd had memory flashes, but they were so jumbled and inconsistent, he wasn't sure what to make of them.

"I remembered Taryn was a fire elemental sorceress before she told anyone, and I vaguely remember two other girls and a guy. I think they were from the Circle as well, but then there are other memories that don't seem to fit."

"Meagan, Amber and Cyrus," grunted Radimir as he took another bite of the tough jerky he was gnawing on.

"I remember wearing an old brown robe and carrying a crooked wooden staff while wandering the woods somewhere with a couple of knights, but I was an old man. There are other fragments too, but they seem like they are scattered throughout different periods of time."

"Better look forward not backward," said Radimir. "See who want to be, not who was."

"I know, but it just seems like my past holds the key to my future." Alex couldn't explain it, but he knew his memories were important. More important than just knowing who he was, something in his past held the answers to finding his future. Time seemed twisted in his mind as if his memories were not following a chronological path.

"Do you remember anything about these dark sorcerers?" continued Sheelin.

"It's not the dark sorcerers that worry me," he answered. "It's the demon lord they serve that is the bigger problem."

"Demon lord?" questioned Sheelin and Radimir almost as one.

"I don't know where that came from," Alex said. He was kicking himself for not remembering that piece of information before. It made him wonder what other critical details he had locked away in the recesses of his scrambled memory.

"Who is this demon lord? Do you know his name?"

Alex shook his head.

Sheelin's eyes drifted to the firelight. "Is it possible this demon is even more of a danger to my people and the rest of the world than the Wendigo? Regardless of my father's instructions, I know now more than ever I need to join the fight against the darkness. We need to find Taryn and return to the Circle. Taryn hadn't mentioned a demon lord so either this was the information she was hiding... or not even the Circle knows about it."

"We get sleep," said Radimir. "Start fresh in morning. I take first watch." Without even waiting for the other two to agree, he changed into a great grizzly bear and started to prowl the perimeter of the camp.

Alex decided to get some sleep. He wasn't about to object while Radimir was in bear form.

20   CHOOSING SIDES

Vincent returned from Mount Helicon to Ravenicon castle through the mirror in the library where he spoke to the Muses. He had been on a mission to gain information regarding the sorcerers trying to overthrow Malcolm as the leader of all dark sorcerers. He found Gollnick sitting nearby pouring over a New York City newspaper.

"So what's new in the Big Apple?" he asked, sitting down across the table.

"Weird weather conditions the meteorologists can't explain—not that they're the best at predicting normal weather patterns. They haven't been right all week. So, what did you find?"

"Veena doesn't have any new information at this point about Malcolm or the other sorcerers in New York. But then, she's the muse of historical literature, not current events."

Gollnick folded the newspaper and gave a command. "*New York Times.*" The print swirled around and when it was done, the banner for the *New York Times* appeared above the fold. He opened it and started paging through again.

"Hank has informed me he can get seven sorcerers from Egypt," commented Gollnick as he scanned the headlines. "Three from Greece and four from Rome will aide us if it comes to fighting this civil war. He's still trying to contact some other people he knows. So far, we've had little response to our call for aid, most are more concerned about protecting their own areas of the world."

"I think I can count on five sorcerers in the Miami area to support us even though they claim allegiance to Malcolm," said Vincent. "It seems Francois LeRain came to New York by way of Canada, but he was originally from France. Veena didn't have much on Duestoff."

"Duestoff is the younger brother of Frederick Von Woonst," Gollnick said. "Apparently he blames Malcolm for his brother's death at the hands—or claws, as it were—of Tiamat in Babylon."

"As I understand it," Vincent said, "each of the two faction leaders have about a hundred followers supporting them. Malcolm has somewhere in the neighborhood of three hundred, which means he still has the best odds of maintaining control... even without our help."

Gollnick laid down the paper. "The question is, what's the likely fallout? How much damage and death will they cause?"

"The better question is, what does Malcolm really think we can do to help? If he has that many sorcerers at his disposal, how are we going to make a difference?"

"I may have a suggestion," said a voice from behind them.

They both spun around to gaze upon the face of Malcolm in the mirror staring back at them. Vincent realized he had been listening in on their conversation. This sudden appearance was unsettling and unexpected.

"Remind me to put a block on that mirror as soon as possible," instructed Gollnick, leaning over to Vincent. "I don't like eavesdroppers."

"So what is this great idea of yours?" questioned Vincent with an obvious dislike and distrust.

"If the two of you were to secretly take out my competition..." started Malcolm, "...say in a surgical strike... then there won't be anyone to challenge me. Admittedly their followers would join me in coming after you, but think of the number of lives you can save by doing this."

Vincent stared at Malcolm's image with bulging eyes. "You seriously think we're going to just walk into New York City, kill two dark sorcerers and walk out without having every sorcerer in New York on our heels? We wouldn't make it one block until we'd be dead."

"If you have a better idea," replied Malcolm, "I'd love to hear it. Either way, you'd better make up your minds soon. There've already been a few skirmishes. The civil war has begun. And you know me, I'll be protecting myself. If innocent people get hurt, it's on you for not acting sooner."

Waving his hand in front of himself, Malcolm's face disappeared, leaving Gollnick and Vincent sitting there still wondering what to do.

Vincent spoke first. "We can't do what Malcolm wants. I say we contact these two sorcerers, get their point of view and see if we can negotiate a truce. If we do what he wants, we're as good as dead ourselves."

Vincent was determined not to do as Malcolm had suggested. He didn't want to see innocent people die, but knew it would be worse if Malcolm gained full control of New York. "I'll contact Deustoff, you get in touch with Francois."

Gollnick scrunched his nose at the suggestion. "It might be better if I contact Duestoff. He may have a grudge against you too, since you were with Frederick when he was killed by Tiamat. We need to make this quick or Malcolm may force our hand."

21 THE DWARVES OF NIDAVELLIR

Arriving on a plateau overlooking a great canyon, Amber, Cyrus and Meagan arrived by way of the Bifrost. The column of multi-colored light gave way to reveal a desolate barren valley below. They were on the side of a mountain with two paths before them. One led off to the left and wound around the side descending into the valley below. The other was a cave opening in the side of the mountain itself. On either side stood twenty-foot statues of what appeared to be dwarves holding great axes. The sky was dark and what little light was available came from torches near the cave's entrance.

After a quick survey, Cyrus grabbed one of the torches and headed between the statues. Meagan followed, but Amber hesitated. They turned back to see her staring into the dark void. Her complexion was pale and she took two tentative steps away. Cyrus knew as an air elemental sorceress, she would naturally not like going underground, yet again. In addition to her encounter with Tiamat and the descent into Fenrir's pit, another journey underground would only serve to reinforce her fear.

He looked at the sky and decided it was late and getting darker by the minute. They needed to find shelter for the night. "Amber, I know you don't like this, but we don't have much choice at the moment. Meagan and I will be with you all the way. You don't have to worry."

Amber continued to stare at the cave entrance for another moment, not saying a word. Finally, she nodded and slowly moved toward them. Cyrus reached out to take her hand and led the way into the cave.

From stories of both myth and modern culture, dwarves were thought to be dwellers of underground caverns and cities. It only made sense this cave would be the entrance to their underground kingdom of riches and weapons. Or at least shelter for the night.

The tunnel led down into the bowels of the mountain, eventually branching off in many directions, but Cyrus kept them on what appeared to be the main passageway, hoping it would lead to their destination. Eventually the tunnel opened up into a large room about fifty feet in diameter. It was completely empty. There were no other corridors, no doors and no objects inside the room.

After examining the space for many minutes, they decided to retrace their steps in the hope they had merely missed a turn somewhere. Cyrus knew they had to be careful. There were many side tunnels along the way leading to numerous twists and turns. It would be easy to get disoriented in the labyrinth. The last thing they wanted was to be lost forever in the underground lair of the dwarves.

The clanking of metal and unsheathing of weapons echoed through the passage. As they turned to make for the exit, they were confronted by a hundred armored dwarves standing ready for battle, bearing great axes, hammers and weapons of dwarfish design. The soldiers made no move to attack, but neither did they look ready to offer safe passage.

Remembering their training with Taryn, Cyrus pointed to the center of the room. Amber positioned herself according to her brother's direction. He wanted to make sure her elemental powers could be used effectively to defend them. Meagan stood next to her, ready to erect an earthen barrier for protection. It was Cyrus who stepped forward to talk with the dwarves, he hoped.

"Hi there. It seems we're a little lost. Any chance one of you can point us to someone who knows how to make powerful things?"

Amber and Meagan rolled their eyes at Cyrus' request. Meagan whispered to Amber, "Leader maybe, but diplomat? No way."

Many of the dwarves started mumbling amongst themselves, but Cyrus couldn't make out what they were saying. It was either too garbled or they were speaking some language he didn't know. The dwarf at the head of the group made no comment and no movement to converse with the others. He stood stock still, staring at Cyrus.

The two men never flinched. Locked in a contest of wills.

After many minutes of the motionless and soundless competition, it was Cyrus who finally blinked. The dwarf puffed up his chest, proud of his victory as Cyrus lowered his gaze.

From the corner of his eye, Cyrus determined the other two had been preparing to defend themselves. He still wore his bracer of fireballs. He may have lost this battle, but he was not ready to surrender just yet.

"I am Kallanir Stonefoot," said the lead dwarf. "You will come with us."

"Where?" questioned Cyrus as he raised his gaze once again.

"The destination is of no concern to you." Raising his overly large axe, the dwarf pointed down the currently blocked hall. As he motioned, the other dwarves separated, creating a path down their ranks to whatever was Kallanir's planned objective.

When Cyrus and the girls started toward the path, Kallanir took the lead. As they passed the dwarven ranks, Cyrus noticed he stood at least a foot or more above the heads of their captors. However, the dwarves were more bulky and their strength could be seen in their arms and legs.

Kallanir led them a third of the way up the passage then turned into one of the side tunnels. After many twists and turns, climbing up and down, Cyrus was completely lost—which he figured was Kallanir's plan.

They walked for almost an hour before entering a large chamber with many guards on either side. At the opposite end stood two gigantic stone doors. They swung open without a sound at Kallanir's approach.

Upon entering the area beyond the doors, the trio emerged into an enormous cavern. Structures were carved into the sides like apartments overlooking a grand central plaza. Ornate Norse carvings decorated almost every surface. Buildings and streets lined the cavern floor. Artificial light from a central point at the top of the cavern made it seem like a bright sunny day even though they were hundreds of feet below the surface.

Kallanir marched them through the city to the far end of the cavern. Many dwarves stopped to watch and stare at the newcomers. Apparently it had been long years since someone other than a dwarf was seen in the city.

Approaching the far end, they came to two more gigantic stone doors flanked by twenty-foot statues. Kallanir approached the guards at the front of the doors and whispered something to them. The doors swung open, and one of the guards raced inside. He looked over his right shoulder. "The dwarf king's palace."

A crowd had gathered to watch the spectacle as Kallanir led them into a large audience hall with a throne at the far end. The crowd poured into the chamber, anxious to observe. Kallanir marched up to the throne then knelt. He immediately glanced back over his shoulder. Cyrus took the hint so he motioned Amber and Meagan to approach. They knelt too, awaiting the king's entrance.

From the right side of the chamber entered ten more guards followed by a stocky figure with a silver cloak. His bushy red beard hung over a broad golden chestplate with a round belly. The crown upon his head was encrusted with many rare gems. He eyed the newcomers cautiously and took his seat on the throne.

"Who have we here?" The question was directed to Kallanir who now rose to speak.

"Intruders into the central tunnel, my lord."

"What are their names?"

Kallanir opened his mouth to answer, but hesitated. Cyrus realized their earlier conversation had been too short. The dwarf leader never asked for their names. After their capture, he'd brought them straight here without so much as a word.

The dwarf pursed his lips with a frown. He turned to Cyrus and said, "Speak."

"My name is Cyrus Marx," said Cyrus as he came to his feet, "and this is my sister Amber Marx and our friend Meagan Strom. We are sorcerers from Earth—or Midgard, as you may know it. We've come in search of your help, oh wise king."

"You have manners for intruders. Welcome to Koldihr. I am king Brodkir Stonefoot. What is it you seek and why come to me?"

"The giant wolf Fenrir has been released and we seek a way to re-imprison him."

"What!" exclaimed the king as he rose from his throne. "How can this be? Our Gleipnir bound him in a deep cavern on the Gioll rock."

"Dark sorcerers discovered his location and freed him." Cyrus then opened his backpack and pulled out the shredded remains of Gleipnir, presenting them to the dwarf king.

"The wolf is loose on Midgard once again," sighed Brodkir as he hung his head. "Alas, the Asgardians are not here to stop the beast this time. Fortunately Fenrir has no way to reach our realm."

"But what about Earth?" asked Cyrus. "The people of Midgard have no way to defeat the beast. We need a new Gleipnir."

"What you ask is impossible. The dwarves who made that binding have long since passed. Though we live longer than humans, we are not immortal."

"There must be something you can do?" Cyrus was desperate for any idea to stop the giant wolf.

"Kallanir, assign them quarters for now and keep them there. I must assemble the council to discuss this situation." Without another word, the king left the room in a hurry.

Cyrus moved to stop the king, but Kallanir blocked his movement then shook his head. Kallanir motioned for them to follow him. As they turned to leave the audience chamber, the crowds mumbled to themselves, perhaps concerned for their safety. Kallanir led them out through part of the city and into a building, then up many flights of stairs.

Finally reaching their destination, Kallanir showed them into their quarters. "Remain here. There will be guards just outside the door if you need anything."

When Kallanir turned to leave, Cyrus asked, "What's going to happen now?"

Kallanir looked over his shoulder at Cyrus. "The king will meet with his council. They will tell him we are safe from Fenrir and should not attempt to aide you in any way."

"But why?" asked Amber.

"Another sorceress from your realm arrived about an hour ago. She told us it was you who were trying to release certain creatures on Midgard—including Fenrir. The fact that you brought the remains of Gleipnir indicate the wolf is indeed free. The only question that remains is who freed him... you or her."

"If we'd freed him, then why are we trying to find a new Gleipnir?" questioned Amber.

"Why indeed?" Kallanir said, then left the room.

"Well, that went better... and worse... than I had hoped." Cyrus flopped down on a stone chair only to realize there was no cushioning. "I wasn't sure what kind of welcome we would get, but no Gleipnir is going to be a problem. And who is this other sorceress?"

"Don't be so sure they can't make another Gleipnir." Meagan looked out a window toward the audience hall. "Dwarves have never been the most sharing of races. They probably just don't want to give it to us. At least not without payment of some kind."

"For now we wait," said Cyrus. "This other sorceress has me concerned, but there isn't much we can do at the moment. We might as well use this time to report in. Meagan, will the mirror communication still work here?"

"No. Mirror communication and transport only works within the same realm, though I should be able to use my mental link with Nick. But I'll keep it to a minimum. I expect the dwarves will be listening in."

"Can they do that?" questioned Amber.

"Not on my mental link, but I'm sure they're listening in on this room somehow."

"You don't trust them?" asked Cyrus.

"I have my reasons." Meagan crossed her arms in front of her and walked out onto a balcony to end the conversation.

Cyrus furrowed his brow. "Then why did you suggest coming here?"

Meagan sighed as she looked out over the dwarven city. "Lack of options."

22   Lost in the Woods

Taryn lay shivering at the base of a tree in the woods. Her dreams were more nightmares as she woke in a cold sweat. Even awake, the nightmares were still running through her mind. Images of the Wendigo, the pain in her left shoulder from its bite, running through the woods and jumping off a cliff to a river far below... but that wasn't the worst. She had caught glimpses of the Wendigo's memories of hunting and killing its prey, of ripping the life out of many different people, but always the hunger, the hunger for the next kill.

Taryn knew part of the curse was to always be starving. No matter how many people a Wendigo would kill, it was always hungry for the next one. Its hunger would never be sated, a hunger she was now beginning to feel. She tried to resist the urge, to pit her will against the hunger. She had no doubt Qaletaqa would seek to kill her, not because of his mistrust of her, but because she had been bitten. Qaletaqa could not allow the creation of another Wendigo and would be determined to kill her to prevent that from happening. Her only hope was that Alex, Radimir and Sheelin would come to her aid.

She stood and shivered, her sensitivity to cold growing. There was that spell Alex had taught her for warmth, but she couldn't think clearly enough anymore to remember it, let alone try casting it. She needed to keep moving and keep alert. Any sign of movement could mean a hunting party or the Wendigo or her friends. She needed to find them, but in the dark and cold of the night, she had gotten herself so turned around she had no idea where she was or where they might be in relation to her.

Taryn vaguely remembered the river was to the west of the camp where they met Qaletaqa and Alex. She couldn't hear the rushing water from her current location, but if she could find the river and then head east, she might have a chance. The problem was where to find the blasted river.

Standing up was challenge enough, but walking was even more difficult and the hunger was growing. Her eyes were bloodshot and her face was even paler than normal. She hadn't gone more than twenty steps before she bent to vomit, then leaned against a tree to steady herself. Her head was swimming and the nausea was getting worse, but she was determined not to let the curse win. She had to find her friends and quickly. She just hoped she wasn't in the mood for a meal when she found them.

Looking skyward she spotted the moon above the tree tops. She remembered seeing the moon earlier at camp, but she didn't know how long she had been out. Thinking was difficult and her memory was foggy. She wondered if this was how Max's memory was all the time. Shaking her head to clear her mind, she tried to focus on the direction of the moon. Thinking it had been behind her as she dove into the river, she hoped moving toward the moon now would take her back.

She didn't know for sure, but she needed to pick a direction and get moving. The nausea welled up in her stomach again, but she fought hard to keep it down. She couldn't afford to waste time stopping every few yards to vomit. Picking up a broken branch, she started using it as a walking stick to help stabilize her balance.

After about an hour of stumbling through the woods, she heard the sounds of the river. The discovery quickened her pace, but nausea forced her to slow again. As she neared the edge of the river, she spotted three sets of footprints in the snow. The hunting parties were in groups of three... but so were her friends unless Alex had returned to hunting with Qaletaqa. She knew she needed help to cross the river. Scaling the cliff was not likely to happen in her current condition. Her best bet seemed to be following the tracks in the hope it was her friends.

She knelt down next to the river and scooped a handful of water into her mouth, trying to relieve her hunger, but the water only served to make her thirstier. Leaning on the walking stick for support, she stood up in disgust that the curse was getting to her. She turned to find the tracks again but a sudden wave of dizziness came over her and she fell to the ground.

A few seconds later, she sat up, again trying to focus on her breathing to steady her nerves. A long, low howl pierced the silence of the night, alerting her to the terrifying fact the Wendigo was near. If her hearing was worth trusting, the creature was on the same side of the river. Her time was running out. If the creature found her first, it would probably just kill her rather than wait for her transformation and have a second mouth to feed.

Dizziness or not, nausea or not, she hoisted herself up and tossed her walking stick aside. At a brisk pace she followed the tracks. The sun was starting to rise and she needed to find her friends as quickly as possible. Tired and weak, she was determined not to become that which they were here hunting. She was going to find her friends, kill the Wendigo and return to being normal, she hoped.

23 THE SEARCH FOR TARYN

The next morning just outside of Manitoba, Alex, Radimir and Sheelin were on the trail of Taryn who had been bitten by the Wendigo and dragged off. She had apparently escaped the creature, but was also separated from the rest of the hunting parties—parties who were now hunting her too.

Sheelin's father, Qaletaqa, had already made his intentions known that he would not risk the creation of another Wendigo. If he had the chance to kill Taryn, Wendigo or not, he would kill her in order to stop the cycle. Their only chance to save Taryn was to destroy the Wendigo before she killed someone herself.

Radimir took wolf form as he, Alex and Sheelin followed Taryn's tracks. After a long journey, they found the spot where she had apparently collapsed for the night. They had gotten an early start to beat the other hunting parties and the Wendigo, but now they were tired and in need of a rest. No sooner did they make camp than they heard the cry of the Wendigo. And it was too close for comfort. Sheelin estimated it was only a mile or two away.

Alex wondered if maybe it wasn't the original Wendigo, but Taryn newly transformed. If so, they were headed right into danger. Deciding the creature was too close for safety, they chose to eat on the go and keep moving. No sense making themselves sitting ducks for a hungry Wendigo.

"I'm sure that wasn't Taryn," said Sheelin to nobody in particular. "But if she did transform during the night and retained her fire elemental powers, she could be very dangerous."

"She's strong," replied Alex. "Stronger than any of us. If anyone can resist the curse of the Wendigo, it would be her." Alex was trying to convince himself as much as the others.

With danger so close, Radimir shape-shifted into a bear for added fighting strength regardless of who they faced.

"She's heading back toward the river," Sheelan said, pausing to examine the tracks. "But she's moving slowly and having difficulties." Sheelin stopped to examine a pile of stale vomit. "She's also not feeling well. The curse must be getting to her."

Alex held up a hand without saying a word. The other two stopped in their tracks and waited to see what had caught his attention. Alex pointed off to the south. Sheelin and Radimir's eyes followed.

In the distance, he spotted another hunting party. They were too far away to tell who was in the party, but he was confident it was Sheelin's father's group. Only Qaletaqa would have pushed through the night in order to stop Taryn from becoming another Wendigo.

Sheelin pointed to the tracks, then in the direction Taryn had gone—east, back to the river. With as little noise as possible, they continued to follow the trail. They had a head start, but it wouldn't take Qaletaqa long to find Taryn's tracks as well. They needed to move quickly, but silently.

Sheelin looked skyward. "A storm system is moving in. If a new coat of snow falls, it will make following Taryn's tracks that much more difficult and obscure visibility. Losing the trail would be bad enough, but with a Wendigo on the loose, it would be dangerous to continue the pursuit much longer."

Alex lowered a hand behind him and the snow moved in to cover both their tracks and Taryn's in the hope of slowing Qaletaqa down a bit.

In the distance, they could see a ridge line where they might find refuge. In less than an hour, it was as Sheelin had feared. The snow storm was intense. Alex had trouble keeping Radimir and Sheelin in sight. They barely made it to the ridge line in time to find a small outcrop of rock. It wasn't as good as a cave, but it was the best they could do with such a storm.

Sheelin started a fire and they huddled under the outcrop as best they could in the hope of waiting out the storm. Alex knew the Wendigo was a creature of cold, and weather like this would not hinder it in the least. He made sure someone was on guard at all times.

They had been clustered under the rocky protection for less than an hour when Alex spotted a shape moving around in the distance. With poor visibility from the storm, he couldn't make out who it was. He dared not call out for fear it may be the Wendigo, but it could also be Taryn or one of the others from a hunting party. However, anyone stuck in a blizzard like that wouldn't last long without protection.

At last, Alex made the decision to call out to the figure. Sheelin and Radimir prepared for a fight in the event it was not a friendly.

Raising a burning log from the fire, he called out, "Hello! Over here!" He continued to wave the burning log for another moment, but the figure had disappeared into the storm. The three of them did not lower their guard, but kept still in anticipation of an attack.

A moment later, three figures were seen making their way toward the firelight. It was Qaletaqa and the two new hunters in his party. He and his hunters looked more like walking snowmen. They dusted themselves off and settled around the fire to warm themselves.

Sheelin said nothing to her father nor he to her. They were still at odds over how to deal with Taryn and neither was ready to give in. The storm forced them to share this refuge, but not a plan of attack.

Alex and Radimir welcomed the others cheerfully, though Alex noticed Sheelin and Qaletaqa not saying a word to anyone or each other. He felt it best to leave them be for now. With this many people in the outcrop, it was unlikely the Wendigo would attack, but not impossible as demonstrated by the previous evening.

After they all had a bite to eat and time to rest and warm up from the storm, Alex made his way over to Qaletaqa. "Your daughter is as stubborn as you."

Qaletaqa made no response, but looked over his shoulder to where Sheelin was sitting. "I'm proud of my daughter and angry with her at the same time. She is standing up for what she believes, but at the same time defying my authority. She takes after me a little too much, I'm afraid."

Alex could see he wanted to speak with his daughter, but something was preventing him from doing so. "We're not going anywhere for a while. Go talk to her."

"I made excuses for not discussing the future with Sheelin, not finding out what she wanted to do with her life. I always assumed she would follow in my footsteps, but this interest with the battle of good and evil has made me see she is interested in bigger things."

Like Qaletaqa, Alex could sense Sheelin was leaving once the hunt was over. With or without Taryn, she was going to join the Circle against the dark sorcerers.

"She'll leave with you and Radimir when the hunt is over?" Qaletaqa said. It was both a question and a statement. Clearly he already knew the truth.

"Yes. She knows she's needed, and so am I." Alex saw no reason to lie about their plans. The sooner Qaletaqa could accept the truth, the easier it would be for them both.

"Have you found any tracks?" asked Qaletaqa.

Alex hesitated in telling Qaletaqa about Taryn's tracks heading back to the river. Yet he also knew Qaletaqa could tell if he were lying.

"Any tracks that might have been out there are snow covered by now," Alex said truthfully. "It's hard to say where either of them may be at this point."

"Taryn will most likely head for familiar ground."

Alex could tell Qaletaqa was trying to reason out where to find their prey, both Taryn and the Wendigo.

"The creature on the other hand will not be fazed by this storm. It's still out there hunting for us."

"Qaletaqa, I know you consider Taryn a threat at this point," Alex reasoned, "but the Wendigo is the greater threat. Let us find Taryn. We'll keep her safe and secure until the Wendigo can be destroyed. Once the beast is gone, she'll be free of the curse."

"And if she's already turned?"

"Then it should be her friends that destroy her."

Qaletaqa held his gaze for a moment. "Fine. We won't hunt Taryn for now, only the creature. But if she does turn, she must be destroyed."

Alex let out a sigh of relief. "Agreed."

A few hours later, the storm subsided and the two groups prepared to exit in search of their targets. Before heading out, Qaletaqa approached Alex, Radimir and Sheelin.

"My team will head further west. The Wendigo is most likely hunting us as much as we are hunting it. My guess is that Taryn is probably heading east, back to familiar territory."

"I agree," said Sheelin with a furrowed brow. "Does this mean you've given up on finding Taryn?"

"No. It just means that the Wendigo is the higher priority. If we can destroy it, we may be able to save Taryn. It'll be up to you to find her and keep her from killing until we can find the creature."

The slightest smile cracked Sheelin's face.

Alex was happy to see Sheelin and her father being more reasonable after some time to think. He was just glad they were in agreement at least for now.

Qaletaqa and Sheelin gave each other a hug then rejoined their respective groups to head out, this time now comfortable in the knowledge they were no longer competing to find the same person.

24 The Impossible Items

After checking in with Gollnick and Vincent back in Baltimore to learn about the dark sorcerer civil war, Cyrus, Amber and Meagan began to think their situation was a lot less stressful. They had been given quarters in the dwarf king's palace and told to wait. What they weren't told was how long.

As Cyrus' patience wore thin, Kallanir returned with news. "King Brodkir Stonefoot has decided that we are unable to aide you in making a new Gleipnir. Because Fenrir is on Midgard, he is no threat to the other eight realms. The Agardians are gone and we must look to protect ourselves from you and other sorcerers now that someone is indeed releasing creatures from their eternal prisons. I am sorry."

"Kallanir," started Cyrus. "Your last name is Stonefoot just like the king, correct?"

"He is my father."

"Then you must speak to him," pleaded Cyrus. "We are members of the New Circle on Earth. It's our job to protect the prisons. We would never intentionally open them."

"Then I would say you are doing a poor job."

"Just like a dwarf to be narrow minded," shot Meagan from the balcony door.

Everyone turned in surprise. Cyrus had never seen her so mad. Meagan was always the calm one who never got excited about anything, but something about this place, or the dwarves in particular, had her fired up.

"I can understand your frustration," replied Kallanir. "I do not feel this is a wise decision, but Brodkir is my father and my king. I must do as he commands."

"You understand our frustration?" demanded Meagan, but Cyrus held a hand up to stop any more comments.

"What about this sorceress Brodkir spoke of?" questioned Cyrus. "Where is she?"

"The king has given her, and you, two choices. Return to Midgard or remain here as our guests for the remainder of your lives. You will be safe here from Fenrir and any other creatures released on Midgard. Alexis Malkin has decided to return to Midgard, but before she does, she has asked to know your decision. It seems she wants to learn if you will be causing any more trouble back on Midgard."

As Cyrus opened his mouth to respond, Amber interrupted. "We wish to return to Asgard. Though the Asgardians are gone, Odin still lives. If the dwarves will not help, then maybe he will."

"We know Odin of Asgard remains, but he is old and lacks the mental or physical capacity to aide anyone. You are not prisoners, you are free to go. Yet be warned... If you bring any harm to this or any of the other eight realms, you will have an army of dwarves to face. And I assure you we are not weak."

The three of them had gathered up their things to leave, when Cyrus turned back to face Kallanir. "You said Brodkir's decision was unwise."

"Yes, but there is nothing I can do about it."

"Maybe there is," suggested Cyrus. "Do you know anyone who might know the spell to create a new Gleipner?"

Kallanir sat down at a finely crafted stone table opposite Cyrus and crossed his hands. "There are elder dwarves in the lower mines, great crafters of magical items." Kallanir pondered Cyrus' question for a moment. "There may be one or two down there who might yet possess the necessary skills to make such an item. But if the king finds out, he will be furious with both you and me."

"Kallanir..." said Cyrus. "This Alexis Malkin is most likely a dark sorceress. And we already know she possesses the spell to get here from Earth. If that's the case, then she has the power to bring Fenrir here as well. Your city is not safe as long as that creature is free. Help us."

Kallanir had to consider this for a few moments. Cyrus could tell that Meagan was getting impatient with the dwarf. He needed to keep her at bay—at least until he could convince the dwarf prince they should work together. With a stern look and a nod Meagan tossed her hair and moved out onto the balcony.

"According to legend," started Kallanir, "there are six impossible items that are needed to make Gleipnir. In addition, Fenrir is no fool. Last time the Asgardians put bonds on the wolf, he demanded someone put a hand in his mouth as a show of trust. When he couldn't get free, he bit off the hand of Tyr."

"Does this mean you'll help us?"

"I fear the dangers of Midgard will spill over into the other realms, including Nidavellir," he said quietly as if trying to keep the conversation a secret. "I will help. And call me Kallan."

Cyrus dropped his voice as well. "So, Kallan, where do we find these impossible items?"

"Don't worry," the prince replied. "They may be impossible on Midgard, but not necessarily in the other realms. The items we need are the sound of a cat's footfall, the beard of a woman, the root of a mountain, a bear's sinews, a fish's breath and a bird's spittle."

"Yeah, sure," said Cyrus with mock enthusiasm, "that stuff should be easy to find."

"Don't worry, my friend," Kallan grinned widely, "any dwarf could find the root of a mountain or be ashamed to call himself a dwarf. As for the beard of a woman, some of our women folk here should have no problem with that. The other items, we may need some help. For now let's go to the lower mines and find the elders who know how to make Gleipnir. Perhaps they will know where to look." Before leaving, he paused and held up a hand. "There is one obstacle we may have. The dwarves who made the first Gleipnir are no longer alive. We may need to visit the elves... they will know the spells. Unfortunately, we're not really on speaking terms with them at this—"

"I will go to the elves," interrupted Meagan, who was once again standing at the doorway to the balcony with Amber by her side.

"Dark or light, elves do not tolerate humans," said Kallan.

"Let me worry about that," she replied, her voice more calm and agreeable now.

"I don't think we should split up," said Cyrus concerned about Meagan's personality change since arriving on Nidavellir.

"Kallan is right about one thing, elves don't normally like humans... or dwarves for that matter... but I can get in to see them."

Meagan seemed confident, but Cyrus was still unsure.

"I'll go with her," said Amber.

"No," replied Meagan quickly. "I can do this alone."

"Look, I'm an air elemental sorceress. I've already been below ground longer than I like and I'm not really wild about the idea of going deeper into the mountain to the lower mines. I need to get above ground. Like it or not, I'm coming." Amber gripped Meagan's arm.

Cyrus could see the pleading look in Amber's eyes. She was doing her best at keeping things together, but it was clear the underground was starting to get to her. The white of her knuckles and the shaking of her hands revealed her nerves were on end.

"Okay," said Meagan relenting for Amber's sake, "Amber and I will go see the light elves. You two go see these elders."

"Before you leave," interrupted Cyrus, "I need you to contact Gollnick. I have a little request." Cyrus had the slightest of a grin on his face.

"I will take you back up to the surface," said Kallan. "From there you can take the Bifrost to Alfheim, home of the light elves. Then Cyrus and I will head for the lower mines. When you return, enter the cave and take the third right turn in the tunnel system. It will lead to a small dwelling site. Wait there for us. As long as we don't die in the lower mines, we will meet you there in two days' time."

"Why so long?" questioned Amber.

"The mines are very deep and much of the distance will be walking or climbing." Looking to Cyrus and smiling, he added, "I hope you can keep up, human."

"Don't worry about me." Cyrus was confident about the physical challenge of the next two days. He was just glad he didn't need to learn any new spells.

25 A Fiery End

It was mid-afternoon when Alex, Radimir and Sheelin stopped for a rest. The weather had cleared and the sun shone bright in the sky. A bitter chill and a new layer of snow reminded them they were still in the frigid north. Sunlight reflected off the newly fallen snow, blinding the trio of sorcerers. They had not seen nor heard any signs of Taryn... or the Wendigo.

Alex wished Taryn were with them to start a fire and keep them warm. But she had her own problems right now. Time was running short. If the creature didn't get to Taryn, the hunger would. When that happened, she would become that which she'd come here to hunt.

Alex pushed back the hood of his winter coat and ran fingers through his disheveled hair. He sat on a fallen tree to rest while they took a drink and grabbed a quick bite to eat. The deer jerky was tough, but anything tasted good right now. Food options were scarce since they needed to travel light. Speed was their ally in hunting this creature, both for offense and defense. For such a large biped, it moved lightning fast.

Radimir had returned to wolf form in an attempt to pick up Taryn's scent, but with no luck. Sheelin found herself in a similar situation since she was unable to spot any tracks left by Taryn.

Alex could see their spirits were low, as were his. They needed some encouragement, even the smallest indication Taryn was nearby. He stood, closed his eyes and cast a spell, "*Searo te-yon maku.*"

The others watched as he turned in place with his right palm perpendicular to the ground as if seeing through his hand. He could feel their eyes on him as they held their breaths. He too hoped for the slightest sign of their friend.

When Alex finally lowered his hand, his head drooped as well. The spirits of the other two sank with him. No one said a word.

He looked from Radimir to Sheelin then brushed some snow from his pants and started walking.

The wolf sprang to its feet, but hesitated. When Sheelin too stood and followed Alex, the wolf quickly moved into the lead with nose to the ground.

Sheelin moved up next to Alex. "Our chances of finding her in time are dwindling. If it isn't already too late."

"We'll find her. We just need to figure out where she would go."

Just then Radimir's head jerked quickly to the left. He sniffed a few more times and took off in a sprint. Alex and Sheelin exchanged a glance then took off in pursuit of their shape-shifting friend. After ten minutes, he and Sheelin came to a stop. They had lost Radimir's trail until he poked his head out from behind a tree.

"Clothes?" he asked.

Sheelin tossed him his clothing and waited for him to dress.

When Radimir finally rejoined the other two he pointed south. "Scent head to river. She follow river south."

"She's looking for a cabin or settlement," said Alex. "The question is, is she looking for shelter... or food?"

Sheelin took a few steps toward the river and knelt. "There are tracks here. Possibly Taryn. Definitely moving slow and dragging her feet. She stumbled a few times. She must be cold and weak."

Encouraged by these new signs, the trio picked up the pace. They followed the trail along the river until they spotted a shape in the distance. It was white, but small. Alex hoped it was just Taryn's snow-covered jacket and not the Wendigo. The figure fell to the ground and they broke into a run toward whatever it was.

When they approached, the figure was curled up in a ball at the base of a tree beneath some low hanging branches. Seeing no movement, Alex carefully pushed back the tree limbs to get a better view. He cautiously reached in and placed a hand on the figure. There was no response to his touch, so he rolled it over to get a better look.

Taryn launched at him with a scream as her fingers reached for his throat. Alex caught her hands in mid-strike. Her face was pale and drained. Her bright red hair was almost white and her eyes lacked pigment.

In her weakened state, she was easily restrained. Hunched over, she sat cross legged on the frozen ground. With her hands tied behind her back, she glared at her three captors. A low growl emanated through her clenched teeth.

Alex, Radimir and Sheelin sat on the opposite side of a small fire. They had built a make-shift camp twenty yards from the river's edge.

Alex was concerned. His friend still resembled Taryn, but she was slowly beginning to look more and more like the Wendigo. "So what do we do now?" he whispered to Sheelin.

"We wait. It's up to my father and the other hunters to destroy the Wendigo. Once that's done, she should be free."

Radimir leaned forward to speak past Alex to Sheelin. "While wait, sitting goose."

Alex smiled. "I think he means we're sitting ducks. If the Wendigo attacks, we're going to have a hard time protecting Taryn *and* fighting off the monster at the same time."

Sheelin appeared to consider the situation. "I could try a signal flare. It would alert the others to our location and let them know we need help. Unfortunately, it would also let the Wendigo know where we are, too. We have no way to know who would get here first."

Alex considered their options. Taryn's pale features and white streaks through her once red hair made her look almost ghost like. He couldn't let his friend suffer, but they were in the middle of nowhere with little protection and in a poorly defensible location. "Time is against us. We have to risk it."

Radimir nodded his agreement.

Sheelin stood and point skyward. "*Sili fir-tor mata.*" A bright red orb shot from her finger and raced skyward. At an altitude of two hundred feet, it exploded into a red globe that hung in the air for many minutes. As it descended, it exploded twice more, indicating their location directly below.

Alex stood. "Now we protect this area until help arrives. Spread out and find some cover. Keep your eyes and ears open. It could be a while."

Later that evening, as the sun set on the distant horizon, the trees cast long shadows and the already cold temperatures began to drop. What little warmth the sun provided had deserted Alex and his friends. They were alone in the cold, and in the world, it seemed. Their hope waned with the diminishing light.

A solitary figure walked out of the darkening woods to approach their meager camp. Alex and the others stood their ground, prepared for an attack.

As the figure neared, Sheelin called out, "Father?"

Qaletaqa stood near the edge of camp, the firelight barely illuminating his features. His eyes studied their captive. A gentle breeze was the only sound against Taryn's low growling. Her whitened eyes locked with Qaletaqa as they held each other's gaze.

Sheelin moved between Taryn and her father. "We did as you requested. We found her and kept her safe, both from the Wendigo and herself."

Without a sound, Qaletaqa briefly glanced over his right shoulder before returning his attention to his daughter. "Unfortunately, we've been unsuccessful in finding the creature."

Within seconds, fifteen other hunters emerged from the shadows and flanked the eastern edge of the camp, all weapons trained on Taryn.

Qaletaqa craned his neck to look around past Sheelin at Taryn as she sat with her hands bound and hunched over. "Surely you can see there is no hope for her. It's only a matter of time before she is strong enough to break her bonds and attack. At the first taste of human flesh, she will become a Wendigo. We must destroy her now before that happens."

Alex and Radimir moved to join Sheelin in blocking Qaletaqa's path. This was what Alex feared, that Qaletaqa would strike out at Taryn once she was a captive. "You gave me your word you would leave Taryn to us. To protect or destroy if necessary. She isn't too far gone yet. There's still time to save her."

"Look at her. She's more Wendigo than human."

"She's also defenseless. I will not allow you or anyone to harm a defenseless person, no matter what potential threat she may pose."

Qaletaqa held up a hand. The hunters lowered their weapons and took a more relaxed stance. "Her strength grows the longer we wait. Soon there will be no other choice." Qaletaqa moved forward and took a seat near the fire, opposite Taryn.

Alex took a seat to his right. "Are you sure there's no other cure, other than destroying the original Wendigo?"

"None that I know."

Alex thought for a few seconds then quickly stood and moved toward Taryn. Twisting from the waist, he threw his right hand forward, fingers extended, toward Taryn. She looked at him with fear in her eyes then froze in place.

Qaletaqa jumped to his feet as Sheelin and Radimir watched in confusion. Qaletaqa took a step closer and saw that Taryn was unmoving. "What did you do to her?"

Alex turned to face Qaletaqa. "You were right, I am powerful. More powerful than anyone realizes. I'm not sure how I did that, but I've frozen her in time. So long as the spell remains in effect, she won't continue to change."

"You froze her in time?" Qaletaqa studied Alex. "How?"

Alex raised himself to full height and announced, "My name is not Alex, and it is not Max either. I am Chronos, King of the Titans and Master of Time."

Taryn started to move a bit, drawing Alex's attention back to her. "Okay, maybe not *master* quite yet. I need to concentrate to keep her progression frozen."

"Chronos?"

Without diverting his attention, Alex explained. "That was what Taryn was withholding. The Circle believes I am the Titan, Chronos, from Greek mythology."

Qaletaqa stepped closer and reached out to touch Taryn's cheek.

"No! You'll disrupt the spell."

Qaletaqa pulled his hand back, but continued to stare in amazement. "How did you do this?"

"Honestly, I'm not sure. It was more by instinct than anything. What I do know is if I break my concentration, she'll return to the normal timeline. And I don't know if I can freeze her again."

An hour later, they heard a long loud howl from nearby. Alex's focus wavered, but he regained his composure quickly. "Please tell me that was just a wolf."

Qaletaqa moved to the outer edge of the firelight as he looked off into the distance. "No. It was the Wendigo and it's headed this way. It's coming." He continued to stare into the darkness then turned to his friends. "Hunters, form a perimeter. We must not let the creature get away."

The fifteen hunters spaced themselves at equal distances around the meager camp. They stood, weapons armed and spells ready. The night grew silent... not even the birds made a noise. The only sound was from the water rippling in the river as it made its way south. Then a gentle breeze caused some leaves to ruffle in the wind and drew a misfired arrow from one of the hunters.

Qaletaqa tried to calm the others. "Steady, friends. Let the monster come to us."

A long minute passed without event. Alex's senses were heightened, waiting for a sound or movement in the woods. The shadows played tricks on his mind while seeing things that weren't there. A quick scan around the camp revealed everyone was experiencing the same thing. The night had grown dark and the cloud cover provided no moonlight to aide their sight.

Without warning two men from the eastern edge of the perimeter called out in pain then came flying into the circle backwards, landing near the fire.

Alex startled, then turned to the perimeter where the attack had occurred.

Taryn screamed in anger. Her bonds were still in place, but her strength and fury had grown.

From the edge of the camp near the river rose a towering figure, over nine feet tall and pure white. Skin stretched over bones with thin lines of muscle underneath. Its ribcage looked like a xylophone while long thin fingers ended in razor sharp claws. The face was humanoid in appearance, with an extended snout and long white hair. A low growl could be heard as it gnashed its sharpened teeth.

Radimir dove behind some bushes. Seconds later a grizzly bear rose to block its path to Taryn. Alex ran to the aide of the bear and using his elemental powers, summoned water from the river. Sheelin stood at his side.

The first tentacle of water froze around the left wrist of the Wendigo who looked down at its immobile hand. It tried to shake it free... then with hidden strength, forcibly broke the icy bond.

When it looked up from its hand it was met by a charging bear. With a bear claw to the face, the creature let out a howl and backhanded the animal with little effort. Another icy tentacle from the river ensnared the right ankle of the creature.

Fireballs from the Hunters with magical powers flew in to hit the monster as Radimir backed away a few steps for safety.

Unfortunately, the heat from the fireballs served to melt the ice bonds and the creature moved forward shoving the massive bear backward.

Alex continued to ensnare the creature only to have it break free... or be freed by flying fireballs. Of course his icy aura prevented the fireballs from doing any harm to the creature either.

Alex looked over his shoulder to Qaletaqa. "This isn't working. Fire and ice are fighting one another and the creature is winning."

Qaletaqa held up a hand. "Hunters, hold."

Alex continued throwing tentacle after tentacle of frozen water at the creature and freezing the water into bonds, only to have the creature break free. It was a stalemate. Alex couldn't form the ice any faster than the creature could smash it.

* * *

Taryn growled once more then snapped the bonds around her wrists. Sheelin stared at her as she freed herself of the remaining restraints.

She turned to see Qaletaqa let loose a fireball at Taryn. The flames engulfed her, but quickly subsided. Sheelin quickly moved to block any further assaults. "Father, No!"

"Stand aside, Sheelin. She's loose and dangerous."

"*Mmm...ooo...rrrr*," said a voice from behind Sheelin.

She turned to find Taryn standing, but hunched over. Her eyes were glazed white and she shook violently. Seeing another fireball hit Taryn, Sheelin turned to face Qaletaqa again and screamed, "Father!"

"Sheelin, stand aside. We've waited long enough. This must be done."

"No!"

Taryn muttered once again. "*Sheee...linnn...*"

Sheelin turned to face Taryn, but kept her father in the corner of her eye.

Taryn's blank stare met hers, but she spoke in a shaky breath. "*Moooo...rrrreee... ffff...iiiiirrreee...*"

Qaletaqa watched as the conversation continued.

Sheelin lowered her head. "She's given up."

Qaletaqa announced, "Hunters, to me." When Sheelin turned to regard him again, he smiled. "I don't think your friend has given up just yet. As a matter of fact, I think she has a plan. Join us."

Qaletaqa signaled to the others. "Hit her with every fireball you can... until I say stop."

He threw the first volley at Taryn followed by two more, then five more, then ten, until Taryn was being pummeled by hundreds of fireballs.

Sheelin cast a pitiful fireball and lobbed it at Taryn, but with little effort and did not quickly cast her second.

The fire had engulfed the center of the camp, with Taryn in the middle. Alex continued to raise up icy water from the river to ensnare the Wendigo. Radimir too, took swats of his massive bear claws at the monster as it endeavored to break free of its restraints.

"Enough!" said a voice from within the flames.

Qaletaqa held up a hand and the other hunters ceased the fireball barrage.

Standing at the center of a flaming inferno, legs spread apart with arms stretched down in front of her, Taryn's flaming red hair whipped around in the fury of a firestorm.

"Take cover! Now!" Qaletaqa called to Alex and Radimir.

Sheelin watched in dismay as Alex and the bear did not hesitate. Radimir dove left and Alex to the right. As the creature broke free of its last ice bond, Taryn turned and ran straight at the snow-white monster whose mouth dropped and eyes widened. With a final lunge she launched herself into the air. When Taryn's fire met the Wendigo's ice aura, the two exploded in a huge fireball reaching the treetops and leveling the grounds.

Smoke and flames engulfed the area for a full minute before subsiding.

Waving her hand to clear the air around her, Sheelin spotted Taryn standing over the burnt and smoldering husk of the Wendigo. The charred remains crumbled under her touch. She looked skyward and took a deep breath then relaxed as she met eyes with her friends. "It's bloody done. The beastie is dead. Can we go home now? I need to get some sleep."

26 The Elves of Alfheim

Arriving in a wooded glen, Meagan and Amber were both relieved to be away from the dwarf kingdom even if it was for different reasons. The glen was bright and green with trees all around. The sun was high in the sky on a beautiful summer's day. The smell of flowers in bloom gave a relaxing feel to the warm surroundings. A cobbled path led into the woods and had overgrowth all around as if seldom used... and perhaps it was. Few people visited the light elves and they rarely ventured forth from their realm.

Meagan and Amber followed the path for about a mile until the woods opened at the head of a valley. Below was a stream that ran through a majestic city of carved trees and arched stonework. More cobbled paths led through groves of trees and homes. Music was carried on the breeze that echoed the soft and gentle sounds of nature. Wildlife roamed the paths as did the light elves of Alfheim. They were tall and graceful figures with long straight hair and handsome robes.

As Meagan and Amber approached, they were stopped by two male elves in lite leather armor carrying gleaming longswords with a natural curve to their blades as if made by nature itself. They crossed their swords in front of Meagan and Amber and said something in their native elven language.

"They wish to know who we are and what business we have here," Meagan translated.

The two elves looked at one another then back to Meagan. "How do you know our native tongue?"

"We are here to speak with your king," replied Amber.

The two elves now examined Amber, realizing only one of the visitors appeared to know the elven tongue and customs.

"You should not have bothered to make the trip. No one will see you. Leave."

The two guards then turned and walked away from the girls to return to their posts.

Before they had gone more than ten feet, Meagan said, "Seelay Tu' Lam."

The guards stopped in their tracks and turned to look at Meagan once again. With questioning glances, they seemed puzzled as to what to do.

"Take us to see the Lady of the Sacred Woods," ordered Meagan.

They hesitated at first, but then complied. "This way."

They led the girls down into the valley. Amber quickened her pace to walk side by side with Meagan. "What did you tell them?"

"My name."

Amber appeared confused. "Was that your name in elvish?"

Meagan sighed before answering, trying to decide how much to tell her. "Amber, you can't tell anyone what I am about to tell you."

Amber nodded her confirmation, her eyes fixed more on Meagan than the path before her. She stumbled, but quickly regained her balance. "Does this have anything to do with your mood change since arriving in the nine realms?"

Ignoring the question, Meagan proceeded to tell her tale. "My father and Gollnick were brothers, which is why everyone knows Gollnick is my uncle. What most people don't know is that my mother was not human." Glancing at Amber, she noticed wide eyes and a gaping jaw. Meagan continued, "She was a light elf. There are a number of light elves living in Yellowstone National Park. That's where she met my father."

Amber just continued to stare at Meagan trying to reconcile the fact her mother wasn't human.

"I'm part elf," confirmed Meagan as she looked Amber in the eyes.

"Well, that explains the somewhat pointy ears," replied Amber still in shock. "But why keep it a secret, at least from the rest of the Circle?"

"Ever since my parents' death at the hands of dark sorcerers, Nick and I have been trying to keep my lineage a secret. We decided that unless it became necessary to reveal, it would be best to keep it quiet, even from the Circle. That's why I originally said I would come here alone. At this point though, I figured you needed to know the truth."

"I understand," replied Amber, "and thanks for letting me come with you. I couldn't take that underground stuff anymore."

"Me either," said Meagan. "For now, let me do the talking. Since I am at least part elf, they're more likely to speak with me. They may still be leery about you. They're very suspicious of outsiders."

They continued along the path behind the guards. Many other elves stared at them, but continued about their business. A few deer stopped suddenly at their approach then dashed away, uncertain of the newcomers. After many minutes, the guards entered a clearing and stood to either side as they allowed Meagan and Amber to pass between them. A beautiful elf woman in a long white dress sat strumming a white harp with golden strings. The music was relaxing and beautiful. The girls just stood at the entrance and listened as they waited for the musician to notice them.

Amber looked around anxiously including a few glances to Meagan who gave no response.

Meagan hoped Amber would heed her instructions and not say a word. Patience was important to their hosts... as was their music. She didn't want to offend the lady harpist, but Amber's lack of focus was unnerving. She grasped Amber's hand and held it at her side hoping Amber would just calm down.

It was almost ten minutes before the musician ceased playing and gently set the harp down, then rose from her seat and turned to greet her visitors. "And who do we have here?" The elf lady seemed pleased... until she realized they weren't elves. Noticing Meagan's ears, she passed her attention to Amber who had a decidedly more human appearance. Finally she turned her attention back to Meagan and resumed her seat.

"My lady," said Meagan, "I am Seelay Tu' Lam. My mother was Alayla Tu' Lam. My friend, Amber Marx, and I are here from Midgard seeking your help. Fenrir has been released by—"

The lady held up a hand to stop Meagan from saying any more. She then dismissed the guards and rose from her seat. After watching the guards depart, she turned her attention back to Meagan and Amber.

"Fenrir was imprisoned deep in the ground of Midgard and bound by the magical ribbon Gleipnir. Who has released this monster?"

"We don't know exactly who released him, but we are sure it was one of the dark sorcerers who—"

"Dark sorcerers?" This seemed to shock the elf woman. "What has happened to the Circle? They were to protect the magical prisons of Midgard."

"My lady," replied Meagan, "we are members of that Circle. At the time Fenrir was released, we were attempting to prevent the release of two other monsters."

"How is it that the dark sorcerers know of so many prisons?"

"I wish we knew," mumbled Amber.

The lady snapped her focus to Amber who immediately gained an intense interest toward a leaf on the ground. The lady held her gaze upon Amber for a long minute before returning her attention to Meagan.

"The dark sorcerers have gained a lot of knowledge about the prisons recently," stated Meagan. "We don't know how, but they have greater resources and seem to be one step ahead of us at each turn."

"What do you want of us, daughter of Alayla?"

"Our friends are seeking the help of the dwarves of Nidavellir to obtain the necessary items and skills to create a new Gleipnir. We come to you in search of the spells needed to create the magical ribbon."

"Dwarves?" The lady raised herself to full height, and straight-faced looked down at the newcomers. "I fear you have wasted your time. Even if the dwarves still possessed the skills to create such an item, our feud would prevent me from ever helping them... even if it meant the destruction of Midgard. You are welcome to join us for our evening meal and rest the night, but you must leave in the morning, without that which you seek."

Meagan bowed to the lady and glanced sideways at Amber, to hint that she should follow suit. Amber bowed her head slightly, but never took her eyes off the tall elf lady. Meagan turned, and grabbing Amber by the wrist, left the clearing.

"Now what do we do?" questioned Amber a little louder than required. "We can't return to Nidavellir without the spell. We won't be able to create a new Gleipnir and we'll never re-imprison Fenrir."

In a quieter voice Meagan replied, "Shh... I know. I'm still working on that. I never said this was going to be easy."

27 The Next Challenge

The first rays of sunlight crept over the mountains and treetops to reveal the start of a new day. Even after the fiery battle the night before, there was a chill in the air. Some of the hunters had started breakfast as Max emerged from his tent. He stretched his tired muscles and walked to the next tent to check on Taryn.

As the light peered through her tent opening, her bleary eyes flickered, but remained squinted. "Is it mornin' already?"

Max smiled as he offered her a hand. "I'm afraid so. How did you sleep?" She took his hand and he helped her outside. Max noticed that her hand was still quite hot, but he figured it was residual heat from the hundreds of fireballs launched at her last night.

"I slept like a log."

Max contemplated her expression as he furrowed his brow.

She smiled. "I slept very well, thank ye."

He watched as she rolled her left shoulder. He remembered that was where she had been bitten by the Wendigo. "How's the shoulder?"

"Stiff, but the healin' spells helped a lot. It'll be back to normal in a few hours."

They made their way to the campfire to get some food and found Radimir already there enjoying his second round of eggs and bacon. "Eat. Good food."

Qaletaqa and Sheelin approached from the far side of camp. Neither looked happy with their pursed lips and downward stares. Max could only assume they had an early morning discussion about Sheelin's future with the hunters, and her father. Max decided it was best to wait for one of them to make conversation before stepping into an unpleasant situation.

Sheelin went straight to her tent and Qaletaqa approached the fire. He didn't speak with Max or his friends, but took some food and wandered off to sit on a log near the river by himself as he ate. The others continued with their breakfast.

After eating, Max wandered over to Qaletaqa and sat on the ground nearby. He stretched his arms and leaned against a tree. It wasn't the most comfortable position as the bark was rough against his back. "Now that the Wendigo is destroyed. I'll be leaving with Taryn to rejoin the Circle."

Qaletaqa gazed into the blue sky as he squinted against the bright sunlight. He held a small smooth stone in his hand that he rubbed gently. "I had a feeling you would." His answer was short and said nothing of Sheelin. He continued to look skyward and didn't make eye contact.

Max looked back to the tents and noticed Sheelin emerge with a backpack slung over her right shoulder. She sat down between Taryn and Radimir, placing the pack to her left side. She then picked up some breakfast and began to eat. It spoke volumes about the results of the earlier discussion between Qaletaqa and his daughter.

He regarded the older man then looked skyward as well. "I take it Sheelin has made her decision?"

Qaletaqa threw the stone as far into the nearby river as he could. "She has."

Max recognized the tone. "I take it you don't agree with her decision?"

Qaletaqa looked over his left shoulder and studied Max. "I thank you for your concern, but this is between me and my daughter. So long as I am her father and leader of the Rogue Hunters, she will remain here with us."

Max didn't want to anger Qaletaqa any further so he stood up and returned to the center of camp. There he found Taryn and Sheelin laughing at something while Radimir watched with raised brows.

Max took a seat next to Sheelin as their laughing subsided. "Taryn has informed me they suspect you and Radimir are the two newest members of the Circle."

Max looked her in the eyes. "Sheelin, I just had a brief talk with your father. And it was brief."

Sheelin's face lost all expression and her eyes drifted to the light of the campfire. "We had a slight disagreement on my future plans."

Max looked back to where Qaletaqa had sat near the river, but couldn't see the older man now. "It sounded like a little more than a slight disagreement based on our limited conversation." He watched her, but she didn't respond. "I don't want to see a family torn apart because of us." He paused again, but still she gave no response. "Perhaps the time is not yet right. Maybe you should stay here for now. Your place in the Circle will be there when you're ready to join us."

Taryn's smiling face lost all its joy. Radimir too lowered his gaze and couldn't make eye contact with anyone.

The light from the fire danced in Sheelin's eyes as she stared at the warm flames. "I'm ready to join the fight now, but I need time to convince my father this is the right thing to do."

Max wasn't sure what kind of response he had been hoping for, but he was disappointed she agreed so quickly. Perhaps the time wasn't yet right for her to join, but he knew one day she would be needed.

The hunters still celebrated their victory over the Wendigo, but the spirits around the fire were momentarily subdued. A tear ran down Sheelin's right check.

Taryn reached over and placed a hand on Sheelin's shoulder. "I'll make sure the mirror in the library of Ravenicon Castle will allow ye through. Ye're always welcome and we'll be waitin' for the day ye join us."

"Indeed, you are honorable people," said a voice from the other side of the campfire. They all turned to see Qaletaqa standing there watching the scene.

Sheelin wiped the tear from her face and stood. She met her father's gaze for a brief moment then took her backpack and returned to her tent.

Max stood to face Qaletaqa. "She will always be welcome in the Circle. And someday she will join us."

Qaletaqa walked around the fire and extended a hand to Max. "I know, but for now, I'm not ready for her to leave. I'm old and there is still much for her to learn. Someday she will join you and there's nothing I can do to stop that. For now, she's where she belongs."

28   The Answer Is No

After many attempts, Gollnick finally got through to someone in Duestoff Von Woonst's organization. However, he grew impatient waiting on Duestoff to arrive at the mirror. He was beginning to think the man was intentionally making him wait when a face appeared. He was thin in the face, but had a full beard. Like his brother, he spoke with a thick German accent. "I'm a little busy here, what do you want?"

Gollnick wasn't in the best of mood after waiting for so long, and the German's attitude didn't help matters, but he reminded himself of the reason for contact. He was trying to prevent the deaths of many innocent people in New York City.

Gollnick put on a smile and spoke as politely as he could muster. "My name is Goll—"

"I know who you are. Speak your mind or be on your way."

Once again Gollnick did his best to be nice. "I wanted to discuss the sorcerer civil war in New York. In particular, if there might be a way to settle this in a peaceful manner."

Deustoff's straight face and serious expression didn't give Gollnick much hope.

"Peaceful? Bring me Malcolm's head on a pike and we can discuss it. While you're at it, I'll take your friend's head as well. Vincent is as much to blame as Malcolm for my brother's death. One way or another they will both pay."

Gollnick knew the circumstances of Vincent's involvement. He also knew that Frederick and all the water automatons had been destroyed. What he didn't know is whether Duestoff knew any of the details. "Malcolm's more to blame than you may realize. While Vincent was present, he was under a binding spell. He had no choice but to follow orders..." When Duestoff rolled his eyes, Gollnick added, "but you already knew that."

"He was present and still to blame. They will both die."

Gollnick decided on a different approach. "Think about all the innocent people who might get hurt in the process."

"No one is truly innocent, especially in New York City. To cleanse this world, it must be purged of the unworthy. If a few thousand people die a little early, so what? You bore me. This conversation is over." Duestoff waved a hand in front of the mirror and his image disappeared.

Gollnick was not encouraged by this brief exchange. Actually, he was more convinced that Duestoff wanted the civil war. Maybe even a little too much. Gollnick couldn't put his finger on it, but something seemed off. He could only hope that Vincent was having better luck with Francois LeRain.

* * *

Back in Vincent's private chambers, he raised a small handheld mirror. The image it showed was of a dark room with only the slightest glimmer of light from the right side. He had been waiting for almost an hour when he heard voices in the background. Finally a person came into view. A man sat down on a chair in front of the mirror and leaned in close. "Vincent, is that you?" he whispered. "It is good to see you, my old friend. Though I wish it were under better circumstances."

"Francois, what's going on? Why so secret?"

"Shh! You've called at a bad time. A group of Malcolm's men are outside my location searching for me as we speak."

"Then it's true, there is a sorcerer's war going on in New York City."

"Yes, my friend. And at the moment, I'm not doing so well. Half my men have been captured or killed in the past few days. Where are you?"

"Francois, I've left Malcolm. I'm with the Old Circle again."

"Then the rumors I've heard are true. You killed Frederick Von Woonst and freed Tiamat. But when you ordered her to attack New York City she abandoned you."

"Wow! That's a story I haven't heard before. No. I was under Malcolm's binding spell. I was forced to serve him. When

Frederick ordered Tiamat to do Malcolm's bidding, she fried him and fled."

"You never truly believed in the dark sorcerer plan to remake the world?"

"Sorry, but no. And this sorcerer civil war makes even less sense. Malcolm has told us a lot of innocent people are dying. Is this true?"

"There are new rules, my friend. The time is fast approaching for the great global purge. It's survival of the fittest now."

"The purge? That wasn't supposed to happen for another two thousand years."

"On the contrary, we recently found out the great seal was created two thousand years earlier than believed. The purge is to happen in less than a year from now."

"Where did you come by this information?"

"Malcolm has a source who provides him with valuable information. Information I need if I'm going to survive this war. Vincent, is there any way you can send aid? Maybe a hundred sorcerers? If I can eliminate Malcolm and gain control of his source, perhaps I may be able to spare your life at the time of the purge."

"There's not going to be a purge. The combined power of the Old and New Circles won't allow it."

"As I understand, there's little left of the Old Circle and the new one is a bunch of inexperienced kids. I don't see you putting up much of a fight."

Vincent studied Francois' face for a moment. There was no evidence of tension, no sweat beading down his face. "Answer me this, Francois. You seem awfully calm for a man who is being hunted by Malcolm's sorcerers. Why are you so willing to share a lot of information with someone who is your enemy?"

"You were once my friend, Vincent. Does that not count for something?" Francois held Vincent's gaze for a moment, then wavered. "I have to go," he said, waving a hand in front of his mirror. The image disappeared.

Vincent couldn't help but wonder how truthful his friend had been. Francois never had the best poker face, but he was familiar with the plans for the great global purge. The fact Francois believed it to be at hand gave Vincent great cause for concern. He would need to discuss this with Gollnick.

* * *

Gollnick could tell by the somber face of Vincent things hadn't gone as planned. His news would be no better. "I take it Francois didn't provide much encouragement for a truce?"

Vincent shook his head and sat at the kitchen table. "No. Any luck with Duestoff?"

Gollnick hung his head. "No. However, he did seem a little off from what I had expected."

"How so?"

Gollnick met Vincent's eyes. "Duestoff sounded like he wanted the civil war with Malcolm. Oh, and he wants you dead, too. He blames you and Malcolm for his brother's death."

"How did he even know I was there?"

Gollnick tilted his head. "I was wondering that myself. When I reminded him of the binding, he dismissed the thought and moved on. It was almost like he didn't know."

Vincent furrowed his brow. "Both Duestoff and Frederick knew I was under Malcolm's control because of that blasted amulet. There's no way it was a surprise for him."

Gollnick considered this information.

"Francois seemed a little off to me as well," Vincent added.

Gollnick's eyes widened. "Why do you say that?"

"He claimed he was being hunted by Malcolm's sorcerers. He was hiding from them at the time of our conversation. Yet, he took the time to talk with me. He appeared calm and willing to share a lot of information. Almost like the situation was staged."

Gollnick pursed his lips. "I'm beginning to think you're right. This is a trap. I'm going to tell Malcolm, he's on his own."

A few minutes later, Gollnick sat down in one of the overstuffed chairs in the Library then called out to the mirror in front of him, "*Mirtor a mirtor tong-la Malcolm.*"

In seconds, the image of a dark room appeared. Gollnick could see paintings adorn the walls in the background with spotlights aimed at each one. The room appeared to be empty. "Hello? Anyone there?"

"One second," said a voice. Malcolm's face appeared shortly afterward. "Ah, Gollnick. I take it you've come to a decision?"

"We have." Gollnick paused to gauge Malcolm's level of interest, but the dark-skinned adversary said nothing. "We've decided not to aide you in this sorcerer civil war."

Now Malcolm's eyes widened. "How can that be your decision? There are hundreds of innocent people here in New York City who will be impacted."

Gollnick made no physical response. "Your rivals gave us cause to hesitate. In addition, I've been checking the news. So far, I haven't seen anything out of the ordinary about incidents in New York City. Either you're doing a really good job at keeping the attacks quiet..." When Malcolm briefly looked away from the mirror before regaining eye contact, Gollnick continued, "...or there haven't been any."

Malcolm pursed his lips. "I have sorcerers assigned to keep all attacks hidden and out of the news."

Gollnick smiled. "I doubt that. Only a week ago, you and Frederick were having a battle of your own. Other sorcerers had to get involved to make it look like a severe storm. Everyone I've talked with has said the rules have changed. Yet you expect me to believe you are now trying to keep these attacks a secret? Your adversaries don't seem so concerned about keeping things quiet."

Malcolm's face flushed red. His breathing became heavy. Gollnick was certain Malcolm was not enjoying the conversation.

"You think you've figured everything out. What you don't realize is, one way or another, I've been ordered to eliminate you as a nuisance from our plans."

Gollnick sat up a little straighter in his seat before leaning closer to the mirror, not so much from the threat, but the implied source of the threat. "Ordered? I thought you ran the show for all dark sorcerers?"

Malcolm's eyes widened once more. He stood and waved a hand in front of the mirror and his image disappeared.

29 SEARCHING FOR ANSWERS

After a brief stop at Ravenicon castle, Max, Taryn and Radimir had made their way to Asgard. Max looked around the great city and though he couldn't remember specifics, he knew he had been there before. The place was in need of a great many repairs. Giant cracks wrecked the perfection of tall spires. Vegetation had overrun large sections of the city, and a few buildings had collapsed into rubble. The streets were covered in dirt and debris. Even the main spire of the city—the palace of the Asgardian king, Odin—had gaping holes. Shields, swords and spears lay strewn about, evidence of a mighty battle... Ragnarok, the fall of the Norse gods.

Max moved deeper into the city with Taryn and Radimir close behind.

As she attempted to keep pace, Taryn called, "Max, we're going the wrong way. We need to get to Nidavellir and find the others. We don't have time for sightseeing."

Without turning, Max pressed on. "We need to find Odin."

"Odin was a sorcerer from ancient times. He's dead."

"No. Now that I'm here, I remember. Odin was one of the immortals. He lives."

With renewed vigor, the three of them continued their journey deeper into Asgard. Max led the way into the palace climbing over and around boulders and shattered walls, through gaping holes in defensive barriers and finally into the throne room. There, upon the crumbling remains of a once majestic throne, sat a withered old man. Mostly skin and bone with little muscle left, his armor hung from his thin limbs. A white unkempt beard covered most of his chest. His stare reached the heights of the audience chamber until their approach drew his attention.

Even after thousands of years, Max recognized the withered old man—Odin, king of the Asgardians. Taryn and Radimir hung back.

Odin pointed a shaky spear at Max and growled, "What are you doing here? I thought I left you with the ring, err the round thing."

"I am once again with the New Circle."

"Yes, the Circle. So what are you doing here? Haven't I babysat you enough over the centuries? Now you come here and disturb my peace once again."

Max could tell Odin was not pleased to see him. "We're looking for our friends. They came here in search of a way to create a new Gleipnir. The Fenris Wolf has escaped and is roaming Midgard."

"What? You fools let that monster escape? The last time it got out, he swallowed me whole. If it weren't for my son Vidarr, I'd still be in the belly of that beast."

"It was the dark sorcerers who freed Fenrir."

Odin lowered his spear and gnashed his jaw as he looked around the floor of the throne room. "Why haven't you put an end to their brutality? Don't you remember what they've done to this world?"

Max hesitated. "Actually, I don't remember much of anything."

Odin slammed his spear onto the floor and it skidded away in an erratic pattern just missing Radimir. "You fool! You lost your memory again? Youth eternal, memory zilch, and powers; who knows? One day you can barely light a fire, the next you've ripped the universe in half. You are the most consistently inconsistent imbecile in all the nine realms."

Max looked over his shoulder at Radimir and then Taryn, who shrugged in response. Max regarded the aged Asgardian king once more. "Odin, we need your help. We're searching for our friends, Cyrus, Amber and Meagan. They must have come this way."

"Well... three children were here the day before yesterday. Or was it yesterday? It could've been last week. I don't think it was tomorrow. It must've been last month. Either way, I think they went to Nidavellir in search of the dwarves." He stared at Max for a few seconds. "But you, you're going to Giza."

"Giza?"

"You must travel to Egypt and find Ra. Maybe he'll be in a better mood to help you with your memories. Just get out of my city."

Max took a step forward. "But our friends, they need our help. They must find a new Gleipnir and re-imprison Fenrir."

Odin paced the dais of the throne room. "Fine! You go to Egypt and get out of my hair. I'll aid your friends."

Max's eyes widened before re-examining the elderly figure. "Are you sure you're up to it?"

"*Go!*"

With some enthusiasm Max questioned, "Okay. How do I find Ra?"

"Start at the Giza Plateau. Find the tomb of Osiris. From there you're on your own. See if there's any memories left in that vacuum you call a mind."

Max, Taryn and Radimir made a hasty retreat from the Asgardian king. As they disappeared out of the throne room, Odin's last words echoed... "Now what was I supposed to do?"

30   GATHER THE TROOPS

After a less than encouraging conversation with Gollnick, Malcolm paced behind the desk in his darkened office. The only glow was from the hundred video screens covering one wall. The darkness suited him right now as he wished to hide forever. His master would be furious with the outcome of the request for aid. His plan for destroying the Circle was quickly falling apart. If he were to save his own neck, he would need to move quickly to come up with an alternate plan, an all-out attack on Ravenicon Castle.

Another man entered the room dressed all in black and wearing a trench coat. He approached within ten feet and waited. Malcolm paced a few more times before acknowledging his presence. A furrowed brow and harsh growl revealed his displeasure. "Call a truce with Deustoff and Francois immediately. I want them both here in one hour. We need to settle our differences if we are to destroy both Circles."

The man didn't hesitate after receiving his orders. He turned and made a hasty retreat.

Malcolm wasn't sure how long he could conceal this failure from his master. How long until he was once again summoned to the depths of New York City? He knew he needed to implement his alternate plan as soon as possible. A way to accomplish his master's task now that the trap had been revealed.

Out of the corner of his eye, he caught some movement. He quickly looked in the direction of the motion, but saw nothing. He lowered his gaze once again, but this time when he spotted the peripheral movement, he saw a small demon-like figure darting from shadow to shadow. He recognized it as one of his master's little pets. He quickly cast a spell, *Magna fir-tor loma.* The fireball shot with a quick snap of his wrist at the little demon, but the creature was too quick for his off the cuff aim. The figure no longer kept to the shadows, but made a mad dash for an air vent. It had disappeared before Malcolm could cast a second fireball.

In frustration, Malcolm slid his arms across the surface of his desk, throwing everything onto the floor. The few pieces of paper he still grasped in his hands were torn to shreds as he continued his tirade.

He was out of options and his master's little spy was on its way to give a full report of his failure. His two would-be opponents were on their way to meet with him and he had no idea how to eliminate his greatest enemy, Gollnick. Depleted of energy and drive, he flopped down in his chair and resigned himself to the fact he had finally proven himself useless to his master. And uselessness meant only one thing.

An hour later, Malcolm was slouched in his leather chair, half awake with a nearly empty bottle of brandy in his hand. His black shirt hung open revealing a white t-shirt underneath. One side of it was still tucked into his black pants while the other hung free. His hair was disheveled and his cheeks were flushed.

Deustoff and Francois entered, strolling in side by side, apparently without a care in the world. Deustoff was dressed all in black including his trench coat. Francois wore black pants, a white button-down shirt and a brown trench coat. Deustoff gave Francois a quick glance before returning his attention to his so-called leader. "We're here as you requested... but I thought the master didn't want us seen together."

Malcolm snapped his head toward the German. "You've been in contact with the master?"

Francois replied, "He's the one who instructed us to start an uprising against you. You didn't know?"

Malcolm straightened a bit. "Of course I knew."

Deustoff smiled. "Irrelevant. What are the master's commands?"

Malcolm chuckled. "Who knows? Probably to kill me. You two blundering idiots couldn't talk your way out of a paper bag. Gollnick and Vincent saw right through you. Neither of you convinced them the civil war was real. They've turned down my request for aid and will not be coming to New York. Which means,

I won't be able to ambush them or kill them. We've failed. And make no mistake, if I'm going down for this, you two morons are going down with me."

Deustoff sneered as he looked to Francois. "I told you this game we were playing would never work. We can't underestimate our enemies. If we wanted to kill them, then why not just do it? Why lure them here to spring a trap? I prefer the direct approach."

Francois regarded his partner for a moment. "And how exactly do you propose to do that? We need to find them first. So, unless you know their hole in the ground, we're stuck with playing these games."

Malcolm stood, still a little shaky, and pointed a finger at Deustoff while his other hand remained wrapped around the bottle. "You are exactly correct. We need to attack them directly. An all-out assault on their castle. While Vincent was under my control, he revealed Ravenicon's location. If I could just remember..." He tapped the bottle against his head a few times trying to remember his conversation with his would-be captive. Then it hit him. "Baltimore, Maryland. Their castle is somewhere in Baltimore. Gather our troops. I want a city-wide search. Find that castle. We'll tear the thing down brick by brick if we have to. I want them dead."

31 THE LOWER MINES

The mines of Koldihr ran deep into the mountains and further below ground than any human had ever ventured. The tunnels were not crude holes in the ground, but clean and well-shaped with stone archways every so often for support. The archways were finely crafted stone embellished in dwarvish runes and scrollwork. Light was minimal except for the torches they carried with them.

Kallan and Cyrus made their way along the crafted tunnel system. On occasion, they descended rope ladders and carved stone stairs. They had been walking for the better part of a day when they decided to stop for a rest.

Cyrus took a seat on the ground and leaned against a wall. He opened his pack and pulled out a bottle of water. He offered one to Kallan who declined and instead drank from a flask from his own supplies.

Cyrus capped the bottle and looked at where they had come and where they were going. "Any idea how close we are to the dwarf elders?"

"Maybe another three hours."

Cyrus took another sip. "So why are you helping us? I know you disagree with your father's decision, but you're going against the wishes of your king."

Kallan took a seat on the ground opposite Cyrus and lowered his gaze. "I have eight older brothers. All of them are dedicated to our father. So much so, they would never question his decision, no matter what. Even in this case they have sided with him. Yet, what affects one world is bound to spill over into the other realms of Yggdrasil. We must have a way to imprison Fenrir or be prepared to defend ourselves. Since no preparations are being made, I feel it is my duty to protect our world. What about you? Your charge is to protect Midgard. Why are you here? With what you have told us about the dark sorcerers, aren't you worried they will release more monsters during your absence?"

Cyrus paused as he considered the past week and his decisions. "This is the third creature the dark sorcerers have attempted to release recently. Max and Meagan succeeded in preventing the release of Cerberus from the Greek underworld, but the rest of us failed to prevent the release of the Babylonian dragon Tiamat. Fortunately, she wants nothing to do with humanity and has since disappeared. Now we find out the dark sorcerers have secretly released Fenrir. We have no way to stop such a beast. Our only option was to find the dwarves and seek your help in making a new Gleipnir. As for other creatures, we still have friends back on Midgard. They'll keep us informed of any trouble."

"The dark sorcerers seem to have a lot of information if they found three prisons in such a short time. How is it you didn't know of their intentions?"

Cyrus put his water bottle into his pack and stood. "Our Circle is new and we only have five members. Well, maybe four, we're not sure yet. The dark sorcerers apparently know more about the prisons than we do. Right now, I feel like we're just playing catch up. We can use all the help we can get at this point."

Kallan stood and slapped Cyrus on the back. "Well, if we survive this, you have a friend among the dwarves."

Kallan led the way down the next tunnel as he lifted his torch high above his head.

A few hours later, Cyrus noticed the tunnel passage had changed. Its fine detail work was gone. These walls were rough and unfinished. Piles of dirt and rubble lay to the sides. They could hear the pounding of picks on stone as rubble became separated from wall, floor and ceiling. A dim glow illuminated the tunnel ahead.

They entered a larger cavern to find thirty dirty dwarves hacking and pounding the stone, examining each piece and sorting it into metals, minerals, gems and dirt. As they entered, the activity ceased and all eyes focused on them.

After a few minutes, one of the elder dwarves stepped forward. He eyed Cyrus and then Kallan. The dwarf pursed his lips upon recognizing the dwarf prince, but made no move to bow or show respect. "Why have you come here, princeling? And why do you bring a human with you? Do you need protection?"

The other dwarves chuckled aloud. It was clear to Cyrus the king had little influence here. And Kallan had even less. As Cyrus looked around he noticed the tools they carried would also make formidable weapons in the right hands. And dwarves were known to be excellent fighters. Though he made no offensive move, he prepared himself for an attack if things went wrong.

The lead dwarf elder eyed Cyrus from head to toe. "Your friend here thinks we mean him harm. Or he means to bring harm to us."

Kallan quickly looked at Cyrus then moved between them. "No. We mean you no harm. He is merely unfamiliar with our ways and doesn't know what he's doing."

Cyrus was uneasy about the situation, but decided it best to follow Kallan's lead for now. He relaxed his hands and held his arms out to each side. "I'm sorry. I meant no disrespect. We need your help."

The brow of the lead dwarf shot up in surprise. "Ha. If you need our help, you truly are desperate. We are old miners. We are of little help to anyone."

Cyrus stepped around Kallan to address the old dwarf face to face. "My name is Cyrus Marx. I am a member of the New Circle from Midgard. The ferocious Fenrir of Norse mythology has been freed by dark forces. The binding known as Gleipnir has been destroyed. We need your help to make a new one or the people of my world will suffer."

The stoic dwarves whispered amongst themselves. The lead dwarf held up a hand and the whispering ceased. "My name is Sturlin Stonefist. I am sorry you have travelled all this way for nothing. The skills and spells needed to make such an item have long since been lost. Some of our number are among the most skilled smiths in all of Nidavellir, but we are no spell casters."

Cyrus knew the relations with the elves was tenuous at best, but he needed Sturlin to know how desperate they were for the magical ribbon. "As we speak, my sister and a friend of ours are acquiring the spells needed to make a new Gleipnir."

Sturlin stared at Cyrus through squinted eyes. "The only ones who know those spells are the elves of Alfheim. And they do not share easily."

Cyrus was determined not to falter in his belief in his friends. "Nevertheless, I trust my sister and our friend will find what they are searching for. But I need your help to make the ribbon."

Sturlin turned to Kallan, then stepped closer to the prince. "King Brodkir has agreed to this?"

Cyrus feared Kallan would admit the king refused to help, but he also remembered how the old dwarf could tell with a mere glance that Cyrus was preparing for a fight. He didn't want to lie to Sturlin, but he was desperate.

Kallan brought himself to his full height, which was still a few inches short of the grey bearded elder. "He has refused to help the humans, but I believe this is a mistake. What affects Midgard will eventually have an impact on the other realms. It is my duty to protect Nidavellir at all cost. This is why I brought the human here to see you. This is why I defy my king and father. To protect my home and my people."

The frown on Sturlin's face only deepened. He glanced around at the other dwarves before returning his attention to Kallan. "Too bad you'll never be king, little princeling. You would've done a better job than your father." His expression lightened as a smile appeared on his face and he let out a loud belly laugh.

The other dwarves joined in the laughter and gathered around the newcomers. Many dwarves slapped Kallan on the shoulder and shook his hand. Though Cyrus was mostly ignored, he took a seat on a nearby stone to allow Kallan his moment of approval.

When the ruckus died down, Kallan motioned for Cyrus to join him amidst his new friends. "I thank you for your kind words, Sturlin, but we need to begin work on Gleipnir."

The cheer on Sturlin's face faded. "Alas, my prince. Even if your friends do retrieve the necessary spells from the elves, there is more to the magical ribbon. In order to forge a new Gleipnir, we must first obtain the six impossible items used to make the magical binding. Plus the great wolf would've grown stronger over the years. We must add one more ingredient. One that will be even more difficult to obtain—water from the well of Urd. In ancient times, the Norns would pour its water onto the roots of Yggdrasil to strengthen the tree."

"What's so hard about getting some water from a well?" Cyrus scoffed.

Kallan placed a hand on his shoulder. "The well of Urd is near one of the three roots of Yggdrasil and is guarded by the Nidhogg, a monstrous dragon-like creature, in addition to other dangers of the well. I fear this may be an impossible task."

Kallan turned back to Sturlin. "Is there no other way?"

Sturlin sighed as his gaze drifted to the floor. Then he raised his head once again to meet Kallan's eyes. "I'm afraid not, my prince. To forge a new Gleipnir without the added strength of the water would be folly. The wolf will have grown too strong."

Cyrus stepped forward in the moment of dismay. "Fine! Then we gather these items and take on this Pig-Hog. What's the problem with finding one more *impossible* item?"

"Nidhogg," Kallan corrected.

Cyrus glanced quickly at him. "Okay, Nib-hob, whatever. The big baddy. We can't let Fenrir run loose on Midgard, Nidavellir or anywhere else. If this is what needs done, then I'm willing to do whatever it takes."

Sturlin smiled at Kallan. "Your arrogant friend here has heart. Perhaps not brains, but he has heart." He then addressed both of them. "I shall send members of my company to locate the impossible items. The remainder will prepare to battle the Nidhogg. We shall summon Ratatoskr, the squirrel of Yggdrasil. He is large enough to carry you all and can navigate the world tree. He will take you to the root where you will find the Well of Urd."

Cyrus leaned close to Kallan. "Let me get this straight, we're going to ride a giant squirrel to find a well near the root of mystical giant tree so we can recreate a ribbon to tie up a giant wolf?"

Kallan nodded confirmation.

Cyrus hung his head. "Sounds like the opening to a bad joke. I'm afraid to hear the punch line."

32   GIZA

Max, Taryn and Radimir walked the streets of Cairo, Egypt, making their way through the crowded marketplace. Merchants aggressively peddled their wares as they pushed through the crowd. The sun beat down on a scorcher of a day. The dry sand blinded everyone as a strong wind whipped through the city. They realized too late their American clothing and trench coats made them stand out. Radimir kept asking of everyone he passed, "Osris? Osris?" But no one understood the harsh accent of the big Russian.

A young man stepped from the crowd and approached Max. "Hello, friends. My name is Tiem. I believe you are looking for the Great Sphinx, are you not?" The Egyptian boy stood but an inch or so shorter than Max, yet looked to be in his late teens. He wore a full length white garment with a white rimless cap. Around his neck hung a thin gold chain with a gold Ankh.

Taryn pushed past Tiem. "No, we're not, but if ye can point us in the direction of the Tomb of Osiris, we'd appreciate it."

"I do not know why you seek the Osiris Shaft, but it is partway between the Sphinx and the pyramids on the other side of the causeway." He pointed to the east. "I can take you there if you like."

"Nah, we can manage. Thank ye." Taryn led the way through the crowd leaving Tiem standing in the middle of the street with a furrowed brow.

"Maybe he could've helped us," said Max looking over his shoulder at the young man fading into the distance.

"Yeah, sure," replied Taryn. "Hey Tiem, any idea where we find the immortal known as Ra? Odin said we could find him somewhere near the Tomb of Osiris. Somehow I don't think that conversation would go over so well."

As they neared the Sphinx, Max stopped and stared at the massive limestone statue. The sculpture stretched over sixty feet high and two hundred feet long. The enormous lion body with a human head carved into the limestone bedrock was a marvel to behold, but Max was transfixed by the face.

Taryn noticed his preoccupation. "Are ye rememberin' somethin'?"

"Not exactly. That's the Sphinx? What happened to it?"

"What do ye mean?"

"This was once a statue of Sekhmet, the lion goddess. She protected the pharaohs and led them into battle. The daughter of Ra and a divine arbiter. She sat in the judgment hall of Osiris. Where the heart of the deceased was weighed on scales against a feather. If the heart was lighter than the feather, the soul was permitted to enter the afterlife. If not, it would be eaten by Ammut, the Devourer of Souls."

"I thought ye were Greek. How do ye know so much about Egyptian history?"

"I'm not sure."

"Lovely," said Taryn. "Shall we continue on to the tomb?"

They split off from the crowds and crept along the causeway in search of an entrance to the Tomb of Osiris. When they came upon a hole cut in the limestone at the base of the walkway, they clambered down the passage only to find a metal gate.

Max pointed an open palm toward it. "*Pug nona—*"

"Wait!" Taryn grabbed his hand and pulled it away from the gate. "We don't want to draw attention to ourselves."

She stepped forward and held a single index finger toward the lock. "*Lo-toc altu rocom.*" The lock popped and the gate slowly creaked open. Smiling, Taryn pushed the gate aside to find a deep shaft. She began the descent down the metal ladder installed by archaeologists for access to the tomb. Max and Radimir followed close behind.

"*Alecto orona na-see,*" said Max. A glowing orb of light preceded Max as they headed down into the shadows.

They descended into the first chamber. There they found another shaft leading further into the depths of the limestone bedrock. Following the second shaft, they lowered into another chamber lined with smaller, but empty rooms. A third shaft led further down into the darkness.

Upon reaching the third chamber at the bottom of the Osiris Shaft, they were greeted by the remains of the Tomb of Osiris. Four large obelisks laid toppled, one at each corner of a giant black stone sarcophagus. The lid of the tomb was shifted to one side. Much of the chamber's base was under water, including the sarcophagus itself.

They made their way into the chamber, staying on top of the ruins, still above water level. The sarcophagus was larger than normal, almost nine feet in length. Max stared into the tomb. He wasn't sure if he was waiting for a memory or searching for a clue, but something just didn't feel right. He realized the place was a mess and figured, like the statue of Sekhmet, it had fallen into ruin. He held a hand over the sarcophagus and muttered, "*Searo te-yon maku.*"

He retracted his hand. "There's magic here. The base of the tomb has a false bottom that only magic can reveal. "*Dim-tar mai secul.*"

A few seconds later the water in the tomb disappeared followed by the bottom of the stone tomb. A stairway led further down into the darkness.

"How down we go?" questioned Radimir, rolling his eyes.

"I wish I knew," answered Max. "This place seems both familiar and wrong at the same time. I'm not sure why, but I get the feeling we're headed in the wrong direction."

"This is where Odin told us to go to find Ra," Taryn pointed out. "Why would he send us in the wrong direction?"

"We're talking about a ten-thousand-year-old schizophrenic sorcerer who thinks Cyrus and the others had visited him tomorrow," said Max. "Which inconsistent imbecile do you trust?"

33 DINNER WITH THE ELVES

The evening hours came quick. Meagan and Amber were asked to join the Lady of the Sacred Wood at her table for dinner. The clearing was circled by trees and fauna of all varieties. Carved wood with natural looking scrollwork along the edges, the table seated twelve including the newcomers. The ten elves spoke not a word. They merely awaited the food and proceeded to eat when it arrived.

Meagan could see Amber eyeing the meal, but not touching it. The food did not resemble anything they had on Earth. Amber leaned close and whispered, "What is it?"

"It's fruit, now eat," Meagan replied.

"It doesn't look like fruit."

Meagan gave Amber a wide eyed glare and placed some of it into her own mouth. Amber leaned away and proceeded to eat her food without further complaint.

Between courses, Meagan took the opportunity to start a conversation. "My Lady, forgive me. I understand you have decided not to aid the dwarves in making a new Gleipnir, but I wish to understand how it is the elves and dwarves have come to such a bitter dislike for one another."

The Lady of the Sacred Wood regarded Meagan before answering. "You have lived all of your life on Midgard, have you not?"

"I have."

"For this reason, I sympathize with your lack of understanding. There has always been a distrust between our peoples since before I can remember. After Ragnarok and the fall of the Asgardians, that distrust grew bitter. Once, the Aesir maintained the peace in the nine realms, now only Odin remains."

Meagan sighed. "We've met him."

"Then you know his mind is fragile and his wisdom has fled. None dare challenge him in Asgard, but outside his realm, his influence has diminished. Without a guiding force to maintain the realms, each have turned inward. Trust and cooperation are no more."

Meagan fell silent in thought before continuing. "My Lady, you know of the Circle on Midgard. You know what we represent. If your trust in the dwarves has faded, I beseech you to trust us. We seek only to protect Midgard and the other realms from the creatures of the Nightmare Realm. Fenrir may be free on Midgard for now, but there is no limit to the lust for power of the dark sorcerers. They will eventually make their way to Alfheim, Nidavellir and the other realms."

The Lady of the Sacred Wood studied Meagan. "Daughter of Alayla Tu' Lam, while your words have merit, I fear I cannot help you. Our feud with the dwarves has grown strong. Allow them to use their own magic. We dare not share any of ours for fear they would use it against us." The Lady placed her hands on the table. "And now, the evening has grown late. I will turn in. And you will depart in the morning."

A guard rushed into the clearing.

The Lady gave him an angered look. "Why do you disrupt us?"

"My Lady." The guard quickly bowed then stood at attention. "One of our scouts reported a fire has been started along the north woods near the tomb of the elders. The wind currents are carrying it in this direction. We must evacuate you to safety."

"How is this possible?"

The guard looked at Meagan and Amber. "Two creatures of stone were spotted moving in the woods near the fire. We have dispatched one of the stone abominations, my lady. The other has escaped. We suspect it is the work of dwarven mystics."

Amber rose to her feet. "That's a lie."

She was about to say more when Meagan placed a hand on her shoulder. "My apologies, my Lady. What my friend meant to say is that we saw no evidence of mystical powers among the dwarves. In fact, it is for that very reason we have come here. They no longer possess the mystical powers to create Gleipnir, so I doubt they have the power to create earth automatons. In fact the only ones I know who can create such monsters are the dark sorcerers of Midgard."

The Lady rose from her chair. "And why would they attack us here? Unless they followed you."

Amber brushed Meagan's hand aside. "Perhaps they did, but if so it was to keep us from getting the spells we need to create Gleipnir. Don't you see? Anyone with power is a threat to them. They won't stop until everyone—including the elves—bow at their feet."

Meagan stepped away from the table and slowly walked around to face the elven queen. "My Lady. The dark sorcerer's war will affect humans, dwarves and elves alike if they are not stopped. The release of Fenrir and the creation of these stone automatons are only the beginning of their attacks into the nine realms. We need your help. Please."

The lady sighed. "The scrolls you seek are no more. They were hidden in the tomb of the elders in the northern woods. I fear the dwarves will not be able to find a way to recreate Gleipnir."

Amber rose from her chair and darted around the table to face Meagan and the elf. "No! There has to be a way. Someone created the spell before. That means there has to be a way to create it again. There's gotta be someone who can come up with a new spell!"

The Lady of the Sacred Wood observed Amber coolly. Meagan wasn't sure if she was furious or just shocked.

When the lady finally responded, she placed a gentle hand on Amber's shoulder. "My child, you are brave and boisterous. I know of no other way to re-create the spell." She paused a few seconds before continuing. Her eyes drifted off into the distance like a thought had occurred to her. "Perhaps there is a way. Odin once drank from the Well of Urd and was gifted with great wisdom, but the price he paid was great as well. It cost him an eye. If someone were to drink from the well... it is possible to ask for the knowledge to re-create the spell to make Gleipnir. However, that person will also be required to pay a price. Be warned, the well can be greedy."

34   Journey of the Dead

Max descended the stone stairs preceded by his orb of light. Taryn and Radimir followed right behind him. The wet limestone walls had eroded badly after thousands of years of water seepage. The damp floor squished beneath their feet with each step they took. The passage went a hundred feet before splitting off into three directions, each new corridor as badly worn as the next. They stood at the intersection evaluating their options.

"This isn't right," said Max. "Ra was king of the Egyptian gods. Why would he hide so far underground beneath a tomb for thousands of years?" Max looked back the way they had come. As soon as he took a step back toward the Tomb of Osiris, a loud grinding noise could be heard. They looked at one another for a brief second then sprinted through the muck back to the tomb.

As they neared the stairs, they saw it. A huge stone slab had lowered, blocking their escape.

Max ran up to it and slapped it with an open hand. The stone slab was solid and thick. He knew they weren't going to move it with brute strength. He stepped back a few paces and pointed an open palm facing the slab. *"Pug nona se ton."*

An energy wave shot from his palm toward the stone slab and rebounded back at Max, knocking him and the others flat on their backs in the wet muck.

Taryn was the first to sit up and look around. "That worked well. Any other bright ideas?"

Radimir stood and shook the wet dirt from his arms. "No back, go forward."

Max raised himself on all fours before pushing up from one knee. "Radimir's right. We can't go back. The problem is, we have three choices to move forward."

"I wouldn't recommend splittin' up, not in this darkness." Taryn lit a flame around her body to burn off all the dampness. The flame died and left her standing in dirty, but dry clothes.

Max looked at his arms and legs and then at Radimir. With a flick of his wrist, the moisture fell from their clothes and returned to the ground, leaving them in roughly the same condition as Taryn.

Max headed back to the intersection and stopped in the center of a ten-foot circular area. He examined their options once again. They could continue forward, go left or go right. "We're gonna need to pick a direction. Any suggestions?"

Radimir looked back then forward again. "No back, go forward." He pointed straight ahead.

"It's as good an option as any." Max took the lead with his glowing orb right above his head.

They walked for a hundred feet and came to yet another intersection. This time, their options were left or right only. Max sighed. "I can see this is gonna be fun."

Radimir looked at Max. "Fun?"

"Sorry, Radimir. Bad joke."

"Right now, I wish we had a Book of the Dead." Taryn examined the walls near the intersection. When she looked back at Max and Radimir, she noticed they had gone silent and were staring at her. "The ancient Egyptians buried a papyrus scroll with the deceased called the Book of the Dead... at least those who could afford it. It contained many magic spells intended to aide in the dead person's journey through the Egyptian underworld, also known as the Duat." Smiling she added, "I know a little about Egyptian history too, ye know."

Radimir looked at Max. "No Egypt history."

Max placed a hand on his shoulder. "That's okay, big guy. I'm not even sure what I know about Egyptian history, or Greek history or any history for that matter." Max took one more look in each direction. "I say we go left."

"Why left?" questioned Taryn.

"Why not? We have to go some direction. Left is as good as any."

They walked fifty feet and arrived at yet another intersection. This time they were presented with four choices. Left, right, forward or down. Next to the passage going straight was a set of stairs leading down.

"This is not good." Max examined the stairs. "Our labyrinth just became multi-layered. Who knows how far down this goes? Right about now I wish Meagan were here—we could use an Earth elemental sorceress to help guide us through this maze."

"What?"

Max looked around in confusion. "Who said that?" He thought for sure he heard another voice.

"Who said what?" questioned Taryn.

"Never mind." Max shook his head.

As they continued their inspection of the intersection choices, a noise echoed through the tunnel system. Halfway between an empty stomach and a lion's roar, it was enough to draw the attention of the dirt-covered trio back the way they had come.

"I don't think we're alone down here." Taryn lit a fireball in her right hand and held it there. After a few moments of no sound, she extinguished the flame. "We need to keep movin'."

They turned back to their multiple choices to find they only had two. The options to go left, right or forward were now gone. They could only go back the way they had come or take the stairs downward.

"What just happened here?" asked Max. "I'd swear there were four choices—five, if you count going back the way we came—and now there are only two. Am I losing my mind?" Even in the dim light, Max couldn't miss Taryn's smirk. "I mean... more than normal?"

"Nah, there were four choices before. Now it looks like we go back or go down. Neither seems promisin'."

"No back, go forward." Radimir pointed to the stairs.

"Wait, there must be a pattern here somewhere," said Taryn. "This can't just be random passages. Do ye remember anythin' about a labyrinth in Egyptian mythology?"

Max stood there searching his thoughts. "Sorry, I can't remember anything. Just that Osiris was the Egyptian god of the dead and Anubis guided the deceased on their journey to the underworld." Max thought about what he had said for a moment then glanced at Radimir. "Big guy, I know you can change into animals, but what about partial transformations?"

Radimir scrunched his eyebrows for a moment. With a quick look at Taryn and then back to Max, he said, "Never try. What you think?"

"Max?" questioned Taryn.

Holding up a hand to forestall her questions while locking his gaze on Radimir, he asked, "Can you transform your head only? Many of the ancient Egyptians had the head of an animal and the body of a human. They practiced partial transformations. That's how they did it. Maybe if you can transform your head into a jackal and keep your body human, you might look like Anubis."

"What good will that do us?" Taryn stepped next to Radimir. "Even if he looks like Anubis, that doesn't mean he can lead us through this maze."

"No, but whatever made that noise might think he is Anubis and hold off on attacking."

"What would be down here to attack us?" Taryn looked from the stairs to the solitary passage back the way they had come.

Max paused, trying to piece together what memories he could. "We went through the tomb of Osiris... Anubis guided the dead to the underworld to be judged. If the person was judged to be unworthy, their heart was fed to Ammut—a creature with the hind end of a hippo, the body of a lion and the head of a crocodile. If this is the journey to the underworld, then at the end of our journey, we should find Ammut."

Taryn sighed. "Don't ye ever think of any good news?"

"I don't know, but what I do know is even more concerning." Max looked past his friends into the darkness. "Odin told us where to find Ra. So... either Ra is now in the Egyptian underworld... or Odin sent us to the wrong place."

35 AMMUT

The roar echoed through the tunnels again, but they couldn't determine the direction of its source. Was it behind them or down the stairs? The air was musty and the walls were damp. Max was no longer sure how deep they had gone... but he was certain it was too deep. This was definitely not the way to Ra. The only problem was they couldn't go back the way they had come.

Radimir stood in the middle of the intersection and concentrated on transforming just his head into a jackal. He worked at it for many minutes. First his entire body became a dog, but when reversed only his hands had turned into paws. On his second attempt, he grew long shaggy hair all over his body. After a third failed attempt where he grew pointed ears and a tail, he collapsed to the floor.

Taryn and Max ran to his side. They propped him up between them and saw he was still breathing.

"Sorry, tired." Radimir was breathing heavy, but he was still conscious. "Not easy. Lot of work. Try again."

"No." Max placed a hand on his shoulder. "The Egyptians had years to practice this transformation. For now, save your strength."

Radimir nodded. "Maybe try later."

They lifted him to his feet. Radimir continued to lean on Max for a few more minutes while Taryn led the way down the stairs. They descended fifty steps before reaching the next level. A long corridor stretched out before them.

A scraping noise from behind drew their attention. Max turned and immediately cast a fireball spell, "*Magna fir-tor loma.*"

Taryn lit a fireball in each hand. Two men covered with dirt in torn black trench coats stepped out of the darkness.

Their faces were thin and the bags under their eyes revealed they had little sleep recently. They quickly approached the trio and fell to their knees. "Help us, please."

Max carefully shifted Radimir to lean against a wall. "Who are you? You look like dark sorcerers, kind of."

"I'm Dakat and this is Turner. We've been wandering these tunnels for days trying to find and release Ammut, but the passages... They keep changing. There's no way out. Please, do you have any water?"

Max pulled a bottle from his pack. The two men quickly grabbed for it. Dakat greedily consumed most of the water before Turner swiped it from his mouth, fighting for every last drop.

Max stood with his arms crossed. "We're members of the New Circle."

"We figured as much," responded Dakat wiping the excess water from his lips. "You'd be the only ones dumb enough to follow us into the Egyptian underworld to prevent the release of Ammut." He shifted his jaw side to side as he lowered his gaze.

"Honestly, we're looking for Ra. But since you mentioned it, we can't exactly let you release Ammut either."

Dakat smiled. "If you get us out of here, we'll never make another attempt at releasing the devourer of the dead."

Max studied the grimy dark sorcerer. "And we have your word on that?"

"I promise."

"Ye'll understand if we don't trust ye," replied Taryn. Turning to Max she offered, "I say we tie them up and leave them for Ammut."

Max considered the idea. Bringing them along would require their constant supervision, but leaving them behind could be dangerous too. "While I'm sure Ammut would enjoy a little snack, I don't trust leaving them out of our sight. At least not until we get out of this place. We can always turn them over to Ra at that point." Max looked at Taryn and Radimir who each shrugged their shoulders before returning his attention to Dakat and Turner. "Fine, you can come along. Unfortunately, we don't know where we're going any better than you."

Taryn faced the dark sorcerers. "Ye wouldn't happen to have a Book of the Dead, would ye?"

The two men exchanged looks before Dakat pulled a slightly crushed scroll from his pack. "It's basically worthless. What looks like a map doesn't seem to match up with any passages we've seen so far."

Taryn examined the scroll. "Can ye read ancient Egyptian hieroglyphics?"

Both men shook their heads as their gaze fell to the floor.

Taryn handed the scroll to Max. "Unfortunately, neither can I. Max, what about ye?"

Max looked at the pictorial writing and without thought began to read out loud in ancient Egyptian the directions and spells to navigate the tunnel system.

Once he reached the end, he looked up to find the others staring at him. Looking down at the scroll again, the hieroglyphics appeared as unmeaning pictures and symbols. "How did I just do that?"

With a perplexed look, Taryn asked, "Better question is, did ye understand a single word of what ye just said? And if so, how do we get outta here?"

Max considered the questions a moment. "These are instructions to aid a recently deceased person through the twelve regions of the Duat on Ra's barque."

With a furrowed brow Radimir interrupted, "What is do hot? Why he bark?"

Max corrected him. "The Duat is kind of like a river running through the Egyptian underworld. Ra made the journey every night when the sun set, and he would return the next morning with the rising sun. Unfortunately, this is not the Duat. We're in some kind of maze beneath the tomb of Osiris. With any luck it will take us to Osiris' judgment chamber along the Duat. If we can find that, then we should be able to follow the underground river back to the surface."

The two dark sorcerers exchanged a glance drawing Max's attention. "The judgment chamber is most likely where we'll also find Ammut. We should get through that section as quickly as possible, no stopping. If I think for one second you're going to turn on us, I'll feed the both of you to the monster."

Dakat raised his hands. "We just want out of here. We'll do whatever you say."

Radimir called to the others. "Look! Find pictures on wall."

Max and Taryn joined Radimir to discover more hieroglyphics. They examined the writing with little luck, until Max noticed a section he understood. "There are statues to Osiris, Anubis, Thoth, Horus, and Hathor in the underworld. The statue of Thoth may provide some help."

Max turned to Dakat and Turner. "Have either of you seen any statues down here? Or a river?"

Turner nodded. "There's one statue on this level and another about two levels down. But I don't know who's who. As for a river, if we'd found that we would've swam our way out of this Egyptian hole in the ground."

Max examined the writing again and spotted another section he could make out. "It says, 'Never look back or your options will change'. Apparently Radimir's idea of not going back and only going forward makes sense."

Taryn looked at Dakat and Turner then extended a hand down the passage. "Since ye two know where to find the statues, we'll follow ye. And that way we can also keep an eye on ye."

Dakat and Turner reluctantly took the lead with Max and Taryn following close behind while Radimir brought up the rear. After a few bad turns and one dead end, they spotted a statue in the distance. The group quickly approached to find it was Anubis.

Max turned to Radimir. "This is what you're shooting for, big guy."

Radimir approached the statue and took a close look at the features of the jackal-headed god while the others examined more hieroglyphics at the base of the statue.

This time, Max couldn't make out the writing. "Sorry, but apparently I'm not fluent in dead ancient languages."

"Ah, jackal head," announced Radimir. "I think."

Max and Taryn turned to see the head of Anubis atop a muddy black trench coat, dirty white t-shirt, and filthy blue jeans. While it didn't have the desired Egyptian look Max had been hoping for, Radimir had certainly accomplished the transformation.

"Great." Max held out a hand toward Radimir. "*Mimno ala tru viso.*" Radimir's clothing was replaced by a truer representation of Anubis as Max remembered him. Radimir's dark bare chest flowed seamlessly into the jackal head. He wore gold bracers and a black Egyptian shendyt and sandals.

"Just remember," Max warned, "don't touch anyone or the spell will be broken. You'll still have the jackal head, but your clothes will return to normal." Max couldn't remember where he'd learned of the spell's limits, but he remembered being in another underground tunnel at the time.

"Now all we need is a quick way to the end of this maze." Taryn crossed her arms as she examined the work of Radimir and Max.

"Maybe we have a way." Max stared at the jackal head of Radimir as he became lost in thought.

He remembered Anubis from an ancient time. A time when the temples and sands of Egypt were new. When the ancient sorcerers ruled the African kingdom as gods. A flash of memory gave Max an idea.

"Radimir," he said. "Anubis didn't use magic to make his way through the underworld. The very walls merely obeyed his command. Recite this spell then order the maze to take us to the end." Max handed the scroll to Radimir as he pointed to a set of hieroglyphs.

Radimir scrunched his brow for a moment. Then shrugging his shoulders, he did as instructed. His pronunciation of the spell left Max cringing. Then the big Russian ordered, "Take us end."

Nothing happened.

Max stood next to Radimir so they could both see the scroll. Max clearly spoke the spell aloud so Radimir could follow along. Max ended by saying, "Tell the maze to take us to Osiris' judgment chamber."

The Russian made another attempt at the spell then ordered, "Take us Osiris judgment chamber." Still nothing happened.

After a few more failed attempts, they decided to continue on their search for the statue of Thoth.

Another hour passed. Finally, they had descended two more levels down when they spotted yet another statue. As they approached this time, Max recognized the head as an ibis, a long beaked bird. "This is Thoth."

They examined the statue's base to find more hieroglyphics, along with three items—a sword, a wheel and a book.

Max read the writings. "Place the greatest weapon in the hand of Thoth."

Dakat picked up the sword, but Max quickly stopped him.

"What are you doing? That's not the greatest weapon."

Dakat pointed the sword at Max. "It's the only item among the three that is a weapon."

Taryn slipped up behind Dakat and grabbed his wrist. With a quick spin, she wrenched the blade from his hand and landed him flat on his back with his wrist still tightly in her grip.

Max bent down to better face Dakat. "Thoth is the god of writing and knowledge. To him, the greatest weapon is the book."

Max took the ancient tome and placed it in the statue's hand. For a few seconds, nothing happened, then with a grinding noise, the statue of Thoth slid aside. Behind it was another set of stairs, but to everyone's disappointment, they led still further down into the depths of the underworld.

Max looked at each of the others, one by one, then entered the staircase. Once they were all inside the passageway, going down into the unknown, the stairs shifted beneath their feet, flattening and turning into a giant slide.

Max quickly lost track of their depth as they slid into the darkness. Dakat and Turner screamed in terror as Radimir put up his hands and called, "Yeah!" At the end of the slide, Max was the first to land in a large room. No sooner did he get his bearings when everyone else crashed into the room one after another as they reached the end.

When he looked around, Max found the walls of the room were clean and smooth, as if built by the Egyptians just days ago. Three-legged raised cauldrons held plates of burning coals, giving light to the room. Behind them ran a raging underground river— the Duat. At the far end sat an empty throne of gold and in front of the throne was a golden set of scales. One side held a large feather. The other, an empty plate awaiting the heart of the recently deceased.

Through a passage behind the throne appeared to be a bottomless pit. "Osiris' judgment chamber," Max informed the others. "This is where he decided who would go on to the afterlife and who would have their heart eaten by Ammut before being cast into darkness."

As if on cue, a loud roar came from a side chamber. Through a large doorway strode a bulky creature. Ammut stood ten feet at his shoulders. The hippo hind end blended into the front of a huge lion. Its crocodile head snapped happily at the prospect of fresh food.

Max looked around for Dakat and Turner who were already eyeing the scales and the feather. "Hold your place, you two, or so help me you will be lunch for that monster."

"Now what do we do?" asked Taryn, already preparing a fireball in each hand. She stood off to the side, arms spread and legs slightly flexed, ready to move in an instant.

"Wait." Max held up a hand. Then looking at Radimir, he nudged his head in the direction of Ammut. Radimir just looked at Max. Max realized the Anubis look-a-like wasn't getting the hint. "Anubis?" he prompted.

Radimir looked blankly again, then recognition flashed in his eyes. He turned toward Ammut. He took a few steps forward and raised his right hand. "I Anubis. Let pass."

The massive creature sniffed the air a few times then started toward Radimir with its jaws wide open, growling with hunger.

Taryn called, "I don't think he's buyin' it."

Radimir quickly touched a wall, breaking the illusion, and shape-shifted his head back to normal.

The quick change caught the monstrous creature by surprise, just long enough for Radimir to dodge the snapping attack of Ammut's huge crocodile mouth.

Max looked around to discover the two dark sorcerers had made their way around the room to the scales.

Turner began to search the throne, but Dakat immediately grabbed the feather from the scales. "I have the feather with which to judge the deceased," Dakat anounced. "Ammut, I command you to devour these three enemies of the kingdom."

Ammut's attention was attracted by the feather. He moved toward the dark sorcerers.

"No, you fool," called Dakat. "Attack them, not us."

Turner cast a fireball spell and threw the ball of flames at the creature.

Ammut charged the two sorcerers, knocking Turner over the throne, through the passage and into the darkness of the pit. The massive head of Ammut then swiveled to follow the feather once more.

Dakat threw the feather at the creature and backed himself into a corner screaming. With a quick snap of powerful crocodile jaws, the top half of Dakat was engulfed, his shrieking suddenly silenced. As Ammut threw back his head, the screaming was briefly heard again as the last of Dakat's feet disappeared down the gullet of the massive creature.

After a lite snack, Ammut turned to the trio for its main course. It took a few steps forward before a bright flash of light in the center of the room stopped all motion. The intense light even forced Ammut to cry in pain.

When Max regained his sight, he spotted a figure standing before the throne of Osiris. He blinked a few times and rubbed his eyes until they cleared enough to recognize the young man named Tiem from the market earlier that day.

The boy spoke a few words in ancient Egyptian. Ammut closed his jaws and looked from Tiem to the newcomers and back to Tiem. The massive creature then turned and strode out the passageway the same as when it entered.

"Welcome, my friends." Tiem spread his arms wide and bowed. "I fear I must ask why you chose to disturb Ammut from his slumber?"

Taryn extinguished her flames and stood by her friends.

Max stepped forward. "We have come seeking Ra, not Ammut. I think we just got some bad directions. Odin told us to come here. Perhaps he knew these dark sorcerers were here trying to release Ammut. He was a little vague on his directions."

Taryn raised an eyebrow. "Or maybe he's lost his mind."

"I see," said Tiem. "Unfortunately, your assessment of the all-father may not be far off."

He then turned to Max. "Ra has been expecting you, Chronos, master of time. This is why I met you in the market earlier. If you will follow me, I shall take you to him."

36   THE WELL OF URD

It wasn't long before Cyrus and Kallan were holding on to the furry scruff of the elephant-sized squirrel named Ratatoskr. The giant grey critter had a long bushy tail where five dwarves clung for dear life. Ratatoskr scurried this way and that around branches, stopping every once in a while to sniff a crevice for nuts... which he never found.

Cyrus wasn't sure how the others were fairing, but he felt like he was about to lose his lunch. It was by far, worse than any roller coaster he had ever experienced. A quick glance at Kallan's face revealed a similar expression of nausea. He could only imagine how the dwarves were doing on the swishing tail.

After two hours of clinging to fur for dear life, they arrived in a dark wooded area. The most notable object was the giant root they had just come down. Ratatoskr held still long enough for his passengers to disembark. After a quick sniff of the air, the giant squirrel took off up the tree and out of sight once again.

Cyrus dropped to one knee and hung his head. "Well, there goes our ride."

"I'm not complaining," responded Kallan as he pursed his lips and held his stomach. "I'm not sure I could stand another two-hour ride on such an erratic creature."

Cyrus looked over his shoulder at the five dwarves. Most were seated on the ground, pale faced and looking just as queasy as he felt.

After a five-minute rest, Cyrus rose and tried to rally his troops. They were sluggish to respond, but slowly got to their feet. Kallan had just joined them when Cyrus heard something approaching. His first thought was the Nidhogg had already found them. He knew in their current condition, they would put up little fight against a supposed monster. But after a brief pause, he realized the sound was actually hoof beats upon wood.

Four giant deer approached down the trunk of Yggdrasil. Landing not far from their position, Cyrus watched as seven people disembarked. They stood and stretched their arms after a long ride. No one appeared pale faced or bent over.

As Cyrus, Kallan and the other dwarves approached, the four deer became spooked and darted away up the trunk of the tree. When they neared the newcomers, Cyrus picked his sister and Meagan out among the crowd. It quickly became clear, the other five were elves, tall slender figures with long straight hair... and well-armed with sword and bow.

Cyrus called out to his sister and their friend, "Amber, Meagan!"

The girls turned around with smiles on their faces. Their joy quickly faded as both dwarves and elves prepared for battle. Heavy dwarven battle axes gleamed in the sun as razor sharp arrows were knocked to elven bow. Both sides were well armored and numerically matched.

"Wait!" called Cyrus and Amber in unison. Cyrus threw his arms out in front of the dwarves, attempting to prevent an unwelcome confrontation. Amber imitated his motion in front of the elves.

Cyrus noticed that Kallan and Meagan did not join in the attempt to stop the misunderstanding. They merely stood their ground unmoving. Cyrus wasn't sure what bothered him more, the fact that Kallan hadn't moved to join him or that Meagan appeared to be siding with the elves.

Both groups were ready for a fight, but neither made a move.

Cyrus looked over his left shoulder. "Amber, what are you doing here? And why do you have five elves with you?"

"I could ask the same of you and the six dwarves," his sister called back.

"We need water from the Well of Urd to strengthen the new Gleipnir. You?"

"The scrolls containing the spell to make Gleipnir were destroyed. Someone needs to drink water from the Well of Urd to gain the knowledge to recreate the spell."

Cyrus directed his attention to their two unmoving friends. "Kallan? Meagan? We could really use your help here. Anytime you two want to jump in, it would be appreciated." Cyrus knew of Kallan's distrust of elves, but Meagan's actions had left him confused ever since arriving in the nine realms.

Kallan stood with his arms crossed. "The elves tricked your friends into coming to get the water for themselves so they could use the spells they learn against the dwarves."

"Unlikely," called Meagan. "Everyone knows dwarves have always been greedy, underhanded thieves."

"Meagan, what is wrong with you?" called Cyrus even more confused than before.

Amber responded, "Cyrus, there's something you don't know and now's not the time to discuss it... but I guarantee, Megan is definitely sticking with the elves."

Cyrus could see they had a stalemate, with him and Amber stuck in the middle. They had to find a way for their two groups to work together, but with two of their friends on opposing sides, he couldn't just let them battle each other.

No one moved for a few long minutes. Cyrus could feel his heart race and he was sure the others felt it too, waiting on the edge of a battle they couldn't avoid. He felt even less comfortable knowing he stood between axes and arrows just waiting to fly, until a loud roar followed by the breaking of tree limbs could be heard in the distance. Reluctant to look away from the dwarf-elf standoff, Cyrus' head turned minutely in the direction of the disturbance. He both dreaded and welcomed the approach of the Nidhogg. At least the two groups would now have a common enemy to deal with rather than each other.

"You know, you people really have some issues to work out," called Cyrus. "Unfortunately, right now is not the time to do it. The Nidhogg is approaching. You can either stay here and kill each other, or you can help us get the water from the well. You can't do both. I'm here to save Midgard so I'm going after the water. What you do is up to you. Kallan, Meagan, time to stow the emotional baggage and come with us."

Cyrus ran from the clearing with Amber close behind. Kallan and Meagan hesitated, locked in a staring contest, but Meagan eventually broke the connection first and ran after Cyrus. Kallan followed at a discreet distance. The remaining dwarves and elves followed suit, each keeping a close eye on the other.

In a few minutes they came across a hollow in the woods where a stone well sat near part of a root of Yggdrasil. Cyrus took one step toward it, but heard the breaking of branches, tree limbs and trees overhead. A large scaled claw crashed down through the brush and dug into the ground less than a hundred feet from their position. He looked above the tree tops and saw the sharp fangs and giant maw of a massive creature.

Its black scales and red glowing eyes left little doubt—the Nidhogg had arrived. Dwarves and elves immediately charged the creature, axes and swords ablaze as they slashed and hacked at its massive claw. It took all of them to attack the single visible appendage of the monster.

A second claw slammed into the ground nearby followed by a howl so loud it deafened Cyrus. Three of the elves and two of the dwarves sprinted for the second claw, slamming their steel into the well armored extremity.

While the others slashed at the monstrous claws, Cyrus, Amber, Meagan and Kallan ran for the well. The hollow provided minimal protection from the battle raging around it, but at least the tree cover kept them hidden from the behemoth.

There sitting next to the well were three old ladies. They made no move to greet their guests except with a dark stare. Kallan and the other dwarves had not mentioned anything to Cyrus about a guard, so this was an unexpected surprise. He stepped forward and mumbled, "Hi, uh, how ya doing?"

Kallan strode in front of Cyrus. "My apologies. My friend is unfamiliar with our ways. I am Kallan Stonefoot, prince of Koldihr. My friends and I have need of water from the Well of Urd."

One of the ladies stood. "We know who you are, princeling. And we know your friends. This is Verdani and Skuld and I am Urdr. We are the Norns. We protect the Well of Urd and feed Yggdrasil."

Kallan bowed. "My lady, I was under the impression there was once a great hall nearby where you resided."

"The Nidhogg saw to that long ago. Now we dwell in this hollow."

Meagan stepped forward. "Forgive us, great ones, but our friends are buying us precious time with their lives. We have need of water from the well for two purposes: to gain the knowledge needed to create a new Gleipnir to once again bind Fenrir, and to bolster that new binding against his added strength."

Urdr bowed her head. "So, it's true, the great wolf has been freed. We feared this would happen. You may draw the water from the well as you wish, but be warned. The well will demand a sacrifice."

Cyrus could see, while Kallan and Meagan were working toward the same goal, they challenged each other, practically stepping on top of the other to speak. He placed a gentle hand on each of their shoulders and pushed them apart, allowing himself to stand before Urdr. "My name is Cyrus Marx. I'll draw the water from the well, but how do I know the price it will demand?"

"As you draw the water, you will know," said Urdr. "You will pay the price or fail to obtain that which you need. The well will not allow a second attempt."

Cyrus swallowed hard and nodded. He stepped forward and placed his hands on the crank that would lift the bucket. Slowly he turned the wheel and the rope began to rise. In seconds, he knew what he had to do. In less than a heartbeat, he dreaded the price. The well had demanded the one thing that gave him the strength to lead. The one thing he needed to protect his friends and defeat his enemies... but he only had one shot at this. His stomach sank as he momentarily held the crank in place with his right hand and untied the magical bracer with his left.

Amber called to him, "Cyrus, no! You need that."

Cyrus continued to turn the wheel as the bracer slipped from his forearm. "It's what the well wants. We have no choice." He dropped the bracer into the well, watching as it disappeared into the shadowy depths. Seconds later, a small splash echoed from the darkness. As he continued to turn the wheel, a bucket of water appeared at the end of the rope.

Urdr stepped forward with a small flask. "Fill this and take the water with you to make Gleipnir. Then take a drink yourself.

The well has deemed you worthy. But be warned again... only *you* may drink of its waters."

After filling the flask, Cyrus took a long slow drink. The water was sweet to the taste, but he felt no different. He looked at the Norns. "It didn't work."

"It will," replied Urdr. "You asked for the spell to create Gleipnir. When you are ready to cast it, the words will come to you. Take heed. Your friends are almost spent and your time runs short. The four deer, Dáinn, Dvalinn, Duneyrr and Duraþrór have returned. They await you in the clearing where you arrived. You must hurry."

Cyrus smiled. "Sounds great. I don't think I could tolerate another erratic squirrel ride. A second time on that critter and I probably would lose my lunch."

37 THE IMMORTAL RA

Once Radimir had returned to a more normal appearance with filthy clothes, Tiem led the three of them to another side room with a mirror. The young man cast the spell to open a mirror portal, *"Mirtor tolanga se-atum."* Max was the last to step through to find they had returned to a little shop in the market. Once again they pushed their way through the marketplace, passing many merchants still trying to sell their wares.

"Start over," commented Radimir.

They made their way to the Great Sphinx as Tiem had originally suggested. It was getting close to evening and the sun was beginning to set. Near the ruined temple in front of the Sphinx, Tiem took a seat on a large block of stone. He motioned for the others to sit as well.

"It's late and the tourists will soon leave. We'll go in the front door rather than sneaking around to the back."

Max took an unpleasant seat on a rock facing Tiem. "So how do you know Ra?"

Taryn and Radimir took equally rough seats next to Max.

Tiem reclined against another rock as if it were the most comfortable seat in the area. "Ra is my mentor. Many from this area know of him. Some still worship him as a god. Others know he is merely a powerful sorcerer. He teaches us the arcane writings he has collected throughout the centuries. A vast library exists beneath our feet. Also, beneath us is his audience chamber. He resides both here at Giza and sometimes further south at the temple of Karnak."

"What can you tell us about him?" Max pressed. He remembered their encounter with Odin which hadn't gone so well. He wanted to avoid another unpleasant confrontation with the only other immortal on the planet.

Tiem smiled. "Ra is a very pleasant person, just don't try to touch him. He's sensitive about that. He's been expecting you... Though your detour through the Tomb of Osiris was a little troubling. We thought maybe you had joined the dark sorcerers. Or perhaps, the two lost in the Osiris Shaft would take you by surprise."

Taryn chimed in, "Trust me, we've overcome every other pain in the frozen butt ye can think of. A couple of skinny and frightened dark sorcerers weren't much of a challenge."

"Frozen? In Egypt?" Tiem's head tilted.

Max waved a hand. "We came here from Canada... by way of Asgard. It seems fire elemental sorceresses don't like the cold." Max pointed to Taryn and added, "Especially this one."

"I've had enough cold to last me until the next ice age."

"Me Russian. Cold not bother. Heat, not so good." Radimir had to have his say.

They continued their light conversation for a few more minutes until the last rays of light crept over the horizon. The tourist crowds had departed as Tiem predicted. A few locals remained seated around the area with Max and the others.

An older man with a long white scraggly beard called to Tiem, "The coast is clear."

Tiem stood, stretched his arms and let out a sigh. "Come, my friends. It's time to meet Ra."

He led them down a short ladder and around a small limestone altar between the paws of the Great Sphinx. "This is the Tothmes Tablet, our entry to Ra's audience chamber." He indicated a large stone slab placed against the breast of the huge monolith. Tiem placed a hand on the tablet and cast a spell. "*Toth les Toth mos une altu.*"

The limestone tablet began to shimmer and Tiem's hand passed through it. He then walked through the stone block and disappeared. Max and Taryn exchanged a glance then followed him through the tablet with Radimir close behind.

They emerged in a small chamber inside the Sphinx. Before them was a neatly carved set of stone stairs leading down. They descended behind Tiem twenty feet into a large chamber. The walls were perfectly straight and well maintained. Curtains hung between support columns to break up the appearance of the solid walls. Tripods with plates of burning embers lit the room with a warm glow. Hieroglyphics on the walls depicted many battles as well as times of peace. At the far end of the chamber sat an empty golden throne with a leopard lying lazily at either side. Golden chains restrained them as they sat up and eyed the newcomers.

Attendants were busy making preparations. Three seats had been placed facing the throne at a distance of twenty feet. Other attendants stood off to the side, preparing food.

"Come, my friends. The great Ra has been expecting you." Tiem motioned for them to follow.

He led them to the three chairs. Once they each took their seat, Tiem took a few steps back and clapped his hands once. Attendants stepped forward bearing plates of exotic foods from all over Egypt. Max accepted a goblet of wine. He looked to Taryn and Radimir with hesitation before eating or drinking.

Tiem stepped forward. "Please, my friends. You must be starved after your journey to the tomb of Osiris."

Max placed his goblet on the arm of his chair. "Shouldn't we wait for our host?"

"Ah, no." Tiem smiled. "The lord Ra does not eat. He has no need of sustenance."

Max furrowed his brow and once again exchanged looks with Taryn and Radimir. With a shrug of his shoulders, he began to eat. The others followed suit. Max hadn't realized how hungry he was until he consumed the first bite.

After Tiem insisted on a second plate of food for each of his guests, they sat back in their chairs.

"Enough. I couldn't eat another date," said Max.

Tiem clapped his hands twice and the attendants moved quickly to clear the plates and refill their goblets. Tiem then moved to stand slightly behind and to the right of the throne. "The master will arrive shortly. In the meantime, some entertainment."

Four scantily clad Egyptian girls with veils around their waists dashed between them and the throne. Music began to play in the background and the girls started to dance.

Taryn turned to Max with a cold stare. He could tell she wasn't pleased, but all he could do was shrug. He had no idea what the customs were and didn't want to offend their host.

She didn't say a word, but crossed her arms and sat with pursed lips, watching the fire burn atop one of the tripods.

Radimir had no trouble enjoying the entertainment, but Max sat in the middle quietly thinking about the tirade he would hear from Taryn once they left the place. With this in mind, he had difficulty enjoying the show.

After about ten minutes of dancing, the flames on the tripods engorged for a second before returning to normal. Tiem clapped his hands twice more and the girls dashed from the room. Tiem bowed and waited.

From behind the throne emerged a bald man with skin as dark as copper. He wore a red sash across his shoulders which left his chest and abs bare. A white shendyt—a form of Egyptian skirt worn by the men—covered him from the waist down. The man passed right through the golden seat like a ghost and stood before them. He extended his arms to the sides and bowed his head.

"Ra," Max whispered to his companions, then hesitantly stood and mimicked the movement. Taryn and Radimir exchanged a glance before doing the same.

Ra lowered his arms and took his seat upon the throne. He placed a hand on each armrest and leaned back. His gaze traveled over each of his guests then settled upon Max. A huge smile spread across his face as his demeanor became more jovial. "Chronos, my old friend. It's good to see you again."

"You know me? I mean you really know I'm Chronos?" Max was excited to meet someone who actually knew who he was and could possibly tell him something about his past.

Ra sighed. "So your memory is gone once again? I figured as much, but I always hope something of your last life will remain for a change."

"My last life?"

"As usual, I suppose I should start at the beginning. You are Chronos, king of the Titans and god of Time. Actually you are the only sorcerer I know throughout the last ten thousand years who has mastered the power of time—one of the few powers I have never been able to master myself. I do believe there was another, but I never met the wizard Merlin."

So many questions flooded Max's mind he didn't know where to begin. He waited patiently to see what else Ra would reveal.

"Some of what I am about to tell you, your friends may already know, but there is more. Ten thousand years ago, dark sorcerers attempted to steal magical energies from other realms. They found one brimming with powerful magic and began to siphon that power from what we now call the Nightmare Realm. This ripped a hole in the fabric of reality... creating a passage between our two worlds. Hundreds of creatures flowed through this rift into our world. Most of the dark sorcerers fled in fear. You, Odin and I each journeyed to the rift in the hopes of closing it. None of us individually had the power to seal it, but together we succeeded. However, in doing so we cursed ourselves with immortality."

Max titled his head. "Cursed? I would think most people would consider it a powerful gift to live forever."

"Unfortunately, as you may have already noticed, our immortality came with a price. Each of us bears the weight of our curse differently. You live a normal life for the most part, but whenever you die, you reawaken as a seventeen-year-old boy with no memory. You get flashes of past lives, information you need to survive or fight, but you never retrieve all of your memories, just fragments. Like hitting the reset button in modern day video games. A few times, these memory gaps have even driven you insane."

Max's line of sight dropped to the floor in contemplation of all the knowledge he must have lost over the years... all the friends he once knew.

Ra continued, "Odin, though blessed with great wisdom, has been trapped in the body of a weak old man for thousands of years. In the past five hundred or so, his mental faculties have also begun to give out. Some days he is very lucid, others a raving madman. Time has not been a friend to him."

Max looked at Ra once again. "And what about you?"

"My curse set in over the first hundred years or so. Since then it has been constant. I live and cannot die, but I have no physical form. I am not dead, but I am no longer tangible. I pass through all that I touch. I am not seated upon this throne, merely holding my position above it. I cannot eat or drink, but I will never starve. You have no idea how much I long for the taste of food or the touch of another human being."

Max considered what it would be like to never be able to touch anyone or anything ever again. The thought scared him. "How do you deal with it?"

"I have no choice. I accepted that fact long ago. It no longer has hold over me. Odin, not so much. He still blames *you* for our curse."

"Me?"

"It was you who came to us with a revelation that the curse of immortality was due to a minor error in the spell you cast to seal the rift. So long as the great seal exists, so do we. If the seal is ever broken though, our curse should end and we would live out normal lives... but it would mean casting this world into the darkness of the Nightmare Realm once again. That is something I cannot do."

Taryn touched Max on his hand. "Odin's pledge to help our friends."

Max thought about their last encounter with Odin. "Before leaving Asgard, Odin promised to help our friends. They're trying to find a way to create a new Gleipnir to re-imprison Fenrir."

"The great wolf of Norse mythology has escaped?"

Max nodded. "A dark sorcerer has released the creature. Our friends went to Nidavellir to seek the aide of the dwarves in making a new Gleipnir."

Ra leaned back and closed his eyes. After a few minutes he looked upon Max and his friends once again. "I have spoken with Odin through our mental link. As expected he forgot his pledge until I reminded him. He is now on his way to aide your friends."

"Do we share a mental link?" asked Max.

Ra sighed. "At one time, but each time you died and were revived, the link weakened until it stopped working altogether. We have never been able to reestablish it since."

Max noticed an older man approach Tiem and whisper something in his ear. Ra looked over his shoulder and Tiem stepped forward.

"My lord," said Tiem, "we have just received word. Ravenicon castle is under attack from dark sorcerers."

"What?" Max rose to his feet followed quickly by Taryn and Radimir.

"It seems our discussion is at an end for now. Chronos, you and your friends must depart immediately. Tiem will take you to the nearest mirror. Since my magic has little effect on the real world, I would ask that you allow Tiem to accompany you in my absence. Even if the crystal does not select him as the newest member of your Circle, he can be of great use to you in this battle."

Tiem faced Ra. "My lord!"

Ra smiled. "You are ready, my son. It's time you faced your destiny."

38 The Challenge of Strength

After a brief thank you and goodbye to the two remaining elves, Cyrus and his friends along with three dwarves returned to Nidavellir to the mines of the elders. The dwarf company bade a peaceful farewell to their two fallen comrades then set out to build a fire in the forge of the lower mines.

Once the fire was hot enough, the six impossible items were added. The dwarves took turns pounding the conglomeration of weird ingredients... from rock to sea water to things Cyrus didn't even want to know about. At the end, they added water from the Well of Urd.

While the elder dwarves worked, Cyrus pulled Kallan aside. "I need you to do something for me while they make the new Gleipnir. A friend of ours should be arriving shortly. He will stay near the entrance to the mines, but won't come in until someone fetches him. Can you bring him to us here? Oh, and he probably won't be very talkative."

Kallan scrunched his brow, but nodded his affirmation and headed off for the mine entrance.

It took many hours of heating and reheating the items until it formed a glowing hot mass of goo. Sturlin summoned Cyrus to the forge. "The time has come, my friend. As we start to pound the glob into a single strand, you must continually recite the spell. You will grow tired as this process can take another few hours." He handed Cyrus a mug of ale then held up his own. "A toast, to good fortune, long life and a swift end to this process."

Cyrus clanked his mug to Sturlin's then took a long slow drink. It would need to last for a lengthy time. He finished his mug, slammed it down and concentrated on the spell. It came to his mind quickly and easily, like he had known it for years and could recite it without even thinking about it. "*Tuglo freela aris midjo almir-altu dolong ertisal prhyetr simglay.*" As one iteration ended, he started again and again... and again.

The dwarves hammered the glowing glob as Cyrus chanted. With each strike of the hammer, the glob formed into a thin piece of glowing mud. As the mud cooled, a ribbon began to form. Each stroke produced a mere inch or two. For a creature the size of Fenrir, they knew the ribbon must reach many hundred yards. It had to be long enough to bind the great wolf's legs, muzzle and body so the creature could never again escape.

Cyrus and the dwarves spent almost three hours spell-casting and working the mass into a thin ribbon. When they finally reached the end, Cyrus collapsed with a dry sore throat. The many dwarf smiths admired two hundred and twenty yards of silky fine material before also collapsing from exhaustion. It was light blue in color with a slight greenish sheen.

Kallan gave a tug on a section of the ribbon. Though it looked paper thin, it remained incredibly strong. He laid it down and gave a sly smile. "The wolf will not be happy to see Gleipnir again."

"You're right," Meagan said. "He won't be happy to see it, but he will recognize it. We're going to need a way to camouflage it."

Cyrus waved as he croaked a quiet response, "I have that covered."

After a few hours rest and a gallon of water, Cyrus felt much better, though still a little hoarse. He examined the length of the new Gleipnir, somewhat proud of the fact he had a hand in its creation.

Kallan rushed into the chamber. "Cyrus, I found your friend. Unfortunately, we have a bigger problem. Fenrir has arrived in Nidavellir. He has entered the mines and is making his way to the city."

Cyrus stared at Kallan and the newcomer. "How did you get out and back so fast? It took us almost a day to get here the first time."

"Oh, yeah. I forgot to mention, the elder dwarves stashed a mirror in a chamber not far from here. Give them a break, they're over three hundred years old. It's a long journey to and from the lower mines."

Cyrus quickly rolled up the new Gleipnir and stuffed it into his backpack before taking the arm of the quiet newcomer who appeared to be in his late twenties. Kallan then led the way to the mirror, then to a chamber in the royal palace of the dwarf king.

Screams and cries of terror could be heard throughout the streets of Koldihr. The glow of fires raging in certain areas cast long dark shadows against the intricately carved stone of the great city. A sustained loud howl could be heard as more screams echoed through the cavern.

Cyrus quickly pulled the magical ribbon from his pack and spread it out across the steps leading to the palace entrance. He held his hand over it. *"Mimnalt nissa vari contra tru-viso."* The visage of Gleipnir was transformed into that of a long length of heavy chain. He bent down to retrieve it.

"Don't touch it," called Meagan. "Hank warned Max that touching something with an illusion on it will break the spell."

Cyrus smiled as he lifted the chain with some effort. "This is a little more advanced spell. As I mentioned before, I have a talent for illusions. Now we just need to lure the beast here and convince him to let us put this chain on him."

Amber crossed her arms. "Oh, and what makes you think Fenrir is just going to let you bind him with a chain?"

"Last time someone attempted that," Kallan added, "he bit off the hand of Tyr. I have a feeling Fenrir's going to be more cautious this time."

Cyrus smiled. "I figured as much. That's why I invited our quiet friend here." He pointed toward the young man Kallan had fetched from the mine entrance.

Amber stepped closer to Cyrus and whispered. "Who is he?"

"Our *ringer*."

Meagan stood on the opposite side of the chain. "And how exactly is this mute going to lure Fenrir over here and convince him to allow us to put the chain on him?"

A voice from behind them replied, "Leave that to me."

Everyone turned to find Odin standing in golden full-body armor. He appeared bigger than when last they'd seen him. Though thin in the face, his armor provided the impression of a more muscular frame.

Cyrus could tell the weight of the armor was all the man could bear, but Odin's mere presence might be enough to entice Fenrir. After all, during Ragnarok, it was Fenrir who had challenged and defeated Odin... swallowing him whole. It was only later than Odin's son Vidarr had set him free. Cyrus figured the wolf would have a score to settle with the king of the Norse gods.

Odin lifted Mjolnir—the legendary hammer of Thor—high above his head. Thunder and lightning crackled forth from it, lighting up the palace entrance and grabbing the attention of everyone in the dwarven city, including Fenrir.

Cyrus recognized the mighty stone hammer, the one he had previously attempted to lift. Yet even in Odin's weakened state, the Asgardian immortal lifted it with little effort.

After a brief pause, the commotion in the city flooded toward the palace. Dwarves ran from the streets followed closely by the fifty-foot-tall black wolf. Fenrir's ears laid back. The snarl on his face revealed huge sharp teeth as saliva dripped from the edges of his mouth.

Everyone at the palace entrance took a step back except Cyrus, the young newcomer and Odin who stood their ground waiting for the great wolf's approach.

Fenrir stalked the edges of the courtyard, examining the scene. His glare fixed on Odin. Cyrus couldn't tell if the wolf was planning his attack or preparing for one from the ancient immortal. Fenrir crouched low to the ground and let out a loud howl.

Odin called out, "Beast, you have once again broken your bonds. You are an exasperating annoyance. But since you are here, I once again propose a challenge."

To Cyrus' surprise the wolf responded. "I have no need to prove myself to you, old man. I will eat you once more and this time no one will set you free."

Cyrus called out, "As I suspected, beast. You still fear the might of Odin."

Fenrir let out a low rumble, shifting an angered glance at Cyrus. "How dare a child such as yourself speak to me. Do you not know who I am?"

"You're the oversized and cowardly son of Loki," Cyrus replied. Perhaps if they could make the wolf angry enough, he would accept the challenge without thinking.

Fenrir took a step toward Cyrus, but a lightning bolt struck the ground at his feet. The wolf quickly drew back his paw and shifted his attention to Odin once again.

"I challenge you," Odin bellowed, "to a test of strength. Hundreds of years have passed. We wish to see how weak you've become."

"I have only grown stronger in captivity."

"Prove it."

Fenrir snarled. "Fine, but this time, I demand that someone stand inside my mouth while I endure your pathetic test. If I fail, I will eat that person alive. Should I succeed, I promise to eat that person last."

Cyrus called out, "We have a deal. My friend here has volunteered to meet your terms."

Fenrir sniffed the air in the direction of the newcomer, but made no gesture to back down. Fenrir merely laid at the base of the palace steps and opened his jaw wide. The newcomer climbed inside and took a seat within the mouth of Fenrir, while Cyrus and Kallan went about binding the legs and body of the monster.

Once finished, they stepped back to watch Fenrir's multiple attempts to break the chain.

After enjoying the struggle, Cyrus waved a hand and the illusion was broken. The visage of the chain faded to reveal the glowing ribbon known as Gleipnir.

The enraged wolf immediately bit down on the person seated in his mouth. A wave of water gushed from between his fangs.

Fenrir leaned back his head to howl, but gurgled on the excessive amount of water. When the wolf finally opened his mouth, a single golden ring fell out, bouncing down the steps and landing at Cyrus' feet.

Cyrus picked up the ring and placed it in his pocket, He smiled at the successful completion of his plan. "For once, one of Vincent's water automatons actually came in handy."

Kallan's jaw dropped. "That was just a water automaton?"

Cyrus smiled and admired his work... both in helping to create Gleipnir and in tricking Fenrir into his new bindings.

Without warning, a fireball slammed into the ground a few feet in front of Cyrus. The wolf cried out, "Sorceress!"

Out of the shadows ran a dark figure dressed in a black pantsuit and trench coat brandishing a sword. The movements of the sword were swift and accurate. With each slice, a section of the Gleipnir ribbon fell to the ground. Within seconds, Fenrir was once again free.

As the great wolf stood, the figure stepped into the light, revealing herself to be Alexis Malkin, the dark sorceress.

Alexis sheathed her sword. "This is becoming tiresome. Please try not to get captured again."

Fenrir immediately lunged for Odin who struck the wolf with Mjolnir. Lightning sparked and the wolf was knocked back, but so was Odin. Though he found the strength to once more lift the mighty hammer, it was all he could do. His strength was now gone and the hammer fell from his grip.

Kallan, Meagan and Amber quickly dragged the limp form of Odin inside the palace while Cyrus tried to pick up Mjolnir, but with no luck. The hammer would not budge.

Fenrir regained his bearings and pounced at Cyrus. Abandoning the great hammer, Cyrus ran for cover. With only a quick swat of Fenrir's paw, Cyrus flew ten feet into the palace entrance and crashed to the floor. After shaking the cobwebs from his head, he regained his feet and joined the others tending to Odin.

Fenrir pawed at the carved stone entrance to the palace. Fortunately the archway was too small for the giant wolf. However, with each swipe, sections of stone were sundered from the building.

Odin grabbed Cyrus' arm. "You must wield Mjolnir to defeat Fenrir."

Cyrus shook his head. "I tried. I can't lift it."

Odin undid his belt and pulled it from his waist. "This is Megingjord, Thor's belt of strength." He handed it to Cyrus. "It will give its wearer the strength to lift Mjolnir."

Cyrus eyed the belt with excitement. He placed it around his waist. He could immediately feel the swell of strength in his arms and legs. However, Fenrir stood between him and the place where Mjolnir had fallen.

Looking out the palace entrance past Fenrir at the mighty hammer, Cyrus saw Alexis Malkin standing over Mjolnir.

Odin whispered, "Call to it."

Cyrus did as Odin instructed. He reached out his hand toward the great stone hammer and called, "Mjolnir."

Odin let out a quiet groan. "No, you idiot. In your heart and mind. Speaking doesn't do anything."

Cyrus tried again. He reached out his hand toward the hammer and closed his eyes. He thought about his desire to hold it. He could feel the need to wield the mighty hammer. He continued to focus on this thought. After a few seconds, Mjolnir first shuddered then flew from its resting place, tripping Alexis in the process, slamming into the side of Fenrir and straight into the palace to Cyrus' outstretched hand.

Alexis let out a curse, followed by Fenrir's loud howl. The giant wolf clutched its ribcage.

Meagan smiled. "Great. We have Mjolnir, but no Gleipnir. Now what are we going to do?"

Cyrus replied, "We'll need to find a new way to imprison the beast. Any suggestions?"

Cyrus and the others thought for a moment while Fenrir continued to smash away at the palace entrance.

Kallan eventually suggested, "In the lower mines, there is a two-mile shaft into the heart of the planet. At the bottom stands about a hundred feet of water. If we drop the beast into the mine shaft, he'll tread water for all eternity since he can't die, but at least he won't be able to escape either."

Cyrus frowned at the thought. "Nice idea, but I doubt there's a large enough mirror to transport Fenrir. It took us an entire day to travel there by foot. How do we get him there?"

"The shrinking spell," Amber called. "We shrink him down to puppy size, take him through the mirror then return him to normal. Even if he somehow finds his way out of the shaft, he won't be able to leave the lower mines because the passages will be too small."

"Okay. So how do we get close enough to cast the spell?" asked Meagan.

Odin pulled himself to his feet. "Use Mjolnir. Surround Fenrir with lightning. It will keep him stationary long enough to cast the spell."

Cyrus ran from the palace and raised the hammer above his head. He willed the lightning forth from Mjolnir. Bolts of energy streaked from the stone hammer. Arcs of lightning cascaded down around the giant wolf.

Enraged, Fenrir reached out for one of the bolts. It singed his flesh. He howled and inched away from the sources of pain. "Release me, mortal, and I will spare your life. Do not and I will destroy all you hold dear."

Cyrus made no movement. He was focused on maintaining the lightning cage until someone could cast the shrinking spell.

Alexis appeared at Cyrus' side. "Finally someone powerful enough to wield Mjolnir. Why bother with the wolf? You and I could rule the world. Good sorcerers, evil sorcerers, it doesn't matter. They will all bow down before us. Lower the hammer and come with me. We will be worshiped as gods."

The lightning stopped and Cyrus turned toward Alexis. "My... queen?"

Meagan ran from the palace. With a clenched fist, she made an upper cut motion with her hand. A column of rock shot up from the ground and slammed into Alexis' lower jaw.

The shock knocked the dark sorceress to the ground, dazed and confused.

Meagan extended open palm hands then closed her fingers into another fist. The rocky soil reached up and solidified into stone manacles holding the enchantress to the ground. A final strand of rock extended upward and encased her mouth... preventing her from further speech.

Freed of her spell, Cyrus turned back toward Fenrir who now launched himself at the sorcerer. He raised Mjolnir once more and slammed it into the jaw of the giant wolf. Lightning shot through the body of the creature, singing fur and causing steam to emanate from its ears. The wolf collapsed to the ground unconscious.

Amber moved to the beast and cast the shrink spell. "*Mino zor-ti redu.*" The wolf gradually shrank in size until it was only one foot long.

Kallan grabbed the wolf cub and ran into the palace. He led them to the closest full body mirror and cast the transportation spell. "*Mirtor tolanga se-atum.*" The images in the mirror swirled around in a whirlpool of color.

Amber knelt next to Odin and whispered to her brother, "You go on. I'll stay with him."

Cyrus placed the hammer next to Odin and removed the belt. "He needs this more than I do." Cyrus then jumped through the mirror, followed by Kallan and Meagan.

Once they arrived in the lower mines, they returned to the chamber where they met Sturlin. "We need to get to the old vertical mine shaft," called Kallan.

Sturlin looked at the wolf cub then back to Kallan. "Follow me."

They raced through eight more tunnels until they arrived in a big circular room with a hundred-foot diameter hole in the center.

The wolf cub awoke and bit Kallan on the hand.

The dwarf prince dropped the wolf to the floor at the edge of the pit.

Cyrus knew they couldn't risk Fenrir escaping so he removed the shrinking spell. "*Dim-tar mai secul.*" Before the creature could reach the tunnel entrance, he grew and grew until he regained his full size.

The dwarves ran from the room, followed by Meagan and Cyrus. Fenrir pawed at the tunnel, which only caused the entrance to partially collapse. Cyrus knew Fenrir was trapped in the room, but they needed to get him into the pit. "Meagan, use your earth elemental powers. Force him into the mine shaft."

As Meagan held out her hand toward the giant wolf, Cyrus watched through a gap in the rubble blocking access to the room. Fenrir scraped and pawed at the sides of the room while the floor gradually sloped downward into the mine shaft. He watched a few crates and tools around the edge of the room also slide toward the center, disappearing into the vast darkness of the pit.

Eventually Fenrir too lost what little grip he had and slipped into the depths with a long echoing howl.

Meagan continued to shift her palms. The ceiling of the room above the pit then lowered more and more until it came to rest on the top ledge of the opening. The hole was sealed.

Cyrus collapsed against a wall and slid to the floor. Unfortunately, to his disappointment, Meagan didn't follow suit. Instead she extended a hand and raised it up. As she did, the ground beneath him shoved him to a standing position. "We have to go. Nick just contacted me... the castle is under attack. We're needed on Midgard."

39 ATTACK ON RAVENICON CASTLE

Gollnick ran into the library to find Vincent seated in front of the mirror. The reflection indicated Vincent was no longer in communication with anyone. "I've contacted Meagan and the others," Gollnick announced. "They've captured Fenrir and are on their way home. Any word from our other friends?"

Vincent's long face was not so eager. "It seems in an attempt to keep our friends at bay, the dark sorcerers have launched attacks in major cities all around the world. I haven't been able to reach anyone who can send aide—at least no one outside the Circle. I was able to reach Hank in Egypt, but no sooner had he spread the word than the dark sorcerers launched an attack near Karnack."

"Have you been able to reach Taryn or Max?"

"Something was interfering with the communication spell, but Hank said he would get the word out to his contacts in the area. Hopefully one of them will be able to reach our young friends."

Gollnick was not happy about this. When last he checked there were fifteen dark sorcerers searching Patterson Park in Baltimore, Maryland, blasting structures, trees, rocks and any other objects they could find. He knew what they were looking for, but hoped they wouldn't find it until reinforcements could arrive. The ground rumbled slightly and Gollnick knew it meant they were getting closer. "As long as the castle remains in its pocket dimension, they won't be able to see it."

Vincent stood from his chair. "Maybe we could cast some illusion spells, keep them occupied until help can get here."

Gollnick pursed his lips. "I doubt it will fool them for long. We'll need to keep it simple and believable or they'll just ignore it."

"How about Tiamat landing in the middle of the park?"

Gollnick raised his eyebrows. "That wouldn't be simple *or* believable. Not to mention it would scare half the population of Baltimore."

"Do you have a better idea?"

Gollnick thought for a moment. "As a matter of fact, yes. We create an illusion of ten sorcerers in the middle of the park and make it look like they are creating a protective shield around a pavilion or something. We'll also need to actually create a shield too to make it look real."

Vincent tilted his head. "I don't know if that qualifies as simple, but it might be believable."

Gollnick hobbled up the two flights of stairs to the balcony above the main entrance of the castle followed closely by Vincent. They looked out on the field of grass, walking paths and pavilions to find nearly thirty dark sorcerers wreaking havoc in the park. Several pavilions had already been destroyed and many more were in danger of collapse. "I'll cast the shield spell. You cast the illusion."

Vincent held out his hands toward the center of the park. "*Mimnalt nissa vari contra tru-viso.*" Ten sorcerers in white robes stepped out of an undamaged pavilion near the center of the park, including figures who resembled Vincent and Gollnick. Raising their hands these white-garbed newcomers appeared to cast a spell.

The dark sorcerers immediately noticed their white-clad rivals and launched an all-out assault.

The real Gollnick meanwhile cast a protective shield around Vincent's illusion, making the situation look more realistic. "*Proto maxil si-ta envelum.*" Gollnick and Vincent were forced to maintain concentration to reinforce their spells after each impact.

Gollnick realized this would be a distraction at best—one they could only maintain as long as they continued their focus. If they faltered or weakened, the spell would fail. Their enemies would realize the ruse and resume their search in a more dangerous proximity. Gollnick could only hope the members of the New Circle would arrive in time.

All of the dark sorcerers in the park converged on the small pavilion from every direction, all except one sorcerer. The ground shook from a coordinated effort by the dark sorcerers below. Fireballs, energy blasts and lightning bolts slammed into the defensive shield. Vincent's characters moved and interacted with one another to maintain the illusion, but it was Gollnick who bore the more difficult task. Reinforcing the barrier required focus, concentration and strength of will. A bead of sweat rolled down his face. He knew they wouldn't be able to maintain the deception for long.

With each attack, Gollnick reeled desperately to keep the illusion protected so he maintained an extended left hand. Vincent's characters mimicked his stance and posture, appearing to regenerate the shield with each attack.

Footsteps approaching from behind raised a concern. Was it friend or foe? Had an enemy found a way in to the castle... or had reinforcements finally arrived? Raising his right hand, he lit a fireball ready to defend against the unknown.

Gollnick and Vincent both turned and found only Cyrus, Amber, Meagan and an unfamiliar dwarf rushing out onto the balcony. With a sigh of relief, Gollnick extinguished the flame.

The momentary lapse of concentration, along with the relief of seeing reinforcements, was a happy one until both the illusion and shield collapsed under constant bombardment. The dark sorcerers exchanged glances and slowly approached the destroyed pavilion. A few kicked the rubble and hefted some beams, but found no sign of their target. The solitary and hooded figure who had made no attempt to assist in the attack called, "It was a ruse. Keep looking. They're here somewhere."

Cyrus stepped forward. "What's going on? How did they find us?"

Vincent wiped the sweat from his brow. "That would be my fault. When I was under Malcolm's control, he forced me to tell him where the castle was located. Until recently we weren't enough of an annoyance to bother with. Now, it seems we have their attention. And not in a good way."

Gollnick scanned the park fields and counted thirty-two dark sorcerers now. The single hooded figure stood almost on the exact spot of their previous illusion. The man kicked a few stones and meandered around, examining the ground. After a few moments, he lowered his hood and his gaze drifted skyward. *Malcolm!* Gollnick's pulse quickened. It seemed the head dark sorcerer himself had come to witness their demise.

Cyrus stepped closer to the edge of the balcony, instinctively pointing his right fist at Malcolm. His gaze drifted down the length of his arm as his eyes lowered.

Gollnick now noticed Cyrus was missing his fireball bracer. "Cyrus?"

"I had to sacrifice it to the Well of Urd in order to gain the knowledge to create a new Gleipnir. It was the only way."

Gollnick placed a hand on the boy's shoulder. "We'll get you a new magical item..." He looked back to the field of dark sorcerers then returned his gaze. "...After the battle is over."

Without warning, a fireball slammed into the energy shield protecting the castle. Then another and another. Gollnick knew this meant the enemy had finally found their location.

"What do we do?" asked Amber. "There's too many of them for us to fight."

Vincent leaned over the balcony to look at the base of the castle. "Well, at least we were right about the sorcerer civil war in New York being a trap. Francois Le Rain and Deustoff Von Woonst are at the front gates working together to break in."

Gollnick ran to the balcony's ledge to see the two conspirators. "They're not trying to break in. There going after the anchor stone!"

Cyrus furrowed his brow. "The what?"

Gollnick focused his attention. "The anchor stone. The castle exists in a pocket dimension, not the real world... that's why they can't see it. The anchor stone is a magically enchanted rock that anchors the castle to the real word. If they destroy the stone, the castle's connection to the real world will be lost. Everyone and anything still inside will be cut off."

Wide eyed, Amber spluttered, "W-w-we can still use the mirror to travel to and from the castle, r-right?"

Gollnick shook his head. "No. Once the connection is broken, we will be trapped in the castle forever."

The dwarf stepped forward. "In that case, perhaps we should make a hasty retreat."

"No," Meagan interrupted. "We can't abandon the castle. There's too much knowledge and power that would be lost. Besides, I've already lost one home to dark sorcerers... I won't lose another."

Gollnick nodded his consent. "We need to retrieve the anchor stone and move it to a safe location."

"How exactly do we do that?" asked Cyrus with one brow raised.

"Simple," replied Gollnick. "We mount a counter offensive while one of us retrieves the stone and gets away. Cyrus, you need to be the one to transport the stone to safety."

"Me? I don't think so. I'm staying to fight."

Gollnick rested a hand on his shoulder again. "Cyrus, the stone isn't exactly lightweight. It's probably a hundred pounds or more. Vincent and I need to stay and fight. We'll need the girls' powers to defend the castle. And, sorry, but I have no idea who this guy is," extending an open hand toward the dwarf. "I would rather have someone I trust get the anchor stone to safety."

Cyrus' determined expression softened as his gaze drifted to the floor. He rubbed the bare skin of his right forearm where he had previously worn the bracer, then nodded in agreement. "So what does this anchor stone look like? And how do I find it?"

Gollnick extended his hand toward the stairs. "It has magical runes. You can't miss it." Turning to his niece, he added, "Meagan, show Cyrus the secret door to the island then meet us at the front gate. We don't want to be in here when the stone gets moved."

Meagan hesitated, looking from Cyrus to Kallan and back.

"Cyrus," Gollnick instructed, "give us ten minutes to get out of the castle before you move it. We launch our attack once Meagan arrives at the gate."

Gollnick noticed Meagan's hesitation as she watched Kallan. "Is there a problem here?"

"No. Come on, Cyrus, it's this way." She then led Cyrus from the balcony.

"Everyone else, follow me," instructed Gollnick. He led the group from the room and down the stairs. Fireballs and energy blasts continued to rock the castle. Candles flickered as more and more magical energy was being diverted to protect the castle from the continuing assault. When they reached the spiral staircase, he commanded, "Stairs, front gate."

The staircase made no movement to comply. Gollnick kicked a few of the steps to no avail. "Stairs, front gate," he commanded once again. With some hesitation, the stairs slowly began to shift. They descended into a large courtyard opposite the front gate. The drawbridge was still up, but the magical energy of the huge beams vibrated irregularly. Gollnick knew the drawbridge couldn't withstand much more. They ran across the courtyard and Gollnick waited by the release to lower the bridge.

Meagan approached from a side passage. "Cyrus is ready for to us to make our move. Then he'll grab the stone and go."

Gollnick reviewed the plan. "As long as the pocket dimension stays intact, they won't see the drawbridge lower. However, once we exit the castle, they'll see us... and then they'll know where the entrance is located. We need to distract them while Cyrus gets away with the anchor stone. We can't let the dark sorcerers have the castle. There's too much powerful magic in here. Once we are in the open, defend yourselves by any means possible. They won't be expecting Vincent and I to launch an attack. Once you see an opening, run for it. Find a mirror nearby and teleport to safety."

Amber half raised a hand. "Where exactly is that?"

Gollnick now realized he hadn't thought about a rendezvous point. "Go to Mount Helicon. The Muses will shelter you until I can arrive."

Meagan's voice cracked. "And what if you don't? There are too many sorcerers out there for the two of you to face alone. I'm staying with you."

Amber and Kallan nodded their agreement.

"No," Gollnick said through pursed lips. "You all need to get away. Cyrus will be carrying the anchor stone. He'll need protection. Go with him and get to the Muses. No more arguments."

Gollnick turned toward the main gates and hit the drawbridge release. The bridge lowered with the creaking of heavy wooden beams and clanking of chain links until it slammed down on the other side of the moat. Gollnick lit a fireball in each hand. With a nod to Vincent, they charged out into the park screaming.

* * *

Max stepped out of the mirror in the library, followed by Taryn, Radimir and Tiem. He looked around at hundreds of tomes before spotting the semi-circular shaped doors. The place looked oddly familiar, but new at the same time. His first instinct was to contact the others, so they raced to the kitchen, but saw no one. A blast from outside shook the castle. Max steadied himself against a wall, then exchanged a quick glance with Taryn.

"Balcony!" she yelled. Taryn led the way out of the kitchen, then took a left and headed for the stairs with Max, Radimir and Tiem in close pursuit. When they reached the spiral staircase, she commanded, "Stairs, up."

Max looked at her, unsure what she was expecting to happen. The stairs made no movement for a few seconds.

She tried again. "I said... stairs, up." The first step vibrated slightly then they slowly raised to the next level.

Max cocked his head. "Interesting." They darted up the stairs, past a suit of armor. The head of the armor creaked as it turned and raised a foot. Max looked back. "Stay!" They continued up the next set of stairs and out onto a balcony.

From there Max witnessed a sight. In the park below, a barrier of twenty giant slabs of stone had been erected in a circle around a small group of defenders. An older man ran from gap to gap throwing fireballs while a second man pulled ice shards from the lake to hurl at the dark sorcerers. Two girls and a dwarf had erected personal energy shields to plug some of the remaining gaps. With the destruction of each stone barrier, the girl with curly blonde hair raised her arms and another stone slab rose to take its place.

Max counted thirty dark sorcerers in black trench coats surrounding the structure, each throwing fireballs or energy blasts at the barrier, trying to defeat the meager force within. He looked at Taryn. "I take it our friends are the small group of defenders who don't appear to be doing so well at the moment?"

"Yep."

Max took a few steps back then looked at Tiem. "Don't think, just follow me. No matter what."

After Tiem nodded, Max took a powerful lunge over the balcony parapet, plummeting toward the water below. He glanced back to see Tiem following. As they neared the bottom, he extended a hand and the water rose up to meet them. Two water spouts caught them and landed them safely on the ground opposite the island.

Max looked back up at the balcony for Taryn and Radimir, but neither were there. Instead, a hawk was just taking flight. *Radimir*. A gigantic burst of oranges and reds stole his attention, as Max then saw Taryn, not free-falling but rather with both hands beneath her and like rockets, flames shooting the length of her arms. The force of the flames propelled her forward until she gently landed next to Max and Tiem.

"When did you learn that?" he asked.

Taryn smiled. "Just now. I pulled a Max—I didn't think about it, I just did what felt right."

"Nice," replied Max. "Now let's go help our friends."

Max ran for the barrier. As he neared, he saw the hawk land in the stone circle. It then transformed into a large grizzly bear. Max entered the perimeter. "Hold up there, Radimir. You won't have protection from fireballs and energy blasts."

Taryn caught up. "Yes, but he can't return to normal shape without these." She dropped a bundle—Radimir's clothing.

Max reached his hands between the stones. "*Proto torum seton*." An energy wave shot from his hand, sending the nearest dark sorcerer flying backward twenty feet, crashing into a nearby tree.

Gollnick called, "Glad you could make it."

Max quickly glanced around. "Is everyone here? I feel like we're missing someone."

Gollnick pointed toward the island. "Cyrus went to get the anchor stone. We need to move the castle."

Max looked back at the little island in the middle of the tiny lake. He could see movement, but he couldn't tell if it was the one called Cyrus or not. He then spotted two dark sorcerers approaching that position from the other side. Reaching his hand out toward the lake, tentacles of water rose. The appendages ensnared the two encroachers and pulled them under. Not even a ripple remained, and neither sorcerer resurfaced.

A fireball blast against the stone barrier near Max's head drew his attention back to the immediate fight. He whipped around and fired an energy wave punch at another dark sorcerer. A few seconds later, Radimir joined Max at the gap. Max snapped his head to where he'd left the grizzly bear then back to Radimir.

Radimir smiled. "Change clothes, hurry."

"Okay."

Taryn covered the side of the stone circle opposite Gollnick so they had a fire elemental sorcerer aiming in opposing directions.

The battle continued for many minutes. Max could see normal folk in the distance watching the ensuing conflict from behind parked cars and peeking out of windows from the safety of their homes. He wished they would just leave the area. The closer they were to the battle, the more harm could come to them.

"Where exactly are we going?" asked a voice from behind them.

Max turned to see Cyrus lugging a basketball sized stone with strange markings on it.

"Get that thing out of here!" Gollnick shouted. "Find a mirror and take it to the Muses."

Max saw Gollnick's face go white. "What's wrong?"

"I just received a telepathic message from Elisa and Hank. They teleported in just before Cyrus moved the anchor stone. They're trapped inside the castle."

Max looked at the boulder still in Cyrus' hands. "Are they okay?"

"Yes, but the mirror that brought them in shattered during that last fireball attack. Once we place the stone in a new home, we'll be able to get them out of there. Until then, they're stuck."

In an obviously coordinated attack, multiple fireballs struck the stone barrier in front of them, shattering the massive barrier and propelling Taryn to the other side of the circle where she fell unconscious. Vincent, Tiem and Kallan were knocked to the ground as well.

Two dark sorcerers entered through the gaping hole, arms raised and pointing at Cyrus.

Vincent called, "Francois, Deustoff. No!"

Instantly prepared, Cyrus dropped the anchor stone at his feet and slammed his forearms together to create a personal shield.

Malcolm stepped into the circle next and clapped his hands. "*Proto torum nese-cola-ton.*" The shock wave rippled through the ground underneath Max's feet.

Max watched as Cyrus' shield did little good. The uncoordinated teenager stumbled and tripped over the anchor stone, falling face first to the ground. Meagan stumbled back until she slammed into one of the rock slabs before hitting the ground. Amber lost her balance and focus on her shield before falling forward and having the wind knocked out of her. Radimir tripped on shifting rubble and slammed his head into a slab before collapsing. Even Gollnick, who was standing near a gap in the barrier, wound up pinning himself there as he slipped between the stones.

Max tried to prepare himself, but as he reached out to the nearest stone slab, a fragment fell on his left shoulder, knocking him to the ground as well.

Once Max regained his sense of balance he saw Malcolm point his hand at the anchor stone. "*Magna fir-tor loma.*"

"No!" called Gollnick wide eyed and jaw gaping.

A fireball shot from Malcolm's hand and slammed into the anchor stone. Its surface cracked then split in two, a wave of light shooting out from the crevice. The color of the stone dimmed from bright white to a dull grey.

After pulling himself from between the giant stone slabs, Gollnick lit two fireballs, one in each hand.

Malcolm backed away.

In pursuit of the leader of the dark sorcerers, Gollnick lobbed both fireballs at once, but Malcolm ducked for cover. Another portion of the stone barrier exploded under the impact.

More dark sorcerers poured through the hole in the circle before Meagan could repair the damage. She yelled, "I won't let you hurt the ones I love!" She ran to the center of their group and raised her forearms together, creating a personal shield just in front of Gollnick and Max.

The others were slower to recover from the shock wave. Max stood on unsteady feet propping himself against one of the barrier stones. Gollnick sat in silence as he stared at the broken anchor stone. A tear ran down his face.

Malcolm stepped from behind cover to face the members of the two Circles. Francois Le Rain and Deustoff Von Woonst stood on either side of him as even more dark sorcerers filed into their midst. Malcolm smiled. "This is the end of the line of Circles. I will give each of you this one chance. Join me or die."

Max peered through the gaps in the stones to find yet more dark sorcerers approaching the outside of the barrier. They were outnumbered by more than four to one at this point. He had no idea how they would escape this encounter or if any of them would even survive.

In the distance, as the commotion of battle eased, Max thought he heard something like a chainsaw. Then it grew louder. He looked around to find the source. Through a single gap in the stone, he spotted something. At the northern end of the park, fifty motorcycles roared across the grassy field toward the stone barrier.

The dark sorcerers outside the barrier turned in surprise. Without warning, fireballs thrown by the motorcycle gang slammed into the ground, barriers and dark sorcerers alike.

Max turned back toward Malcolm who was straining his neck to see the cause of the commotion.

Radimir shook his head to clear the cobwebs then looked at Max. "Before leave Sphinx, mirror call Sheelin. Ask for help."

Max let out a little chuckle before smiling. "Good thinking, Radimir." He turned his attention back to Malcolm. "The game's up, Malcolm. The Hunters are looking for their prey."

With pursed lips and a furrowed brow Malcolm seethed, "Not soon enough. *Magna fir-tor loma.*" Malcolm held Max's gaze while loosing the fireball at Radimir.

The big Russian was unprepared and had no time to respond. The fireball slammed into his chest, propelling him backward into a barrier stone. He slumped to the ground dead.

Max stepped forward wide eyed. After a quick glance at Malcolm then back to Radimir, he raised his hand toward the Russian and concentrated. Time stopped for a brief moment. Only Max could move and see what was transpiring—Malcolm's sneer at eliminating his Russian friend, the fire burning through the clothing and flesh of Radimir's chest. He then focused on rewinding time five... then ten, finally twenty seconds. The fireball flew from Radimir's unharmed chest back into Malcolm's outstretched hand, then disappeared as Malcolm spoke the spell in reverse. Once the damaged was undone, time resumed normally. Radimir once again shook his head to clear the cobwebs then looked at Max. "Before leave Sphinx, mirror call Sheelin. Ask for help."

This time Max replied, "Radimir, shield up." He then pointed toward Malcolm.

Radimir obeyed instantly. He slammed his forearms together to form a personal shield just in time to protect himself from the fireball blast.

This time it was Malcolm who looked at Max with wide eyes. "That wasn't déjà vu! You turned back time, but how?"

Max reached out his left hand toward the lake.

Malcolm watched as a large block of ice rose up out of the water. "Not this again."

After removing a finger from his temple, Francois leaned closer to Malcolm. "My lord, the master commands that we bring the one called Max to him, dead or alive."

A sneer crossed Malcolm's face. "That works for me, but I would prefer dead. Get him now."

Hands reached between the stone barriers and grabbed at Max from behind. Max quickly let the block of ice fall and stepped away as he glanced at the flailing hands. A fireball slammed into Max's back. The searing pain lit his nervous system on fire as he dropped to his knees.

Twenty feet away, Gollnick had crawled to the fragments of the anchor stone. Malcolm moved in behind him, but Meagan attempted to block. The head dark sorcerer shoved her out of the way roughly. She tripped over a stone and fell to the ground. As Gollnick touched the largest chunk of rock, Malcolm stepped in behind him and drew his sword.

"*No!*" Meagan screamed. A one-foot wide column of stone rose up between Malcolm and her uncle.

Malcolm's eyes widened, but it did not deter him. He reached around the column with sword at the ready.

Max knew what was about to happen, but he was unable to do anything about it. His memory flashed back on the past week. It was Gollnick who had found him in the hospital and brought him to the Circle. He'd offered Max a home within Ravenicon. It was Gollnick's patient training that helped Max prepare for the battle in the underworld.

Now all Max could do was watch as Malcolm speared Gollnick through the back and out his chest. Pulling his sword free, Gollnick collapsed to the ground.

Max struggled to stand, but couldn't find the strength. He saw Meagan crawling toward the lifeless body of her uncle. Their eyes met and Max called her name weakly, "Meagan!"

Still near the blast site where they entered the stone ring, Francois cast a spell, "*Destro assor rectu.*" The base of the nearest stone barrier exploded. Rocky shrapnel scattered everywhere and the concussive force deafened Max. He was weak and injured and lacked the strength to make a quick response. All he could do was look up as the massive slab came crashing down on his crippled body. The weight of the impact deprived him of consciousness providing the only relief from the overwhelming pain.

* * *

Cyrus stood just in time to witness the stone slab smash down on Max, crushing him to the ground. His senses were shaken and his balance was out of sorts, but Cyrus struggled to walk a few steps. He tried to make his way to Max when a hand grabbed his shoulder from behind. The hand spun him around and almost to the ground. The straight face of Francois Le Rain met his eyes. "If you want to live, sit down and shut up." With a shove, Cyrus landed on the hard ground still trying to get his bearings.

Fireballs hit the ground near Francois and Duestoff who had been flanking their leader, causing them to leap for the safety of the stone barriers.

An older man with long white hair tied back in a ponytail and a teenage girl approached the circle with four other motorcycle riders, each with another fireball at the ready. After Francois backed off a bit, Cyrus stood and faced the two dark sorcerers.

He watched as Radimir stood near the barrier's gap, still rubbing his head. Amber regained her breath and stood beside him while Tiem, Kallan and Vincent moved to encircle their tormentors.

Taryn leaned against a stone slab with a fireball casually in one hand. Francois and Duestoff were trapped between the New Circle and the motorcycle riding Hunters.

Cyrus was both pleased and disappointed when the dark sorcerers raised their hands in surrender. He was hoping to find a release for his anger.

Cyrus turned to confront Malcolm, but found the leader of the dark sorcerers had disappeared through another hole in the barrier wall.

Tiem examined Gollnick and hung his head. "A great sorcerer has passed from this realm to the next."

Amber spun to find Meagan passed out on the ground. She knelt by her friend's side and found Meagan was still breathing. Amber shook her and called her name multiple times, but with no luck. Meagan was not waking up.

Reluctantly, Cyrus made his way over to the stone that had crushed Max. As he knelt to view the remains of his friend's body, Cyrus' breath caught. Quickly, Cyrus stood and scanned the area. "Malcolm's gone... and he took Max with him!"

40 Aftermath

Patterson Park was in shambles. Giant stone blocks formed an irregular circle in the southeastern corner of the park with huge sections shattered into debris. Hundreds of scorched earth potholes littered the area. Most structures were gone or stood in ruin. Forty-eight motorcycles flanked the standing stones.

Inside the gathering, members of the New Circle took stock of their loss. Many were injured but they faced a few fatalities. Four members of the Hunters lay still and Vincent held vigil over the body of his friend and mentor, Gollnick.

As the others searched around for wounded enemies, Cyrus realized another of their number was missing. He scanned the area before calling out. "Where's Meagan?"

Heads turned this way and that until Amber signaled for help. "She's over here."

He rushed to her side.

"She's still breathing, but she won't wake up," Amber whimpered.

Qaletaqa, leader of the Hunters, stepped forward. He placed a hand over her forehead. "*Hema toe-zie fume.*" He lowered his hand and tilted his head then placed his hand on her head once again. "*Inlecto telepa mon see-tor.*" After a few minutes, he turned to the others. "Physically, she is well, but her mind is a jumble. I have no explanation for it. Until her mind settles, she will not wake."

Amber faced her brother, wide eyed and shaking. "We lost Gollnick and Max, we can't lose Meagan, too. And without her, how are we going to fix the anchor stone to get back into Ravenicon castle? As far as we know, Elisa and Hank are still trapped in there. We have to get them out!"

Cyrus put a hand on her shoulder. "We will. We'll find a way to repair the anchor stone and get our friends back. We'll also find a way to get Max back. For now, we need to find a place to stay."

Tiem stepped forward and bowed. "I'm sure my master will provide shelter for the New Circle."

Cyrus raised an eyebrow then looked to Taryn.

Taryn nodded. "It's okay. This is Tiem. And I suspect he is the newest member of the Circle. I believe his master will provide shelter for us. At least until we can get back on our feet. I will warn ye though, ye've never met anyone like his master."

Cyrus looked at the boy for a moment before responding. "So who is your master, Tiem?"

"The immortal Ra."

Everyone except Taryn and Radimir looked around in surprise. Murmurs finally broke the silence. Even Qaletaqa's eyes widened as he rose to his feet.

Cyrus raised a hand. "In that case I suggest we gather our fallen friends and head to Cairo."

Sheelin stepped forward. "Cyrus of the New Circle. My father and I must return with the Hunters to our own home and continue our work. Taryn has informed Radimir and myself that we too are members of the New Circle. If you ever need my help I will come. I might even be able to convince my father to send the Hunters again if needed."

Radimir stepped next to Sheelin. "I going Sheelin for now. I come when called."

Cyrus shook their hands and thanked them.

Kallan next approached Cyrus. "It is time for me to return to Nidavellir as well."

"Until we can see the Crystal again, I can't be sure, but I believe you too are a member of the New Circle, my friend."

Kallan nodded and shook Cyrus' hand. "Call me if I am needed."

After everyone departed, Cyrus picked up the pieces of the anchor stone.

Tiem carried Gollnick's body and lay it next to Meagan. "*Levas mon see-tor,*" the boy chanted. Both Gollnick and Meagan levitated a few feet above the ground.

Amber looked around before focusing on Cyrus. "Without the mirror in the castle library, how are we getting to Cairo?"

Taryn placed her trench coat over the fallen body of Gollnick. "Don't worry, Amber. We'll find a mirror large enough to teleport through to Egypt. And we will find Max. I didn't travel to Canada and almost become a Wendigo just to lose him now."

Amber scrunched her brow. "Okay. I think I missed something."

Taryn smiled. "We'll have plenty of time to trade stories later. Let's get movin'."

* * *

In the depths of New York City, Malcolm stood before the throne of fire awaiting acknowledgment of his presence by the winged creature within the flames. The heat radiating from the throne made him perspire. As the sweat ran down his lowered face, a drop of moisture hit the floor.

The booming voice echoed through the room. "You have succeeded in eliminating Gollnick Strom, though not quite in the way I had planned. Nevertheless, he is gone."

Malcolm's voice quivered, "Thank you, my lord. I have also brought the body of the whelp who defeated me in the Greek Underworld. He will bother us no more."

"On the contrary, my feeble friend. He is the power we seek to remake this world."

Malcolm turned his head to look at the body resting on a stone table next to the open pit of magma in the center of the room. The glow of the molten rock behind Max made his silhouette dance on the wall of the chamber.

The voice boomed. "He will rise again."

About the Author

Edward Eck lives in Pennsylvania and works as a network administrator and computer programmer. His love of fantasy emanates from stories such as *Star Wars*, *Lord of the Rings* and the mythology of various cultures. His hobbies include dancing, reading and writing.

In high school he lost his interest in reading, finding it boring. It wasn't until later in life that his love of reading was rekindled when he discovered fantasy and sci-fi novels. He realized that he hadn't grown bored with reading, he just wasn't interested in the same material he had been required to read in school. Since then he has read many books and found a love for writing as well.

"Reading is an escape from the boring and mundane. Let your imagination soar!"

ALSO BY THIS AUTHOR

CHRONOS
— AND THE —
NEW CIRCLE
EDWARD ECK

Max awakens – with no memory of who he is – to find that magic is real and the ancient gods of myth were mighty sorcerers. When he is recruited to a group of young magic-wielders, the safety of the world is on the line.

The enemy threatens to release powerful mythical creatures from their prison bonds, and only Max and his friends can stop them. But Max has a secret not even he knows. Can he remember in time?

www.ingramcontent.com/pod-product-compliance
Lightning Source LLC
Chambersburg PA
CBHW071302250626
47159CB00004B/1278